"You—" DJ strolled close "—are going to learn how to hunt."

"Hunt? Hunt what?"

"The enemy."

Dom's face, and all the months of pain and anger, filled Tammie's mind. It must have shown on her face. DJ nodded and sat at the table. "Oh, yeah. You're gonna do just fine, mama bear."

She fought the smile at his unintended compliment. She'd do anything for Tyler, and she liked knowing DJ knew it.

"What's this? My last meal or fortification?"

"Definitely fortification." He took a bite of the thick burger, and Tammie stared. "Oh, don't worry. I remembered you don't like onions—I left them off."

A wisp of memory joined them. She didn't dislike onions, but at the time she'd said that she'd been on the beach with the cutest boy she'd ever met and was hoping he'd kiss her... Her face warmed.

Dear Reader,

When dreaming up the Hawkins clan, youngest brother DJ stepped out of the mist first. A wild child, and an avowed bachelor, I wondered how this dedicated marine would handle suddenly becoming a father. Living in a military community, I witnessed men and women combine home and duty, so I knew he could do it. But the woman he was destined to love wasn't someone I understood.

How does a mother abandon her child? I'd fallen in love with Tyler in *A Family for Tyler* (Harlequin Superromance, February 2014) and thought maybe he was better off without her. So I auditioned several women for DJ, but none fit like Tammie. The only way I could imagine leaving *my* kids would be to protect them. Once I understood that about myself, Tammie's story unfolded.

The Marine Finds His Family is the second book in this series. I'm having such fun writing about the Hawkins siblings! Readers can contact me at angel@angelsmits.com, or visit me at angelsmits.com for links to Facebook, Twitter and Pinterest.

Happy reading!

Angel Smits

ANGEL SMITS

The Marine Finds His Family

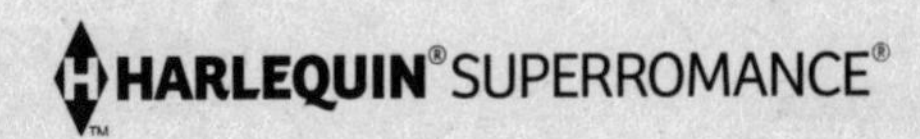

Recycling programs for this product may not exist in your area.

ISBN-13: 978-0-373-60888-1

The Marine Finds His Family

This edition published by arrangement with Harlequin Books S.A.

For questions and comments about the quality of this book, please contact us at CustomerService@Harlequin.com.

Printed in U.S.A.

Angel Smits lives in Colorado with her husband, daughter and puppy. Winning the Romance Writers of America's Golden Heart Award was the highlight of her writing career, until her first Harlequin book hit the shelves. Her social work background inspires her characters while improv writing allows her to torture them. It's a rough job, but someone's got to do it.

Books by Angel Smits

HARLEQUIN SUPERROMANCE

A Message for Julia
Seeking Shelter
A Family for Tyler

Other titles by this author available in ebook format.

This is for my editor, Karen Reid, who somehow gets my vision and makes me strive for my very best. The creative process is not always easy, but she makes even the painful parts enjoyable.

Thank you to Paul and Caleb, who lent me Hamlet and Pork Chop.

And as always, Ron.

CHAPTER ONE

"AW, MAN. IS THAT what I think it is?"

Captain DJ Hawkins heard his buddy Colin's words the same instant he spied the bright red-and-white postal box. He hoped—just as he knew Colin hoped—it was from his sister Addie. Getting a closer look, he saw that the return address confirmed it. *Yes.* Cookies.

The box rattled and Colin reached over and tried to swipe it. No way. DJ wasn't sharing. Not yet, anyway. Not until he'd stuffed himself to the gills, and then only maybe.

Stowing the last of his gear, DJ ripped open the box, yanked out the plastic bag Addie had wrapped the cookies in and stuffed one very broken, very delicious peanut butter chocolate chip beauty into his mouth. He sank to his bunk in pure bliss.

Just to torment Colin, he groaned aloud in near ecstasy. For a minute or two he was no longer in this godforsaken hole in the world, waiting for the next enemy attack. He was a five-year-old whose big sister made the world's best cookies.

"You gonna share?"

"Not a chance." DJ laughed. He could feel the disappointment rolling off Colin. "Don't pout about it."

He tossed the plastic bag to Colin—it wasn't as if the crumbs could get any more busted up.

"She should just pack a spoon." Colin reached into the bag and scooped out a handful of the sweet, gooey mess.

Most days DJ really did love his life. He hadn't joined the military with the notion that he'd stay safe all the time. He'd figured out a long time ago that he wasn't a stay-at-home, family kind of guy. He'd watched his older siblings shoulder too much responsibility after Dad's death. He'd seen the life go out of them when they were just kids. He would never let that happen to himself.

But that didn't keep him from missing his family.

The care packages helped. And his three sisters were great about sending them—cookies, toothpaste and really bad books were the norm. His two older brothers managed to send emails every now and then. He laughed at the image of either Wyatt or Jason baking. Yeah, their expertise ran more in the area of picking out a bag of Oreo cookies.

Expecting the package to include a letter, DJ wasn't disappointed, though the feminine handwriting didn't look familiar. For an instant he wondered if he'd gotten the right package.

His taste buds confirmed these were Addie's cookies, though. Plus, his name and his last stateside address, Mom's house, were clear on the envelope. Then he noticed Addie had written on a little yellow sticky note and stuck it on the outside. "This came in the mail. Thought I'd send it along." Yep, it was his.

He tore open the seal, surprised in this day and age of email and computer-printed letters to see the old-fashioned lined school paper. Several drugstore-printed photographs fell out.

Slowly, he unfolded the letter and stared at the date. Two months? This had been sent, or at least written, two months ago?

The words flowed in pretty curls of blue ink.

DJ,

You probably don't remember me. I don't know why you would. It was only one week. A single week in your life that completely altered mine. I can't blame or regret it…though it saddens me to think of it that way.

It's time you know. You have a son. I've stuck in pictures of him. He looks like you. So much like you. You'll see. But that isn't the purpose of this letter.

His name is Tyler. He's in Texas. I can't do this anymore.

The name Tammie was scrawled across the bottom of the page, the ink smudged.

He stared at the pictures. What the…? A boy and a familiar young woman smiled at him from the dozen images.

Distant, banished memories rushed in. Eighteen.

He'd been a grand total of eighteen years old. Fresh out of high school, prepping to head to basic training in two months. He and three buddies had packed a car and headed to the Gulf Coast beaches of Florida. He couldn't recall why they'd picked Florida. Someone's harebrained idea.

Two weeks of no school, no parents and no commanding officers. Heaven. Pure heaven.

DJ's memories, foggy and age-worn, flickered. He recalled the pretty blonde, too much beer and a long night on a sandy beach. He smiled. Those carefree days seemed so far away.

Picture after picture. His mind raced. How long had it been since he'd been with Tammie? Eight… nine years? The baby photos didn't show him the resemblance, but the others… Three years old, four, six, eight…

DJ's vision narrowed and nearly went black. The whole world moved in slow motion around him. The tent flapped in the wind and the scrape of blowing dirt against the canvas sounded like a lion fighting to get in.

Despite the desert heat in this outpost, a chill shot through him, icicles instead of sand particles cut across his heart. This wasn't possible.

He had a kid?

A kid he hadn't even known about?

He scooped up the pictures scattered across his bunk. As he stared at the boy with the wide grin, he couldn't deny it. The boy looked exactly like him at that age.

My God. The words in the letter tumbled through his mind over and over again.

What the hell was he supposed to do now? His brain was mush half the time these days, what with the long hours, the heat and all the energy he gave his job. He couldn't wrap his mind around any of this.

"Hey," Colin said around a mouthful of cookie as he lounged on his bunk. "What gives?"

DJ paced, his eyes staring at the child—his child—in the pictures. His heart pounded and the desert heat washed over him. Words? He was supposed to be able to say words? Think words?

His stomach revolted and Addie's sweet cookies threatened to return to the world. He couldn't speak. He simply shoved half the photos into his buddy's hands.

"What the...?" Colin looked first at DJ, then back at the picture and back at DJ again. "Whoa!"

DJ cursed again. What was he supposed to do now? He needed to get back to the base and see if he could get ahold of Wyatt, or Jason, or Addie. Someone. Tyler—was that his name?—was in Texas. They needed to find him—he needed to see his son.

His son.

He looked up just as his commanding officer, Major Dixon, walked into the tent, a cloud of dust on his heels.

The frown on the older man's face didn't bode

well, and DJ knew he wouldn't get the chance to call home anytime soon. He stuffed the pictures and letter back into the envelope and shoved it all into the cargo pocket of his uniform. He had to go to work now.

But later—

Meanwhile, halfway across the world...

TAMMIE EASTON DROPPED the tattered curtains back in place. The old, fragile lace didn't so much waft as thunk against the frame. Vaguely, she wondered if Cora had ever had them cleaned. Looking around at the tiny, old house, Tammie shook her head. Of course she hadn't had them cleaned. Cora could barely afford to feed herself.

Even though the curtains hung over the window, Tammie could still see what was happening across the street.

Tyler, her son, at all of eight years old, the only person who mattered to her in the world, was leaving. Never mind that she was the one who'd set all this in motion. Never mind that she was sending him to live with his dad's family to keep him safe. Never mind any of that. Her heart hurt and she doubted it would ever stop. Even if...no...*when* she got him back, she'd never forgive herself for sending him away.

The images blurred, and she blinked furiously to clear her eyes. She couldn't bear to miss even an instant of his life. She might never... No, she reminded herself again, she *would* see him again. She *was* coming back. He'd be with her again. Soon. She'd promised him.

Footsteps came up beside her, and Tammie glanced down briefly to see the diminutive older woman come up beside her. Cora patted Tammie's arm and gave her a warm hug. "You're doin' the right thing, hon. He'll be fine."

"I know. I'm the one who's a wreck." Tammie wiped her eyes and watched as the man she knew was Wyatt Hawkins helped Tyler into the passenger seat of a big black pickup truck. He was taking Tyler home with him since DJ was deployed overseas.

Maybe she should have waited. But she knew the answer to that, too—she couldn't have waited. And she'd sent DJ a letter before learning he was overseas. Doing it all over again—writing a letter to his brother—had torn her apart. Tammie had thought she and Tyler had escaped when they came here to Texas. But the other night someone had broken into the apartment she'd just moved them into. Nothing was missing. The intruder just tore the place up, looking for something. Just as they had at the last two places.

That's how she'd ended up here with Cora.

She looked down at the coworker who'd become her friend. "I'm sorry to put you in the middle of all this."

"Don't you go apologizin' again. I told you, that's why we got Rufus." The old coon dog lifted his head at the sound of his name. "And Bubba." Bubba was the twelve-gauge shotgun Cora kept propped up beside the front door. She didn't need one at the back kitchen door, as it was nailed shut with easily a hundred tenpenny nails.

Tyler loved Rufus, and the dog lavished love on the boy every chance he got.

Tammie hoped Wyatt had animals for Tyler to play with. He loved animals. Her mind filled with all the images of things her son loved. Dogs and cats. Horses. Stories about monsters. Video games. And snuggling while she read to him on cold rainy days.

Could she actually die from the pain of her broken heart?

The truck's taillights glowed, and Tammie leaned closer to the window to watch until they vanished around the corner at the end of the block. Finally, Tyler was well and truly gone.

Tammie lost it. Burying her face in her hands, she gave in to the sobs. Cora rubbed Tammie's shoulder, making all the soothing noises that people made when they didn't know what else to do.

THEY WERE ON the hunt. This was the province where intel had placed the terrorist cell they'd been tracking for months. It was right in DJ's backyard. The team had assembled quickly with Dixon's orders—not surprising since they stood at alert around the clock. Now, slowly, methodically, the four-man team moved through the backstreets of the small town DJ knew intimately, having lived here for over a month.

Silence was thick. A strange silence, unlike the norm of a small town. In the middle of the night the few residents who remained were, hopefully, asleep and tucked away safe.

Safe? DJ would have laughed if it weren't so important to maintain that silence.

He knew the other men were nearby, moving slowly, quietly like him. He sensed rather than heard or saw them. Even with the night-vision goggles they were mere shadows.

A trickle of sweat slid down the center of DJ's back, like a finger of foreboding.

Something was off, but he couldn't identify it. This operation felt different. With the next step, he acknowledged it. Life, work, the mission wasn't different—*he* was different.

The sharp edges of the photos had dug into his thigh all the way here. Twice, a bump in the road had thrown him into the edge of the truck, and the packet. A sharp reminder of all he had to lose.

A son.

Where was Tyler? DJ glanced at his watch. Probably just sitting down to dinner? Where? With who? If Tammie couldn't do this anymore, had she dumped him somewhere?

He had a son. Over and over again that thought bounced around in his brain. He wanted to see him. Hear what his voice sounded like. How tall was he? The pictures gave little in the way of reference points.

DJ had promised long ago that he wouldn't let

himself be bogged down by family. Not like the other guys who carried pictures of girlfriends, wives and kids. Distractions. Enemy leverage. Vulnerabilities to be exploited.

Focus! He mentally swore and blinked to shift the gears in his mind. He had a job to do. The others needed him to be 110 percent.

Footsteps broke the silence and, thankfully, jerked him back to sanity. He shut out everything except his awareness. The others did the same.

Silence returned. Too silent. DJ stood, his finger on the trigger, sensing the others on the team moving into position. No one else on this side. Nothing.

The sound of hasty footfalls broke the night, shattering the quiet. Shots rained down. The shadows disappeared, finding cover.

Images flashed in DJ's mind of a little boy's smiling face. His eyes burned. *No.* Not acceptable. He forced the faces of the men around him into his mind. Tyler was part of the *why* of their mission—the shadows with DJ were the *how.*

Silence returned. No sounds of pain or injury. Shadows moved. One, two, three. All here. All whole. DJ breathed an instant's relief.

Seconds later, noise erupted everywhere around him. DJ dropped to the ground, knowing he'd crawl out if he had to. Wouldn't be the first time.

Gunfire broke the night and tufts of dirt and pieces of rock shot up into the air. He felt the sting of a dozen cuts across his face.

No. Not now. He didn't know if he said the words aloud or not. A soft click echoed through the streets. "Oh, shit!" DJ froze.

The air shifted and time slowed. The roar behind him shattered the quiet. A ball of fire shot up the street. Language, his and others', blistered the night.

Searing pain tore a scream from his throat and ripped DJ from his feet. His back, his shoulder, his legs roared with agony.

Light surrounded him, and in the glow, he saw a pair of startled eyes. So far away. So damned far away. DJ tried to speak, but the heat stole his words and burned in his gut.

The night returned. Pure silence. Nothing but pain engulfed him.

"Tyler!" A name that sounded strange in this land, so far from home, echoed down the deserted streets. A name DJ whispered into the darkness that took him.

And then the nothing was simply blank.

CHAPTER TWO

Two months later

MORNINGS WERE THE WORST. DJ lay there, listening to the ranch come to life, not moving, because once he moved, reality and pain came back. For those first few minutes, he could pretend that he was still normal.

And then he'd do something stupid, like breathe, and the pain would shoot through him with a knife's vengeance.

He cursed, long and loud, before forcing his body into a sitting position and swinging his legs over the edge of the bed. He didn't know how long he sat there trying to convince himself that getting up was a good idea.

"Dad?" A small voice came through the door, reminding DJ that he didn't really have a choice. DJ closed his eyes and let the sweet sound rattle around in his head. He didn't think he'd ever get tired of hearing Tyler call him Dad.

It had taken months to build a relationship with his son. Tyler had called him DJ at first.

"Yeah?" he croaked, then cleared his throat. "Just a sec." He grabbed the jeans he'd tossed over the back of the captain's chair that now sat in his room, and yanked them on with the chair's support.

The sturdy chair had been his father's and the extra leverage the arms provided was a huge help when his scarred legs didn't want to cooperate. Half-dressed, he called, "Come on in, buddy."

Moving around, while it hurt like hell, loosened up the damaged muscles and skin of his back and legs.

Tyler came through the door slowly. A stab of concern overrode the pain in DJ's legs when he saw Tyler's furtive glance up, then back down. *Uh-oh. What's going on?*

"What's up?" DJ tried to be nonchalant, but curiosity was killing him. He focused on trying to get his boots on.

"I wanna ask somethin'."

"Ask away." DJ watched Tyler out of the corner of his eye. His son was holding a notebook from school, the wire binding bent sideways in places. Tyler climbed up on the foot of DJ's bed. Sitting a minute, he began swinging his legs to kick the edge of the mattress.

"Well, ya know. My birthday's coming up."

DJ fought the grin. "Yeah. It is. In a couple weeks, right?"

The smile on Tyler's face made DJ's heart hitch a little.

"Yep. Less than a month. I'll be nine. I was sorta thinking maybe I'm big enough for this." Slowly, reverently, Tyler reached into the notebook and pulled out a pristine magazine picture.

A picture of a dirt bike. Bright green.

"Whoa!" The kid had taste. The bike was top-of-the-line. "It's a beauty."

"It's a Razor Dirt Rocket, and Morgan in my class has one. It's so cool."

"I don't know, buddy." His brother Wyatt, who owned this ranch, would kill him. Kill them both.

"Aw, come on." Tyler slid off the bed and came over to stand beside the chair. "All the guys were talkin' about it at recess. And everyone's gettin' 'em."

DJ doubted that, but didn't say anything. "We'll see. I don't think Uncle Wyatt would be too thrilled with you riding it near the horses."

"He doesn't say nothin' about you and your motorcycle."

"That's different." DJ pulled on the first worn combat boot and took a deep breath. "And he says plenty, believe me." Boot two coming up.

"How is it different?" Tyler's voice rose in frustration.

"It just is."

"That's not fair."

"Who told you life was fair, kid?" DJ mumbled, his back aching from bending over to struggle with his boots. The silence grew long, and DJ looked up when Tyler didn't say anything more.

"Mama always said to play fair." There was a sheen in Tyler's eyes, but DJ didn't dare point it out.

Nearly two months had passed and there was still no word from Tammie—no sign of her promise to Tyler to return. And while Tyler seldom spoke of her, when he did, the pain was sharp in his voice. That pain made DJ ache.

"Look." DJ left his second boot untied and turned to face Tyler. "I won't promise anything right now. Let me think about it, okay?"

"'Kay."

"Keep that picture in a safe place, though. Just in case I need a reference." DJ winked at Tyler and the smile that bloomed on the boy's face warmed his heart.

"When Mama says she'll think about something, that's almost always a yes." Tyler turned and ran from the room.

"Hey, now wait—"

Yep. Wyatt was gonna kill him. With a sigh, DJ followed Tyler downstairs. While the kid ran, DJ took his time. He could move much easier these days, especially after loosening up with the past few weeks of physical therapy, but it was still slow going.

Finally, he reached the ground floor and breathed a sigh of relief. Another day without a tumble down the stairs. It was looking good.

The old ranch house was big, with four bedrooms upstairs, a huge kitchen and several living areas on the main level. DJ's grandfather had built the place, and they'd all come out here in the summers as kids to visit, and later in life to work and play—in his case mostly play. Of the six siblings, Wyatt was the only one who took to ranching. It seemed only natural that he take over after Grandpa passed.

Wyatt was just where DJ expected to find him. In the big country kitchen, at the counter pouring himself a cup of coffee. Though it was early, DJ would bet this was not Wyatt's first cup. "Mornin'," they spoke in unison and both laughed.

DJ bypassed the coffee and grabbed a hunk of the ranch cook Juanita's always-amazing coffee cake and stuffed it in his mouth. He poured himself a glass of orange juice before sitting down at the huge ranch table.

"You weren't dumb enough to promise you'd get him the dirt bike, were you?" Wyatt wasn't known for being subtle.

"No." DJ's hackles rose. The younger brother in him wanted to remind Wyatt that Tyler was *his* son, and he'd promise whatever he wanted. The adult in him knew that was childish. Besides, this was Wyatt's home, Wyatt's ranch, and they were living here at his discretion.

"But?"

Wyatt knew DJ. His brother patiently waited—they both knew there was a *but*.

"I have an idea."

"Uh-oh." Wyatt grabbed a chair, scraping it away from the table to sit across from DJ. "Spit it out."

"He wants the bike, right?"

Wyatt nodded.

"I need him to tell me about Tammie." He met Wyatt's gaze.

"You think that's a good idea? Bribing him?"

DJ shrugged. He couldn't think of anything else at this point. Tyler refused to talk about his life with his mother. He wouldn't share even the smallest details. The first bit of information they'd had was, of course, the house where Wyatt had picked up the boy—and they'd figured out that was a lie, too. Tammie and Tyler hadn't lived there. No one had for years. Tammie had found an abandoned house and borrowed it.

"You don't think that dredging all that up will hurt him?" Wyatt said, his voice thick with concern.

They'd had this discussion a dozen times already. Maybe Tyler had been so badly abused that the horrors returning would be too difficult. But DJ didn't think that was the case. Tyler didn't behave like an abused kid. Concerned, scared at times, but not abused.

"That's the thing." DJ decided to share his thoughts with Wyatt. "I think he's not talking because he's protecting his mom." DJ would bet his Harley on it.

"From us?"

"No." DJ took a deep swallow of the juice, buying time to organize his words. "Something or someone else."

"That boyfriend?"

DJ shrugged, not really wanting to go there in his mind or this conversation. But he knew what Wyatt was talking about. Before DJ had returned home, Wyatt had taken Tyler to the emergency room when he'd cut his hand. That was the only time Tyler had let anything slip. Some guy named Dom had hurt Tyler. Hurt him bad enough to warrant an earlier ER visit that scared Tyler for life. But other than that, he hadn't said anything about his mom.

And now they finally had a key to get Tyler to talk.

Wyatt's simple nod was all the go-ahead DJ was going to get. He'd take what he could.

THIS TIME OF NIGHT was the worst time to work. Tammie liked it better when the dinner crowd was in full swing, or when the late-night-after-the-movies-and-the-bars-were-closed crowds came in. She didn't have time to think…or feel.

This dead, middle-of-the-night calm between the two rushes was almost painful. She'd already rolled all the silverware, filled the saltshakers and stacked the dishes in the front stations.

"Take a load off." Cora pointed at the diner's ugly green counter. Her feet throbbing, Tammie didn't question the older woman's instruction. Who was she to argue with seniority?

Cora poured coffee into two plain earthenware mugs, leaving enough room for cream. Cora had been the one to teach Tammie the perfect way to pour a cup of coffee. "Just enough cream to watch it bloom to the top. Not a drop more." It was how Tammie served it all the time now. And her increased tips from customers proved the value of the woman's advice.

Now, though, Tammie was serving herself. She tipped the silver-topped sugar dispenser, counting to five before she stopped the white stream. She needed the energy to get through the rest of the night.

She tossed her order pad and pencil on the counter beside her coffee, waiting for Cora to join her. The steam of the second cup swirled upward, and Tammie watched it with tired, nearly unfocused eyes. The shape morphed and swayed in the air conditioner's breath.

"What's that?" Cora leaned over the counter, peering down at Tammie's order pad. "It's pretty."

Tammie stared in horror. Her fingers had instinctively picked up the pencil and sketched the steam, creating flowing waves and pockets where her creativity planned to settle precious stones. It was a good design. She could take the gold and fold it just here—

No! Tammie ripped the page free and tore it into tiny pieces. If she had a match she'd have burned it. Instead, she scattered the pieces into the bus tray behind the counter, watching, painfully, as they sank into the dumped ice waters and coffee. The pencil lead disappeared into the damp.

"What'd you do that for?" Cora wasn't accusing, just curious, as she climbed up on the old vinyl stool and settled.

Tammie shrugged, knowing that would be answer enough, at least for Cora. She couldn't let Cora see her work, and she couldn't let anyone ever know what she could do. Not until she figured out a solution—until she figured out a way to escape for good.

"It was just silliness." She dismissed the design with a wave of her hand, but cringed when she saw the spark of curiosity linger in Cora's faded blue eyes. Despite having destroyed the drawing, Tammie still saw it in her mind, felt her fingers itch to pick up the pencil and finish it, felt the longing to hold her tools and work with the materials she'd so loved.

They finished their coffee in silence, both women fighting exhaustion as their shift stretched out.

"I'm gonna get a quick breath of air," she told Cora. "Be right back." Tammie needed, just for a minute, to be alone. And while the alley out back was the last place in the world she wanted to be, with its hefty thick stink and dirt, it was dark and empty. At least for now.

The back door was heavy metal but it was never closed. A supposed fire door, it gave little protection. The screen door was all that separated the kitchen from the alley. She let it slam closed behind her, needing something to separate her from this life she'd been forced into.

She looked up at the sliver of sky she could barely see between this building and the filthy one across the alley. She could almost make out the sparkle of a single star beyond the city lights and clouds. Closing her eyes to seal in the damp that threatened to fall over the edge of her lashes, she let her mind have its silence.

She'd been little when her mother had taught her to make a wish on her first star. "Star light, star bright," she whispered. The rest of the words rushed through her head, but not past her lips. Not here. Tyler's little face flashed into her mind, but she refused to let it go any further. She'd taught him the silly rhyme. Did he remember it? Or would he soon forget it, and her?

She forced her thoughts elsewhere. He was not a part of this world, of the level she'd sunk to. No, he was safe and in a good place. She'd made sure of that.

Never here.

She needed to get back inside. Blinking rapidly, this time not because of tears, but the bright fluorescent lights of the kitchen, she hurried inside. There were voices in the dining room. A couple, half-drunk, had settled in the front booth while two young men stood at the door waiting to be seated.

"And here we go." Cora whipped by Tammie, a tray in one hand and the perpetual coffee carafe in the other.

Tammie grabbed her now-bare order pad from where she'd left it on the counter and shoved it back into her apron pocket. She seated the two men and headed back to the kitchen with their order, hearing the door open again. Yep, the rush was back. Thank goodness.

DJ STARED OUT the window at Brooke Army Medical Center. The whip-snap sound of the flags outside came through the glass and took him back. Too far back. He cursed and turned away from the sight of the fabric dancing at the end of the thick metal poles. That was not why he was here.

"Tell me straight, Doc." He knew what the doctor was going to say, but he wanted to hear the words.

"I think you know what the answer is," the doctor guessed.

"Yeah, but humor me. Say it."

The silence in the exam room was heavy, and DJ wanted to fill it with cursing. Instead, he sat still, meeting the doctor's hesitant gaze with a glare.

"You've reached a plateau. At this point I don't foresee any measurable improvement."

"So the discharge stands?" DJ said through clenched teeth.

The doc looked at him and simply nodded. He didn't move. He seemed to barely breathe. He didn't like being here any more than DJ did. DJ knew that, but dang it, it wasn't his life that was going down the drain.

Without another word, DJ slowly, stiffly stood, then walked to the door and threw it open. He stepped out into the hall, his gait uneven as he moved down the narrow hallway. He knew it was hotter than hell outside, but he walked out into the late afternoon anyway. He wasn't coming back here, and he couldn't wait to escape.

The huge Harley he'd ridden in on sat just where he'd left it, the frame baking in the sun. The bright blue paint on the tank and fenders glistened in the leftover sunlight, the chrome winking at him. If he had "plateaued," why the hell could he drive this monster? They'd told him he couldn't do that. They'd told him he might not walk, yet here he was. How did they know he couldn't still be a soldier? They wouldn't even let him try.

He straddled the bike and kicked it to life, filling the air with the throaty roar of the engine and all the curse words he hadn't let fly inside the hospital.

He wasn't in the mood to go back home. *Home.* Was that what Wyatt's ranch was? It wasn't really. It never would be, even with all the family memories that lurked within its walls. The only thing even slightly homelike there was his son, Tyler. And Tyler seemed at home there as anyplace else he would be.

DJ was the one who didn't know what home was.

He headed east, in the general direction of the ranch, but when he hit the freeway, he passed the regular turnoff and instead headed north…and kept going.

The hot wind slid over his skin. Heck, now he could let his hair grow out. He could dress more like himself, instead of in the endless parade of ugly camo. He could… His thoughts ended. All he saw ahead was emptiness.

The machine ate up the miles. He knew what he had to do. He knew where he should go. He knew… But before that he needed space, time to himself and a drink.

The Lucky Chance Bar was technically only fifteen miles away from Wyatt's ranch—if you were a crow. It took DJ the same two hours to get there over the winding roads. He pulled the bike into the dirt parking lot and let the engine fall quiet for a while before he climbed off.

The rough country bar was where DJ had cut his drinking teeth as a young man. Since he'd been home, he'd avoided the place, too afraid that the lure of oblivion would be too strong to resist. Tonight, he knew he'd failed. There was no more resisting. All his nightmares were coming true.

By the time DJ was settled in the booth at the back of the bar, alone, where he'd sat countless times back in the day, his mind was full of memories of the recent past.

Decisions needed to be made and DJ was avoiding making them. He knew that. Medical discharge. He'd have a couple months of terminal leave before it was all final, but it might as well be today. He was done.

"You still like warm beer, I see."

DJ looked up. Standing beside the table was a tall, lanky cowboy. He couldn't see the guy's face, what with the shadow of his hat brim and the dim lights, but there was something familiar about the guy… The comment was what seemed more familiar.

"Yeah, guess I do." The beer and oblivion had seemed so appealing until the reality was right here in front of him.

"Your memory get killed over in that desert?"

The man's thick Texas drawl rang a few warning

bells in DJ's brain. DJ frowned. He'd only known one guy— "Lane?"

The other half of that troublesome teenage summer when Granddad had nearly killed DJ stood there, proud as can be.

"About danged time you woke up." Lane grinned and slid into the seat across from DJ without waiting for an invitation.

They shook hands over the scarred table as DJ's brain filled with a wave of memory. *This couldn't be good. Not good at all.* But he leaned back in the booth and looked at the man who'd been a boy the last time he'd seen him.

A very drunk boy if memory served. DJ smiled.

Lane took off the worn cowboy hat, setting it on the table. He looked rough around the edges. DJ hadn't seen him in a couple of years, since the last time he'd come home before his last deployment.

"So, how's your family doing?" Lane asked.

DJ smiled. "That'll take a couple of hours. Next topic. How's your dad?"

"Fair enough." Years ago, probably at this same table, they'd sworn to keep their messed-up, convoluted families out of their intent to have fun. Seemed not everything had changed over time.

"So, whatcha doin' here?" Lane looked up. "Haven't seen you since you got back. Heard you were injured."

"Yeah. Trying to heal." DJ didn't want to go into details and the waitress came over just then and saved him from doing so. He bought a round, but DJ realized he'd lost his appetite for bars and hangovers. Lane's appearance reminded him of how miserable the aftermath always was. They'd nearly killed each other too damn many times.

They drank their beers slowly, in silence. "Damn, we're old," DJ finally said.

Lane laughed. "Speak for yourself, old man." He became serious quickly. "I guess I've spent too much time sobering up my dad lately. Takes the fun out of it." When the waitress returned, Lane ordered a round of coffee and they both laughed.

"Here's a surprise for you." DJ leaned forward on the table, hoping to take some of the pressure off his back. The bench was hard. "I got a kid. He's eight."

Lane stared. "No kidding." Something other than surprise flashed in Lane's eyes, but DJ couldn't tell what it was. "How'd that happen?"

"The usual way." DJ shrugged. "He's staying with us at the ranch house. You should come meet him sometime."

"I might do that. I've been meaning to get over to see Wyatt. So, when do you go back?"

Damned reality. "I'm not." DJ hadn't told anyone about the doctor's final decision. He hadn't called Wyatt or any of his siblings. He'd come straight here.

"What?"

"They just told me today. I'm being medically discharged." There, he'd said it. It didn't sound nearly as bad as it had echoing around in his head.

"That's why you're here tonight?"

"Yeah."

"That it?

"What's that supposed to mean?"

"Just seems like a stupid reason to be drinking." Lane stood, grabbing his hat from the table. As if uncomfortable with the conversation and needing distraction, he gathered up the empty bottles and placed them on the bar.

The door opened just then and a much older, worn version of Lane stumbled in.

"Ah, right on time." Lane turned back to DJ. "Go home to your boy. Now you've got the time to be a dad."

The one thing that had made them such good friends as boys was the fact that they'd each grown up with a single parent. Lane's mother had died the same year as DJ's dad. But where Mom had taken up the reins, Lane's dad dived into a bottle. Apparently, nothing had changed.

DJ watched them leave, knowing any offers of help wouldn't be appreciated. Instead, he stood and headed out to his motorcycle. Lane was right.

He headed home, where he should have gone in the first place.

Twenty minutes later, headed toward the front steps of the ranch house, DJ heard a voice quietly echo in the darkness. He stopped and listened for a minute. Nothing. He needed to get to bed. Even if he wanted to he couldn't sleep in. Life around here started just after dawn in a loud, raucous, let's-get-to-work way.

Most days, DJ liked that. He'd learned, early on in the military, to find a way to fill the void, to keep his brain busy and away from the what-ifs.

And there were plenty of what-ifs these days. What if the military actually medically retired him? He laughed. That wasn't *really* a what-if anymore. They were going to. It was only a matter of paperwork and time.

What if Tammie never returned? Was he ready to support a kid for ten or more years? How? His wounds were still healing. Would he ever be able to hold a job? What could he do to earn enough to support himself and Tyler?

His head spun, not from the two beers he'd nursed through the visit with Lane, but from pushing himself so hard. From exhaustion. He tried to focus on the steps in front of him.

DJ heard the voice again. He hadn't had *that* much. Two beers did not constitute drunk. His muscles had stiffened up on the ride home so he moved carefully, walking over to the side of the house.

There wasn't anyone there. A noise, something cracking, sounded overhead. He looked up and saw something—someone—in the old cottonwood tree.

Tyler.

"I can see you," he said softly. No response. "I can still see you, son." DJ leaned nonchalantly against the corner of the porch rail. He didn't want to startle

Tyler. Despite the fact that DJ had climbed that same tree often enough as a kid and knew it was fairly safe, Tyler was still perched a good fifteen feet up.

"Am I in trouble?" Tyler mumbled.

"Depends. *Why* are you in the tree in the middle of the night?"

The silence stretched out and DJ let it. He'd learned patience was important with Tyler, especially when he was thinking.

"I like the tree. I was lookin' at the stars." A long silence again. "Mama likes stars. Says they look like jewels."

DJ took a deep breath. "Why don't you come down and look at them from the porch with me?" Closer to the ground.

Tyler seemed to be thinking again, and then DJ heard movement. He went to stand beneath the tree just in case Tyler fell, then laughed at himself when Tyler hopped down and crawled back over the windowsill and into his room. A few minutes later, the screen door squeaked open softly.

If nothing else, Tyler was unpredictable. He climbed up onto the porch swing and set it slowly in motion. DJ took a seat across from him in one of the wooden rockers.

"Did you think about the dirt bike?" Tyler grinned.

"I'm still thinking about that." He ignored the crestfallen look. Diplomacy had never been DJ's forte, but he drew on every memory he had of Wyatt's and his friend Colin's skills. He'd worked too hard to gain Tyler's trust. He didn't want to screw it up now. "Besides, if I told you my decision, what kind of birthday surprise would that be?"

"I suppose." Appeased, but not happy, Tyler swung his legs to get the swing moving again.

He didn't say anything else, and DJ racked his brain to come up with a topic of conversation. "So, your mom likes stars and jewels, huh?" he ventured.

"Yep. She makes jewelry. Or she used to…" His voice faded off.

"Why do you think she stopped?"

"'Cause of Dom."

He still didn't think Tyler was abused, not over the long haul, but he knew the jerk had done something to him. Tyler's fears were real. "Your mom's boyfriend, right?"

Maybe DJ could learn more in the shadows tonight. He treaded lightly. "What'd he do? *Make* her stop?"

The swing creaked. "No," Tyler whispered.

Great. Open-ended questions, he reminded himself. "What did he do?"

"I dunno, but she didn't like it. She cried. A lot."

DJ didn't pursue what might have happened between the adults. He'd leave that for later. "Did she have a lot of stuff?"

"Yeah. It was cool. She used to let me watch her. She had real gold and silver. And a hot thing that melted metal and made it all stick together."

"Sounds pretty complicated."

The swing creaked again, and DJ watched Tyler nod.

"She used to let me play with some of the jewels," Tyler said softly. "Not the 'spensive ones, though."

"Expensive? Like what?"

"Diamonds. She had other real pretty ones she liked best, even more than diamonds. She called 'em moonstones." Tyler paused. "I like them best, too."

"Wow." DJ was shocked and impressed. "Diamonds. And moonstones. Must be pretty good money in that kind of work," he mused aloud.

Tyler was silent. "I don't know." His voice sounded distant, confused.

Maybe the boy's mind was going the same place as DJ's—if she had that kind of money, why hadn't she kept Tyler? Or, hell, if she needed the money, why not sell a diamond?

DJ frowned into the darkness. So many things about Tammie didn't add up. Wyatt had told him about the old, dilapidated house where he'd picked up Tyler—maybe that topic would get the boy talking.

"That house in Austin where Uncle Wyatt picked you up. That where you guys lived?" He thought he knew the answer but wanted to hear what Tyler had to say.

Silence came out of the darkness. No swing creaks. No soft words. Just pure nighttime.

DJ leaned toward his son, waiting.

"No." Tyler paused. "We just borrowed it for a little while."

"Where'd you really live?" DJ watched as Tyler looked around, glancing into the night with wide, nervous eyes.

"Different places."

DJ tried to remain patient. He knew that his son had gone to several different schools, and he was only eight. "That's not much help, buddy."

Tyler turned wide eyes to DJ. Tyler jumped off the porch swing, sending it swaying wildly, nearly hitting the edge of the house. "Help with what? Not like you're gonna find Mama or help her."

DJ stuck his arm out to stop the boy and only managed to connect an elbow with the flying wood. He cursed.

"Tyler, stop." The boy was already up the stairs before DJ could struggle to his feet. He stopped at the screen door and let him go. He wasn't going to solve anything tonight. He shoved his fingers through his hair. Growing out already, it was driving him crazy. Slowly, he paced back and forth over the worn boards. Help her with what?

At the edge of the porch, he stopped and stared out at the land beyond the yard. The horizon to the east was just starting to glow a faint red. He sighed. He hadn't realized how late it had gotten…or rather, how early. He didn't have anywhere to go today. His therapy had been cut down to twice a week. But Tyler had school in a few short hours.

Despite the fact that Tammie had dumped Tyler on Wyatt's doorstep without a glance backward, the boy was eternally loyal to his mother.

DJ froze, staring at the red glow on the horizon. Loyalty wasn't something a person could *make* you have. It was earned. It was given. Never taken.

He turned to look back at the screen door, seeing the shadow of the stairs beyond. Once inside, he took the steps slowly, carefully. He didn't think he'd ever take the ability to climb stairs for granted again. It ticked him off, though, that it was such a struggle, especially when he was in a hurry, like now.

Finally, at the top, he paused and caught his breath. Then turned toward Tyler's room, which was across the hall from his own. The door was closed. DJ slowly pushed the old wood panel door open, the original hinges squeaking softly in the near-dawn air.

Tyler was huddled on the bed, curled in a ball, his shoulders silently shaking. DJ didn't hesitate. He walked across the room, his footsteps incredibly loud in the sleeping house. "Hey, buddy." He settled in the chair beside the bed and felt the stab of regret when Tyler scooted away from him, closer to the wall.

"I'm sorry. I didn't mean to upset you or make you think I don't care about your mom. I liked her once, remember?" No answer.

DJ racked his brain for the right thing to say. "I need to ask you something," DJ finally said. Still no answer. "You see, I realized something—you wouldn't be so worried about her if you really thought she'd abandoned you, would you?"

This time Tyler turned his head and looked over his thin shoulder at DJ. His expression was far from trusting, but he was interested. DJ ventured further.

"So, if she didn't leave you…do you think she's in trouble?" DJ moved, and though it hurt like hell, he knelt on the floor beside the bed.

The silence stretched out and he tried to guess what Tyler was thinking. Finally, DJ had to speak up. Damn, he hated feeling so inadequate.

"You know—" DJ leaned back to see Tyler more clearly and tried to shift the mood to relaxed and comfortable "—when I first met your mom, she was fun and pretty and smart."

"In Florida, right?"

"Yep. On the beach." DJ let his mind fill with the memories of that night. God, it felt like a million years and miles ago. "We had a good time together." Obviously, as Tyler was the result, he added silently. "I get the feeling she's not having fun anymore."

Tyler shook his head slowly.

"If she's scared enough to send you away, we need to find out why. Help her."

"No." Tyler vehemently shook his head, surprising DJ when he sat up and launched himself at DJ, wrapping his arms around DJ's neck to hold on tight.

Disentangling the boy's arms, DJ peered down at Tyler's face, hardening his heart to the damp on the boy's cheeks. "I can protect her from whatever or whomever she needs protection from. You know I'm a marine. We're tough. You saw what Uncle Wyatt and I can do to protect the people we love."

DJ still had nightmares of that night Wyatt's girlfriend, Emily, and Tyler had been attacked. Her nutcase stepbrother had tried to use Tyler to get to Emily. She'd handled it all really well—the best she could—but if they hadn't shown up, who knew what would have happened. Tyler had thought of him as a hero ever since, and DJ had to admit, he liked it.

"Yeah," Tyler murmured. "But—"

"But what?" DJ carefully prompted.

"She made me promise."

"Promise what?"

"Not to tell." Tyler shook his head again. "Not to tell *anyone*. Ever."

Something told DJ even the lure of the dirt bike wasn't going to budge this kid. He had to admire him…and hurt for him.

Damn, Tammie. What the hell have you done?

CHAPTER THREE

WYATT WAS IN the barn, exactly where DJ expected to find him. With the weekend's arrival, the big farmhouse was overrun with women, and DJ was as uncomfortable with it as the rest of the now-scarce men. Big family gatherings had always been the norm. Heck, with six kids, dinner was a big family gathering.

But today DJ wasn't in the mood, and neither, apparently, was Wyatt.

The jangle of metal and leather told DJ that Wyatt was cleaning tack. DJ stopped in the doorway of the small room and watched Wyatt rub the glycerin soap onto the leather.

"What's up?" Wyatt asked.

DJ took a deep breath and stepped into the room. He hadn't planned what he was going to say, but he had to tell Wyatt the truth. Had to let him know about the decision he'd made.

"The other night I caught Tyler sitting up in the old cottonwood," DJ began. "I don't think it was the first time."

That made Wyatt whip his head up and his hands stopped moving. "What was he doing?" Dread filled Wyatt's voice.

"Just sittin', staring at the stars."

"You know why?" Wyatt relaxed a little, returning his focus to his work.

"I think so. He eventually came down and we talked." DJ tried to wrap his brain around the information, or rather, lack of information, Tyler had shared with him.

Wyatt waited.

"I'm worried," DJ finally admitted.

"About Tyler?"

DJ paused before shaking his head. "No. About Tammie." Wyatt's frown reflected his confusion. DJ moved to sit on the bench near Wyatt. "I know she's in trouble. Big trouble. She made Tyler swear not to tell anyone anything, and he's sticking to that promise."

Wyatt paused, thinking for a long minute. "I've wondered why he doesn't say much." They had both tried to get info out of him, with no luck. "You think he's afraid?"

DJ pondered the question. Sitting still was killing his back and legs. His muscles were tight from lack of sleep lately. He needed the rest, but the stress of his worry was eating him alive. He gave up and paced.

"I need to find her," he finally said. He didn't have to wait long for Wyatt's response.

"And do what? Let her have Tyler back?" Wyatt's anger was controlled, barely. "Emily said you'd mentioned doing that. What if there's nothing to find? Sounds like she doesn't want to be found."

Wyatt watched him, waiting. The silence was deafening. DJ gritted his teeth. "No. Tyler's my son. Her wishes aren't what's important. But Tyler is."

Wyatt shook his head and resumed his work. "What makes you think you can find her? The private investigator didn't discover much."

"Tyler knows something. I just have to get him to talk."

"How? I don't think the bribery you had planned will work."

"No." DJ paced back and forth a few more times. "That's what actually made me realize I have to do this. His loyalty is solid. Too solid for a kid not wanted by his mother."

Wyatt didn't respond. The sound of his work and a stray whinny from the direction of the stalls filled the heavy silence.

DJ couldn't take it anymore. "Okay, get it over with."

"What?"

"I don't know. Yell at me. Do that whole older-brother thing. Tell me I'm making a mistake. Something!"

Wyatt remained silent, staring down at his own hands for a long minute. DJ tried to guess what he was going to say. Then Wyatt looked up.

DJ barely remembered their father, who'd died when DJ was six. But while he didn't remember the man that much, he remembered that look. DJ swallowed. Why had he started this whole conversation?

"Deej, I can't tell you what to do this time. I wish I could."

DJ cursed. He'd been counting on Wyatt to guide him.

"I'll admit I'm not happy about this." Wyatt's voice shook. "I've watched you work too hard to recover, and to build your relationship with Tyler, to just—"

"Just what?" DJ asked after several seconds of quiet passed.

"Risk losing it all for a woman you don't even know."

That's where Wyatt was wrong, and where DJ had to admit he'd been wrong, too. "I knew her once," he whispered. Contradictory memories filled his mind. "I can't put that woman together with someone who'd abandon her son."

Wyatt nodded, and DJ wasn't sure if it was in agreement or submission.

"When will you tell Tyler?"

"I don't know. I'm not sure how." This was a new role for him. Here at home, he'd always been the younger brother, taking orders from half a dozen wannabe parents. In the military, his commanding officer and the mission told him what to do. He looked over at Wyatt, hoping he'd give him some direction.

"When your commanding officer called, it nearly killed me to think of you hurt. But it was worse knowing I had to tell Tyler. Deej, that's the hardest thing I've ever had to do." Wyatt looked down and

DJ turned away, looking out over the row of stalls instead of at his brother.

"Sorry." He didn't know what else to say.

"That's not what I meant." DJ heard Wyatt's footsteps behind him. "What I'm trying to say is, I understand. I—" Wyatt swallowed. "I hate to admit it, but I agree. He's a tough kid, but he needs this done."

"Yeah." DJ knew both those things.

"And so do you." Wyatt's big hand clamped DJ's shoulder reassuringly. "You need this, too." DJ didn't even want to think about that piece of the screwed-up puzzle.

"Dad! Uncle Wyatt!" Tyler's voice broke the quiet of the barn. DJ looked back at Wyatt. He hoped that Tyler hadn't overheard what they were talking about—he wanted a little more time to formulate the words.

"In here," DJ called, watching as Tyler came running into the tack room, his too-big cowboy boots clumping against the packed dirt. Tyler was out of breath and tried to talk and breathe all at once. "Slow down, buddy."

"I… A…hawk. It just—" Tyler flapped his hands in the air, imitating a bird. "Swooped down. Like this. It got one of the doves!" His voice cracked. "It was cool. But—" The boy struggled with the contradiction between the wonder of life and death.

Wyatt didn't speak, staying quiet, letting DJ take the lead. While it thrilled DJ to be able to deal with his son…it also scared the hell out of him. What if he messed up? What if he said the wrong thing? He tried to remember being eight.

"It's cool and creepy all at once, huh?"

"Yeah." Tyler nodded and settled on the bench next to Wyatt. "Whatcha doin'?"

Wyatt glanced up at DJ, then back down at the boy. "Cleaning tack. Want to help?"

"Sure."

Carefully, Wyatt explained what to do. Tyler was awkward, but eager. And Wyatt simply waited and guided. DJ wondered if he'd ever have his brother's patience and skill with the boy. He shook his head. "Ty?" he asked.

"Yeah."

"The other night, when we were talking on the porch, I know you were tired. But you remember what we talked about?"

Tyler didn't speak or look up from the strip of leather—it looked huge in his small hands.

"Well, I was talking with Wyatt about it."

That made Tyler look up. The panic in his eyes tore through DJ, but instead of making him rethink his decision, it only strengthened his resolve.

"Do you remember what I said?"

Tyler nodded and looked down. DJ heard him sniff and almost changed his mind. Wyatt held back, which he knew was killing his older brother, but DJ appreciated it. Slowly, painfully, DJ hunkered down beside his son. The dirt dug into his injured knees but he endured the discomfort. "I can't ignore what you told me." DJ settled his big hand on Tyler's leg. "I just told Wyatt that I'm worried about your mom. I bet you are, too, right?"

Tyler simply nodded and shoved a fist across his eyes before looking up, his gaze bouncing back and forth between the two men.

Wyatt remained quiet, his jaw clenched. DJ wished he could be the silent one. Dread washed over him.

"I was hoping you'd help me find her."

Silence stretched out. "What if she doesn't want to come back?" Tyler finally whispered. "She shoulda been back by now."

"Maybe." DJ thought the same thing, but heck, who knew why she'd left Tyler. Maybe she couldn't come back. He didn't want to think about that, and he certainly didn't want to voice his concerns to his son. "Let's cross that bridge when we get to it, okay?"

"'Kay. What are we gonna do?"

The silence was heavy, and DJ briefly worried that he might not be able to find her. That was a scary prospect and one he wasn't willing to accept. He'd found devious militants hiding in remote caves in the mountains. He could find one woman.

"*We* aren't." DJ hated himself for the disappointment that took over Tyler's young face. "I am." He knew Tyler thought he and Wyatt were the cavalry, and that they could do just about anything. He hated shattering that hero worship.

"You can't go without me!" Tyler cried and jumped off the bench. "I won't tell you anything unless you let me go with you." He stomped an oversize cowboy boot with little effect.

"Tyler." Wyatt finally spoke up. "Listen to your dad for a minute."

"I don't want to."

"*Want* doesn't have anything to do with it." Wyatt's voice grew stern and Tyler quieted.

Slowly, Tyler trudged back to the bench. His bottom lip quivered, but he didn't give in. "How will you know where to look?"

"I'm gonna start with everything you know. Then I'm going to call a couple of my marine buddies to help."

Tyler's eyes lit up. "You're gonna call in the marines to find my mom?"

DJ met Wyatt's gaze. It wasn't quite what he'd meant, but if it worked to get Tyler's cooperation, he'd let him believe anything.

"Cool!" Tyler said, then he surprised and pleased DJ with a hug before running out of the barn.

Wyatt waited until Tyler was out of earshot before he spoke again. "I'm okay with it, but you'd better tell everyone else. I'm not filling them in."

"Afraid of Addie's wrath, are you?" DJ only halfway teased—they were both aware of their oldest sister's strong personality.

"Damn straight I am. You'd better be, too." They both laughed and followed Tyler to the house. "He's probably already told them all. Be prepared."

Wyatt's farmhouse was big enough for the whole

Hawkins family. The oversize country kitchen was loud with all the voices. No one said anything to him as he entered, but DJ saw the sideways glances. He wasn't even surprised when everyone settled expectantly in the living room after dinner.

As a kid, DJ had hated the big family meetings, so it was with a healthy dose of chagrin that he realized he was the cause of this one.

The last time they'd all been together had been at Mom's funeral, though most of them had managed to show up at the meeting when he'd been discharged from the hospital.

Poor Emily. He glanced over at the pretty judge who was perched on the arm of the couch next to Wyatt. The whole bunch of them had probably scared her half to death at first. Though she seemed used to them all now and didn't seem too spooked. Maybe it was because she only had eyes for Wyatt these days. And the sappy look on his brother's face said he was pleased about the whole thing.

DJ dragged one of the dining chairs from the kitchen, knowing there weren't enough seats, and he couldn't sit on the soft couch and stand back up without the help of the solid chair. He settled just inside the doorway.

He took in everyone around him. They all looked good. The big homemade meal the girls had put together was delicious, with Addie's famous cookies to cap it off. Tyler had gone to the barn with Chet, the ranch foreman, to help put the animals down for the night. DJ knew what was coming next, and he wasn't disappointed.

"What's Tyler talking about?" Addie started the conversation. Her gaze found DJ.

"What do you mean?"

"Don't even try to act innocent, David James. He said you were going to look for his mother?"

DJ looked around. Every eye in the place was on him. Despite the fact that he loved each one of them, his stomach flipped. He really didn't want to get into this. He'd been on his own for years—hell, he'd been overseas fighting a war. Why did facing off with Addie scare him more than staring down a terrorist?

He sat up straighter and looked directly at his oldest sister. "He's right. I'm going to find Tammie."

"Why?" Addie's voice was full of anger. "What for?"

"It's not up for negotiation, Ad," DJ said softly.

"Surely you're not taking Tyler with you?" Mandy said, trying to sit up in the overstuffed chair. Maybe he should have given her the wooden chair. Seven months pregnant—and still keeping mum on who the father was—she was already struggling to move.

"No. He's staying here with Wyatt."

Wyatt nodded but didn't speak up. DJ frowned at him in a silent thanks-for-nothing-buddy way.

"What will you accomplish, besides getting Tyler's hopes up, and hurting him?"

"I think there's more to this situation. Something's not right."

"So why do *you* have to go fix it?" Mandy asked. "She gave him up." She rubbed her rounding belly as if caressing her unborn child. "She abandoned him. She doesn't deserve to have him back."

"I didn't say I was giving him back to her." DJ's anger erupted. "He's my son and he's staying with this family, but Tyler needs this."

"Why?" asked Tara, his youngest sister, sprawled on the couch on the other side of Wyatt, her sneaker-clad feet propped up on the scarred coffee table. Her head tilted just a bit to the side as she tried to understand him. She'd always been DJ's biggest supporter; never angry, never judging, she'd quietly listened to dozens of his harebrained schemes growing up. Though he knew she'd shook her head at him many times.

"Tyler believes in her." DJ lifted a hand to stall any more comments. "He wishes on stars to be with her." DJ cleared his throat. "I owe it to him to at least try to figure out what's going on."

Jason sat forward, his forearms on his knees. "Help us out here, Emily. This could jeopardize custody. What if she does want him back? Have you considered that, DJ?" Always the lawyer, Jason thought too legally at times.

Emily frowned. "We'd need to talk to Warren." Warren Litchfield was the judge who'd taken over DJ's custody case once it became clear Emily had lost her objectivity as far as the boy and Wyatt—mostly Wyatt—were concerned.

"Right now, that's not the issue. First we need to figure out what the situation is. And then decide what's next," DJ said.

Suddenly, half a dozen voices filled the room. Every single one of his siblings had an opinion. That was nothing new. And it also wasn't new that he ignored them all. He'd stopped doing what they told him around the time he'd turned sixteen and realized he could drive away in a car.

"Stop it!" Tyler's voice cut through the din. He stood in the open doorway—no one had heard or seen him come in. How long he'd been there was anyone's guess. But from the look on his face, he'd heard plenty.

"She's my mom. Dad *has* to find her." His voice cracked. "'Fore she gets in more trouble. That man might hurt her. Like he hurt me. I know it."

DJ rose to his feet and walked over to his son. Tyler looked up at him, imploring, with tears in his eyes. "Please, Dad. Don't change your mind. Go find her." Tears fell down the boy's cheeks. "I want my mom." Tyler threw his arms around DJ's waist, holding tight.

Slowly, DJ took a step back so he could awkwardly kneel down to peer into his son's face. "Don't worry, buddy. I'll find her. Everyone's just concerned."

"They don't like Mama." Tyler glared at his aunts and uncles. "But she's the best mom. She's just scared. She took care of me the best she could." He hiccuped. "I just wanna go home."

"I know." DJ didn't think this was the time to remind Tyler that this was his home now. Instead, he wrapped his arm around the boy's thin shoulders and turned to face the room of people. His gaze traveled to each one. So familiar to him, but virtual strangers to Tyler. He felt Tyler lean into his side.

"As I said, this isn't up for negotiation. It's a done deal. I'm just letting you all know what we're planning. You can either help, or not. Your choice. But we'd appreciate at least your support."

The room fell silent.

Wyatt spoke first. "You got it. Whatever you need," he said softly, holding Emily's hand. She nodded, too.

Wyatt nudged Tara in the ribs. "Hey, I've always supported him, even with the insane things." Everyone, even Tyler, laughed.

"I'll do whatever you need on the legal end. Just let me know." Jason nodded.

"You got it." Mandy smiled. "Though, in this condition, I'm not much help to anyone." She ran a loving hand over her tummy again, smiling. "Hey, little one, soon you'll get to meet all these aunts and uncles. And a cousin, too," she whispered to the baby.

Addie was the only holdout. And she was the only one besides Wyatt who Tyler really knew. *Don't let him down,* DJ silently pleaded. DJ hugged Tyler, then walked over to face his older sister.

"You…you just be careful, okay?" She stood and

faced him. "I know you think you're the mighty warrior, but we just got you back." Her voice broke.

"I'll be careful, Ad." He looked down at his older sister and saw the sheen in her eyes. "I promise." He glanced back at his son. "I have a whole lot more to lose now."

THE EVEN MOTION of the late-night city bus nearly lulled Tammie to sleep. When something hard hit her shoulder, she jerked awake. Her arms tightened around her backpack the same instant a skinny arm snaked over her shoulder. Dirty, clawlike fingers grasped the strap and tugged hard.

Tammie was worn-out but not stupid.

The would-be thief got more than he bargained for when she yanked hard. "No!" she cried, ripping her backpack free.

"Bitch." The boy spit out the word easily and lunged over the seat.

"Hey!" the bus driver yelled. "What's going on back there?"

"Mind your business, old man."

Tammie took the opportunity to stand and wobble through the aisle, the backpack clutched to her chest. She settled in the seat right behind the driver.

A bus stop loomed ahead and the driver pulled over to the curb. "Off!" the driver yelled. The boy stood, cursing as he exited through the rear doors. She heard his steps fade away in the darkness.

"You, too, lady."

"But—"

"I'm done for the night. Don't need no more trouble. Go on."

The old man glared at her and inclined his head to the open door.

"But my stop's the next one."

"Then you won't have far to walk. Move it."

The dark night was thick outside the lights of the bus. She knew where she was, but that didn't lessen her fear of walking through this neighborhood at night. Alone. Heck, she didn't walk it in the daylight. She normally got off right across the street from work.

The doors squeaked shut and the strong smell of diesel filled the air as the bus moved away. No time for standing around. She had three blocks to go. Three long, dark blocks.

Her footsteps seemed loud in the darkness as she nearly ran, glancing over her shoulder several times, just in case the thief was still lurking in the shadows.

Tammie clung tight to the backpack she'd filled all those months ago in Florida, cataloging what was inside with each step. Her toiletries. Her underwear. Two pairs of jeans, one set of sweats and three T-shirts. Her wallet. A set of keys that now belonged to nothing since she'd sold her car and had abandoned her house. Two sample pieces of the jewelry she'd made that had been in the pack from that last, fateful show. They'd still been in the pack when she'd tossed in everything else.

And there was a book.

The hardcover copy of *Wuthering Heights* wasn't just for reading, though it was good for that, too. Nestled in between the pages was all she had left of Tyler. His baby pictures. His first school photo. The awkward goodbye note he'd written when she'd told him to go with his uncle Wyatt. And all the money she had in the world stuck in different pages. Five hundred and forty-six dollars. The thirty-three cents at the bottom of the backpack jangled every once in a while when she moved.

Everything else was gone.

Stolen by Dom. Destroyed by his thugs. Or just plain used up.

She refused to cry. Absolutely refused to give in. Her father had always accused her of being stubborn. Maybe for once his being right was a good thing.

The fleeting thought of her parents was like a speed bump and she nearly stumbled. Righting herself, she leaned on the wall of a darkened building to catch her breath. She just wanted to find a hole and crawl into it.

Tammie had no idea what to do next. No clue how to get her life back. She'd tried confronting Dom. But that's what had caused him to turn on her in the first place, made him destroy everything she'd worked so hard for. She'd tried going to the authorities to ask for help. What a joke. She had no real proof. No clout. Nothing. They'd told her there was nothing they could do.

Despite the frightening warning she'd been given by his buddies, she'd filed a report anyway. But it hadn't done any good.

A copy of that police report was nestled between her book's pages, as well.

She'd done everything she could think of, only to lose over and over again to him.

And so she'd finally run.

And he'd followed. Always finding her. Always destroying what little she'd managed to build.

Belatedly, she'd figured out that he found them whenever she registered Tyler for school. She couldn't take him out of school—she wouldn't do that to him—yet changing cities and schools every couple of months was damaging and a waste. His education had definitely suffered and that had been another reason to give him up until she could figure out how to fix her situation—and keep Tyler safe.

Her throat ached, clogged with tears of frustration and loss.

She just wanted to go home. All the places she'd lived over the past year flashed behind her closed eyelids. The tiny bungalow she'd bought in Florida hurt the most to think about. Her studio. Tyler's bedroom full of his toys. Her room with the soft mattress and her favorite blue decorations. She even missed the leaky pipe in the bathroom.

All of it gone.

Anger replaced the threatening tears. She wanted it back. All of it.

She'd do whatever she could to get it back.

Slowly, wiping her eyes on her shoulder, Tammie stood away from the wall. She took a deep breath and started walking again. One way or another, she was going home.

When she rounded the corner where the diner sat, the bright lights of the block eased her fears. The diner. The liquor store. The pawnshop…

She'd met the owner of the pawnshop when he'd come into the diner a couple weeks ago. Nice, older guy. Tipped good.

Stepping inside the brightly lit store, Tammie noticed that the pawnshop was huge. Every last corner was filled with pieces of furniture, electronics galore, some odd stuffed animal heads on the wall and cases of jewelry. She'd never seen anything like it. Tammie ignored most of it, especially the jewelry cases—it would hurt too much. Instead, she walked purposefully to the cases at the back. Five hundred and forty-six dollars wouldn't buy her a new gun. It wouldn't buy her a big gun.

But it would buy her a working one.

Her hands shook as she held the cold metal…thing in the palm of her hand.

"You know how to shoot that, lady?" the kid behind the counter asked.

"Not yet," was all she said.

She knew she was taking a risk, filling out all the paperwork, but if Dom were following her—maybe he'd think twice knowing she was armed.

Her resolve and anger slipped into place and she calmed. Carefully, she counted the precious bills out onto the counter, leaving herself with barely enough money to eat until she got paid on Friday.

She headed out into the artificially lit night toward the diner. She'd be early—again—but Cora didn't mind her crashing in the tiny break room, as long as she was ready and on her feet in time for the rush.

She hefted her backpack, its newly added weight comforting. She was ready.

CHAPTER FOUR

DJ PULLED WYATT'S truck over to the curb and killed the engine. The worn streets and should-be-condemned houses reminded him too much of an Afghan village he'd been to once. A lifetime ago. Despite the Texas heat, he shivered and stared at the house beyond the wire fence.

A good hundred years old, it was probably an old farmhouse that the urban sprawl had engulfed. It didn't look like the rest of the block. Older. Worn.

The porch ran downhill and a coonhound rested on the uneven boards. DJ climbed out and crossed the street. He opened the gate, and the hound lifted its head. DJ didn't hear a growl or see much other movement. A good sign.

He'd worn his fatigues and driven the big black truck today on purpose. He wanted Cora—was that her name?—to be able to figure out who he was. Tyler seemed to like the old woman and her coonhound—Rufus? Yeah, that was his name. Rufus. Tyler had said they'd been really good people.

DJ knew the dog wasn't a threat. Tyler had told him that and had given him info on the dog treats the hound liked best. His pocket was packed with a bagful. So far the dog hadn't moved except to swish an ear at the fly that buzzed him.

"Hello?" DJ called, hoping someone would step out and greet him. Yeah, right. He'd more likely get his head blown off. Slowly, he took a couple of steps. Waited. Another two steps.

"That's far enough," an old woman's voice called from an open window.

"Cora?" he called out.

"Yeah. Who's askin'?"

"DJ. DJ Hawkins." He had nothing to lose at this point. This woman was a good person according to Tyler. She'd helped Tammie hide from whatever or whomever she was running from. She'd been the one to find Wyatt and help Tyler get to him. She cared, and for that DJ respected her. "I'm looking for Tammie Easton."

"Yeah? Well, she ain't here."

Despite the negative responses, DJ felt as if he was making progress. "Well, I know she was a friend of yours. Do you know where she might be?"

"Why should I tell you?"

He knew what he wanted to say. Should he? What the hell. "Tyler wants his mother back." He took a step forward. "And I agree." Well, mostly he did, but admitting that part wouldn't get him any answers.

The elderly woman who stepped out onto the tilting porch wasn't even five feet tall. The shotgun she held in her hands looked huge in comparison and was aimed straight at his chest. Not the first time he'd stared down the barrel of a gun. A trickle of sweat sneaked down his back.

Tyler had said Cora would know who he was. If Tammie was here, he hoped she'd recognize him and speak up. Preferably before the shotgun got seriously involved.

"Afternoon, ma'am." He knew he'd have to draw on every ounce of his Southern charm and manners. Cora was old-school. Slowly, the tiny woman made her way down the steps, the gun barrel never wavering. He extended a hand, but she didn't take it—she'd have had to take one off the gun to do so. He let his hand drop back to his side.

The silence stretched out. DJ could almost see the wheels turn in the old woman's head.

"I know who you are, young man. If I did know where..." Her voice lowered, and she and the gun moved closer. "Why should I tell you?"

"'Cause Tyler's birthday is coming up and he's not too happy about his mom missing it."

"That boy." She fought a smile, and then, shaking her head, she sobered. "He doing okay?"

"Yeah. Real good."

"Look here." She shook the shotgun as if to emphasize her point. "You didn't hear this from me, but you might want to have yourself a nice big piece of pie at the Half Cup Café, sometime after ten p.m."

"She workin' there?"

"I can't say any more." The woman glanced around and shook the gun again for good measure. The softened look on her face no longer held the same threat, though. “You give that boy a hug for me, you hear me?” She leaned in for added emphasis.

DJ lifted his hands in surrender, completing her show for whoever she believed was watching. “I’ve got a gift for the dog from Tyler—in my pocket.”

“Reach for it real careful.” She waved with the gun and DJ fought the urge to smile. He slowly reached into his pocket and pulled out the bag. “Now drop it on the ground.” He got the distinct impression this woman had seen a few too many Westerns in her day. But he’d play along. She’d given him the info he needed.

“Thanks for your time, ma’am.”

She didn’t say any more, but he didn’t hear her move away, either. DJ went back to the truck and climbed in. It wasn’t until he stopped at the end of the street, and glanced in the rearview mirror, that he saw the gun lower. She bent and picked up the bag, stuffing it into her pocket before scurrying back to the front porch. He smiled when he saw the old dog rise up and follow her inside. Tyler would be happy.

But how would Tammie react when she saw him?

Eight hours later he was close to finding out. DJ leaned against the brick wall of a closed thrift store. It was late. Really late. Maybe too late.

Across the street, the Half Cup Café sat like a beacon at the end of the darkened street. None of the other businesses were open at this hour, and the flash of the open-twenty-four-hours neon sign bathed their darkness with flashes of red.

DJ had gone back out to the ranch after talking to Cora. He'd strategized with Wyatt and swapped the truck for his bike and a duffel bag. Parked at the broken curb, the bike took its turns bathing in the flashing lights.

The diner's glass walls gave him a clear view of the staff and customers inside. The ratty old diner was the last place he wanted to find Tammie. Despite what Cora had told him, he'd hoped somehow that she wouldn't be here, doing this. So far from her dreams—the dreams she'd told him about all those years ago.

He stood there, watching, waiting and wondering for a long time.

Tammie wasn't the only waitress working tonight, but DJ focused solely on her. She moved around, swerving between tables, filling a coffee cup here, a water glass there. She'd been working in an ice cream parlor when they'd met—the years of experience since showed in her easy movements.

Otherwise, she looked like hell. The girl he'd spent a sweet week with nine years ago was long gone. A flash of memory brought her back. A bikini and tan lines.

So beautiful and vibrant—a dreamer of big dreams. That was partly what had drawn him to her, what kept her in his memories and what brought her back so vividly when he'd learned about Tyler.

DJ shook his head. Dozens of questions swirled around him in the night as he continued watching her.

Had *he* been the one who'd broken her dreams? If not, who had?

Lord, they'd been young. He shook his head. Too young to understand the consequences—and too damned stupid.

What had she thought when she'd found out she was pregnant? What would he have done if she had gotten in touch with him back then? He did a little calculating—he would've been smack in the middle of boot camp.

An alternate universe of marriage and diapers flashed in his mind. He shuddered. They'd have never made it. *He'd* have never made it, he amended. She had managed, he begrudgingly admitted, if Tyler was any indication.

He wondered yet again, why *hadn't* she contacted him? He'd given her his mom's address. He remembered the moment clearly, that last night…on the beach…just before they'd…

Frustrated, he shut out the past, reminding himself that she *had* managed to find the info when she'd wanted to dump Tyler.

His anger returned as he thought of his son. DJ forced himself to stay put, out here in the dark, until the urge to storm in and demand answers passed. He figured, from what Tyler had shared, that she'd probably be skittish. Scaring her half to death would not help matters.

Slowly, DJ headed across the street. His steps mea-

hanging limply down her back. Did it still feel as soft…and smell like roses…and the ocean?

She wasn't wearing any makeup and the sad, orange uniform she wore had seen better days, but her smile was warm as she served. The dimple he remembered so vividly flashed in her right cheek, giving him faint hope that maybe the girl he remembered was still in there somewhere.

He remembered her wearing orange once before—a bikini that hid all the right stuff, and not much else. Shaking his head to dispel the memory, he focused on the here and now.

Without mishap, she distributed the plates and carted off the tray. She snagged the coffee carafe from the burner before heading toward him. She didn't look up, focusing on pulling an order pad from her pocket.

DJ held his breath. Waiting.

Two feet away, Tammie finally saw him—and froze. She stared, her eyes growing wide. Somewhere in the distance glass shattered and the coffee carafe lay in a zillion pieces on the tile floor.

TAMMIE'S HEART POUNDED in her chest as she met DJ Hawkins's cold stare. She recognized him immediately. The long blond hair she remembered all too vividly was gone, as she'd expected. But the face was the same—the same one he shared with Tyler.

Breathe, she reminded herself. *Think.* She'd known this could happen—that she'd be found. She'd run through every scenario a dozen times in her mind, but none of those scenarios had starred DJ. Not like this, anyway.

"Hello, Tammie." His voice came out deep and gruff, cutting through her daze. "We need to talk."

The serious tone of his voice sent fear shooting through her. How had he found her, and why? He was angry. That was obvious. She'd expected that, too, considering she hadn't told him about Tyler. But why was he here now?

"Is Tyler okay?" Her fear turned to panic.

DJ frowned. "If you consider how much he misses his mother, and the fact that his dad, who he just met, left him to go find her, yeah, he's okay. Miserable, but okay."

Her heart hurt. She couldn't tell DJ, or anyone, why she'd left Tyler. She didn't dare share the details of the danger she'd put Tyler, and herself, in. A dose of humiliation and a lot of fear kept her quiet.

Reality interrupted as Lindsey wheeled the mop bucket out of the kitchen. Tammie knew the other waitress wasn't coming out to help her. She was being nosy.

Tammie straightened her shoulders, shoring up her determination now that she knew Tyler was okay. "I'm...I'm working. It's not break time yet." Looking around, she knew she could avoid whatever he had to say with all the customers and her coworkers listening.

"I'll wait."

Why did those words scare the hell out of her? She trembled, then grabbed the mop handle as much to give herself an excuse to not talk to him as to clean.

"I'll take a cup of fresh coffee, when you get a minute," he drawled.

Of course, it took her twice as long to clean up the mess with him watching. At least the other diners had gone back to their meals and ignored them. Lindsey, however, was leaning over the counter, watching the scene with interest.

"One coffee. Coming up," Tammie said automatically, moving with stilted, hesitant steps, like a sleepwalker on the verge of waking up. In the back room, she put the bucket away and paced the kitchen. What was she supposed to do now? She glanced at the back door. Only the old, battered screen door stood between her and the alley behind the diner.

She called herself every kind of stupid. She shouldn't have stayed here in Austin. She'd known that, but the idea of leaving, really leaving Tyler behind, was more than she could bear—he was her world. So she'd stayed. Lot of good that did.

Every instinct told her to run now. Run fast and hard while DJ was occupied and not expecting it. Run and hope he'd only found her because Tyler had said something.

Tyler. She missed him so much. Closing her eyes, she pictured him as she'd last seen him. How much had he changed in the few months she'd been away? Curiosity and determination to not give in to her fears had Tammie grabbing the fresh coffee and heading back to DJ's table. "I… Is…Tyler…settling in okay with you?"

"He's fine."

Her hand shook as she poured the coffee.

"I'm not going anywhere." His voice sounded almost reassuring. He didn't say any more but instead looked pointedly around the room. "We'll talk when we're alone."

Alone. She gulped. She didn't dare let him get her alone. He'd ask questions she couldn't—wouldn't—answer. "Can I get you anything else?" She forced herself to shift gears. Distant-waitress mode was safest. It was where she'd lived for months.

"No, that'll do." He looked up, his gaze hard. "For now."

She shut off her thoughts and made her decision. *Move, feet, move.* She prayed she could get out of here before he caught up to her. Probably a stupid notion, but she had to try.

Tammie walked slowly toward the kitchen, returning the coffee carafe to the burner, and as nonchalantly as possible, she bent down and scooped up her battered backpack. She kept walking, right through the kitchen to the back door. She ran out into the night, not bothering even to think about where she was going. Just out of here. Away.

The light from the diner's kitchen was all that illuminated the alley. And it lit only the first few feet. The shadows swallowed the rest.

She knew there were creepy crawlies and evil trash in the world, and probably half of them lived in this neighborhood, but she told herself she could handle all of them. What she couldn't handle was being found. Not by DJ—and certainly not by the man who would follow. If DJ had found her, Dom would, too.

Her heart pounded and her soul dropped to her knees as she hurried through the alley, toward the street. *Please don't let him notice I've left. Not yet.*

She was nearly to the light at the mouth of the alley when a shadowed figure stepped into her path, blocking her escape. Silhouetted in the streetlight's glow, DJ looked dark and ominous. Once, he'd been a friend. He'd been her first lover. He'd been kind. But time had a way of changing everyone. She shivered, not sure *who* she was really facing.

"I won't hurt you, Tammie," he called to her, sounding a lot as though he was trying to cajole, not harm her. But she couldn't trust him. She didn't dare trust any man. Not ever again.

"I know," she lied. She'd learned a lot of tricks in the past nine years. She kept walking slowly, purposefully, hoping to convince him she *was* headed toward him. She could just as easily be the one doing the cajoling, then slip past and run. Run as she'd never run before.

Thankfully her ugly waitress uniform included tennis shoes. Lightweight, worn tennis shoes. Escape was doable.

"Good. So where are you going, Tammie?" He remained where he was, his arms crossed over his massive chest, trying to look casual. And failing.

His features were stiff, what she could see in the slashes of light. His eyes glowed and she wondered if he was angry. She edged along the wall, facing him and tracking her progress by running her fingers on the ridge between the bricks. She tried to ignore the filth she knew darkened the once light-colored stone. She was nearly there.

"Talk about what?" She hoped to distract him from her progress.

The silence grew heavy and he waited all too patiently. It made her shiver. What did he have in mind?

Finally, he spoke. "Our son. Tyler."

Her heart broke. She missed Tyler so much and it was almost too painful to think about him.

"He wants to know when you're coming to get him."

The knife twisted in her chest. She didn't dare think about how long she'd been away from him. Her eyes stung. She couldn't give in now, though. Too risky. She hardened her heart and shut off all emotion.

Her fingers met the corner brick. She breathed in, and after only an instant's pause, turned the corner and ran like hell.

The rubber soles of her worn shoes slapping against the pavement were loud, too loud. He'd follow the sound. It couldn't be helped. She had to outrun him.

Two blocks, just two short blocks. That was all she had to make, then she could duck into another alley and hide. No footfalls sounded behind her, but maybe her harsh breaths were drowning them out. The alley she'd been aiming for loomed ahead. Nearly there.

A motorcycle's roar shattered the night. Glancing over her shoulder, Tammie nearly screamed. The streetlights illuminated DJ. The bike was huge and he looked right at home on its back. Anger wasn't even close to what she saw on his face now that he was out of the shadows—it was much scarier.

The machine responded to his every command. She'd never outrun him now.

Still, she kept going, half expecting him to mow her over and knock her to the ground.

She didn't expect the sound of squealing tires or the smell of burning rubber. And most certainly not the grind of metal on cement as the bike tipped. She yelped and froze as she watched him fall.

And then there was silence. Not the kind of silence that indicated she'd successfully escaped. No. This was the silence of impending doom.

DJ wasn't under the bike, for which she hated to admit she was thankful. Instead of being splattered on the pavement, he'd managed to roll away from the machine and land a few feet away from her.

She stood there, staring. DJ cursed, his words blistering the air and her ears. He glared at her and rose to his feet. He was limping. Oh, God, she hadn't meant for him to be hurt. Really, she hadn't. But she had to get away.

She turned to run again, but before she could get far, his strong hand grabbed her arm and nearly gave her whiplash as he yanked her around. The rough brick wall cut into her back as DJ pushed her up against it. He'd been much kinder the last time he'd grabbed and imprisoned her. She fought. She was not giving in easily. Not this time. And never again.

She shot her foot forward, her shoe connecting with the hard steel of a shin. He didn't even flinch. She mentally cursed. "Let me go."

"Not a chance," he growled, his face close to hers. Too close. "I have questions and I want answers."

"Let me go."

Silence hung thick over the night. The only thing she could hear was her lungs struggling to breathe, and her heart pounding in her chest. She wasn't even sure he was breathing. He'd grabbed her without any effort, which just plain ticked her off. She tried to kick him again. His grip tightened.

"Do that again, and I won't ever tell you a thing about Tyler."

Dead silence filled the air. She wilted. He knew her Achilles' heel…her son…their son.

"You going to run, or can I trust you?"

She didn't answer, but her silence must have suggested she'd consider staying. His grip loosened and he leaned even closer. His breath brushed her cheek.

The brick wall felt cool against her back, a contrast to DJ's warmth washing over her.

This close, she took in the differences and similarities in him. He was older, bigger—angrier. Nine years was a long time. When she'd seen him last, he'd still been a boy getting ready to head to boot camp.

He wasn't a boy anymore. No, he was a man. A powerful, ticked-off man. She swallowed her apprehension and fought the overwhelming urge to struggle. And then a thought crossed her mind. What if he'd lied to her just to get her to listen? He'd said he wouldn't tell her about Tyler if she didn't cooperate. It wouldn't be the first time someone had done that.

"Is he really okay?" she whispered.

DJ reached down to the thigh pocket of his fatigues and pulled out a piece of paper that she immediately realized was a photo.

She impulsively reached for it. He shoved it back into his pocket, but not before she was able to identify Tyler as the person in the photo. How could she not recognize that sweet, beloved little face? "What's he holding?"

"Baby pigs," DJ said. "Wyatt took it yesterday."

"P-pigs?" she whispered.

"Yeah. We thought they might give him something positive to focus on. But guess if you don't care—"

He stepped away, the cool night air replacing the heat of his body. Too casually, he bent to check out the bike without giving her another glance.

He was trusting she wouldn't run? Or was he leaving her with that taunt? "What do you mean, if I don't care?" She shoved her pack impatiently onto her shoulder.

DJ slowly straightened from where he'd crouched. "You tell me. You left him." His gaze bored into hers, hot and angry, and she heard the rest of his unspoken message. *And you didn't even tell me that he existed.*

She leaned toward him, as he seemed to dismiss her again, refocusing on the fallen bike. "You don't understand," she said. Her words made him look up. The intensity of his gaze made her take a step back.

"Then start talking. Explain."

She wanted to scream, not in fear but in frustration. "I can't."

"Can't? Or won't?"

"There's no difference."

"Oh, yes, there is." He bent again, using his weight and strength to lift the bike from the pavement. Even in the dim streetlight, she saw the play of thick muscles across his back and the flexing of his thighs. She swallowed the sudden dryness in her throat.

Once the bike was upright, he circled it like a predator, rubbing a scratch here, a scrape there. Ignoring her. Ultimately, he seemed satisfied with its condition, and his shoulders visibly relaxed.

Tammie slumped back against the brick wall, trying to be as nonchalant as he was, and failing to ignore all the questions racing in her brain.

She was fairly certain he was debating something more than the bike, but she didn't really know him,

ning, slowly backed away. “I can’t go with you. I won’t.”

The dim light blurred and she nearly stumbled on a broken concrete chunk she couldn’t see through her tears. She righted herself, and instead of crumbling, she lifted her chin and watched her step, hoping she looked more determined than scared.

The deep throaty roar of the motorcycle startled her, but she quickly recovered, keeping her stride steady and sure. He’d gotten the message. He wasn’t coming toward her. He was leaving. Going back to Tyler. She almost stumbled once more. In a couple of hours he’d be seeing her baby again while she’d still be here, waiting tables.

An ache settled tight in her chest.

Then the soft rumble came closer rather than fading. She looked over, expecting him to ride past. Instead, he left the engine running as he sat on the bike, using his booted feet to keep pace with her as she walked.

“You have your reasons?”

She nodded but didn’t explain or stop. He reached into his pocket and withdrew the picture, this time handing it to her.

He was going to kill her emotionally. She ignored him as she drank in the sweet image.

“Get on and you’ll see him once I’m satisfied with your answers.”

She had no intention of going anywhere near Tyler until she knew it was safe. “And if I don’t?”

He stopped, pinning her with that glare again. Except now the anger was replaced with a hard glint. "He's my son. I have full legal custody. I'll use every legal trick in the book, and then some, to make sure you never, ever see him again."

He was serious.

She'd never planned on this. She'd sent Tyler to him to keep him safe, fully intending to go back and get Tyler once she'd solved the danger she'd put them in. She'd known DJ would protect him…but she hadn't expected this. This possessiveness. This territorial protectiveness.

Panic froze her. Never see Tyler again? Never read him a bedtime story? Never hear him whisper, "I love you, Mama"? Never again smell that sweet little-boy scent mingled with dirt as he hugged her?

Her knees threatened to give way. She struggled to breathe. In slow motion, she slipped the precious picture into her backpack then settled the bag back on her shoulder. She stopped and turned toward the big man on the even bigger bike. Its rumble made her think of a tiger and its throaty roar vibrated through her bones.

She had no choice. She knew it. He knew it.

Slowly, Tammie shook her head. Tears blurred her vision and spilled over her cheeks at the movement. "I'm not getting on that gawd-awful motorcycle. Never." She didn't have to fake the shiver. "I can't," she whispered.

She'd rather lose Tyler this way, knowing he was safe, than lose him to the danger following her.

Slowly, Tammie backed away, one painful step at a time.

CHAPTER FIVE

"WHAT THE—"

DJ had never hurt a female, not since he was five and his sister Mandy and he had gotten into a slugfest in the backyard sandbox. That was one of the few memories DJ had of his dad—the talk about never hitting a girl.

DJ had taken it to heart, but right now?

Tammie would have strained even Dad's legendary patience. She didn't run away from him this time. She just purposefully walked away. DJ watched until the darkness swallowed her.

What was he supposed to do now? He'd worked too hard to find her. He'd been so sure his threats would make her agree to come with him. It would have worked on his sisters. Okay, maybe not. His sisters weren't that easy to manipulate, either.

But he couldn't just let her go. Tyler—and he—deserved answers. He'd promised his son that he'd find her and bring her home.

Besides, what kind of mother abandoned her son? Especially one who'd raised such a great kid. What was going on with her?

DJ sat on the bike, leaning back against the leather seat, frowning. She didn't make any sense. Tyler's face came to mind. His faith in his mother was unshakable. Faith like that wasn't automatic—it was earned. Tyler staunchly believed in her. Staring into the darkness, DJ once again wondered why.

What were her reasons for leaving Tyler? And why wouldn't she tell him? Did she expect to just disappear?

Suddenly, he no longer heard her footsteps. "Oh, hell no," DJ whispered and kicked the bike into gear. The low rumble broke the quiet night as he followed her.

TAMMIE HEADED BACK to the diner. Probably a stupid idea to walk alone in this part of town at this time of night, but once again she didn't have much choice. Where else did she have to go? She'd turned her back on DJ and—her heart hitched—she'd just given up Tyler. Probably forever. A sob broke from her chest.

The sound of footsteps from behind reached through the fog in her brain—and blessed anger cut through her pain. She spun around, ready to give DJ a piece of her mind. "Just leave me alone," she snapped before she saw the shadowed face of a stranger.

He was a big man wearing dark clothing and a smirk that didn't say, "Have a nice day." She stumbled as she backed away from him.

"Well, hello there." His deep growl of a voice made her shiver.

She caught her balance and started walking faster, hoping that the threat she saw in his face wasn't real.

Wishing that all of this—this place, this situation, this mess of her life—would just go away. Then it occurred to her that the darkness in his eyes could mean exactly that.

Still winded after running from DJ, Tammie doubted she could outrun this guy, but she had to try. And she almost made it.

Until his meaty fist grabbed hold of her ponytail and yanked her backward. "Not so fast," he said in her ear, then paused. *"Tammie."*

Panic shot through her. How did he know her name? She didn't remember him coming into the diner. That's the only place she met anyone and she'd have remembered him. There was only one other answer…

He laughed, and she nearly gagged at the thick cologne he wore—cologne that barely covered the other odors cloaking him.

"Who are you?" She pulled away from him, feeling hair rip from her head.

"Let's just say a friend sent me."

A friend. She knew who he was talking about, but Dom was no friend.

"Go to hell." She turned to run.

"No need to be nasty. Let's do this easy." He lunged, catching her arm and sending her off balance. She fell and landed on her knees. Pavement ripped through her skin and tiny rocks tore into her palms.

The snarl of a motorcycle cut through her cries

and a new anger bubbled up inside her. She mentally cursed. She didn't want to need anyone. She didn't want a savior, but, damn it, right now she needed one. DJ would do.

The roar grew louder. She looked up. DJ and his bike appeared out of the darkness. Bathed in the streetlight's glow, he brought the bike up on the curb and raced toward them. Tammie screamed.

DJ used the bike to chase the thug away from her, the tires spinning toward the man's legs and driving him back. Knocking him into the street.

This time, DJ kept control of the vehicle and righted it before it fell. He spun the bike around, the smell of burning rubber thick in the air. Revving the throttle, he faced the thug, silently daring him to try something. The look on DJ's face made Tammie shudder—was this her DJ? The light in his eyes was not warm and soothing.

It was frightening. *He* was frightening.

She tore her gaze from DJ and realized her attacker had disappeared. In the distance, hurried footsteps receded into the night. Bowing her head, she took in deep gulps of air. Trying to keep the panic at bay, and think straight, she longed to figure out how to gain control of her life. But once again, nothing came to mind.

Silence reigned as DJ shut down the engine. She didn't hear his footsteps, didn't hear anything except her heart pounding and her breath ripping through her lungs. She couldn't do this anymore. She just couldn't.

She was done.

"Tammie?" DJ's voice actually sounded hesitant. She looked up. Where had his anger gone?

Hers returned on an adrenaline rush. "Where the hell did you learn to do that?" She crawled to her feet, refusing the hand he offered. "And why would anyone in their right mind *know* how to do that?" She stalked toward him. "What if you'd lost control like you did before? You could have hit the wall, or wrecked, or…or…or…" She hiccuped as horrific images of DJ splattered on the pavement blared in her mind.

DJ looked entirely too pleased with himself. He had the audacity to grin. "Hey." He shrugged. "I grew up on a ranch. Cutting horses and bikes. Same difference."

"You idiot!" She went at him, poking his chest with an angry finger. "Is that what you were trying to do earlier? To me?"

"Yeah." He grinned. "Did it right this time, though."

Anger bubbled up inside her. How dare he! "Don't you dare teach Tyler anything like that."

"A simple thank-you would do just fine." He took a step back, his eyes moving, assessing her—and not with appreciation.

She knew she looked awful. The ugly orange waitress uniform, her hair falling around her face from where the jerk had tried to pull it out of her head, blood trickling from her knees and smeared on her palms.

"Stop following me." It was all she could come up with. There was no way she was thanking him, despite the fact that she knew she should.

"Oh, excuse me for trying to help." He stalked over to her and grabbed her hands, turning them palm up and cursing. "Come on. Let's get you taken care of." He didn't let go and they were nearly to the bike before she tried to pull away.

"I already told you I am not getting on that thing."

"I don't think you have a choice," he mumbled, looking past her shoulder.

She followed his gaze. The big shadow was back. And he wasn't alone. Two other men walked beside him.

DJ hopped onto the motorcycle and kicked it to life. "Get on."

"I—"

She hated motorcycles. The idea of riding on one scared her half to death, but the shadowed figures scared her more.

"Get. On," DJ said again, this time through clenched teeth. "Now." Footsteps pounded toward them. DJ had a point. She jumped on and DJ sped into the night.

She hung on tight, knowing she was in for one hell of a ride.

DJ SPED THROUGH the city streets. There hadn't been any vehicles around, so he didn't think they were being followed. But he wound around, just to make sure.

He should take her back to the diner, or maybe to Cora's house, but if he let her off the bike, he'd never get her back on. And she'd run again.

It didn't take long to get to the city limits since they were already on the ratty edges. Streetlights flashed past until they reached the two-lane highway. The moon hadn't yet risen, so the headlight beam and light from the stars were all that showed him the way.

"Where are we going?" she finally asked.

"Someplace safe." He turned his head just enough to see her out of the corner of his eye. Her ponytail waved in the wind, the loose strands whipping across her face. He needed to get a helmet for her.

He turned his focus back to the road, but no matter how he tried, he failed miserably at ignoring the extra weight on the back of the bike. The feel of Tammie's arms tight around his waist was entirely too real, and warm.

Tammie didn't speak. She didn't even shift. She clenched her fists in his shirt whenever he squealed around a corner, but otherwise, she didn't move.

She'd obviously ridden on a bike before. With who? There was so much he didn't know about her.

What he did know was where they were headed, but he wouldn't share the details with her—not yet.

By the time they reached Edgerton an hour later, the sky was turning a bright orange on the horizon.

Nothing more than a few buildings in the middle of nowhere—something Texas had in abundance—the tiny town was a welcome sight. Three houses, a gas station slash convenience store and a motel with a flashing neon vacancy sign that broke the darkness. DJ had stayed here several times when he'd traveled back and forth from Wyatt's place to San Antonio for therapy. It had provided a bed to lay his head and some much needed space away from his brother.

He almost wished he was on one of those trips. His body was already telling him he'd pay for *this* trip—for chasing Tammie and certainly for dumping and lifting the bike off the pavement. His damaged back and leg muscles burned from the abuse. A nice soak in the gym's whirlpool tub would be heaven right now.

He slowed and turned off the highway into the dirt parking lot. When he killed the engine, the silence was thick around them. No one else was here, except George, the manager, owner and purveyor of everything for twenty miles.

"We'll stay here for now."

"What?" Tammie stared in shock.

"I'll check us in."

"I can't go with you. Take me back to town."

"Nope."

Tammie climbed off as if to follow him and nearly stumbled. He caught her arms, steadying her, and the night warmed. He stared at her face. She looked beat. Defeated.

"Listen." He stepped closer. "You're exhausted. You're hurt." He paused and made sure her gaze met his before he spoke. "And whoever you're really running from seems to have found you." He wished she'd tell him who that person was. "Just let me help you." As he headed to the office, he looked over his shoulder and said, "Wait here. I'll be right back."

She looked around at the miles of open space surrounding the tiny pseudo town. "Yeah, like there's anywhere *to* go?"

He actually smiled. He recalled that her dry humor had intrigued him in the past. He was glad to see remnants of it. Maybe there was hope. Maybe the ghosts of their past weren't so dead, after all. He had to believe that.

"Ain't seen you in a while," George greeted him with a smile and a yawn as DJ slipped inside the tiny office.

"Yeah. How you been, man?"

"Fair to middlin'." George automatically filled out the paperwork and ran DJ's credit card. "Usual room?" The old-fashioned metal key slid over the scarred counter with a soft whisper.

"Thanks. Oh, by the way, there're two of us," DJ told him.

Only the single eyebrow lift indicated the man had heard. George glanced out the side window and

DJ knew Tammie was there, standing by the bike, waiting, when George nodded.

"That'll be extra."

"I figured." He paid but didn't explain further. It was none of the old man's business.

DJ knew he was being a paranoid jerk getting only one room. But Tammie had obviously ridden a motorcycle before. While she didn't like it, she undoubtedly had skills. He could very likely be stuck here without his prized bike come morning. No way. He wasn't letting her go, and he certainly wasn't letting her get the better of him.

"Come on." He led her to the farthest room, away from the road, away from George's curious stares. The door squealed when he pushed it open, and the closed-up dusty scent wafted out over them.

"Where's my key?" she asked behind him.

DJ knew it would tick her off, but he did it anyway. Maybe it would spark some life in her.

He walked into the room, lifted the single key and shook it before pocketing it. Her growl should have made him nervous. It only made him laugh as he turned to face her.

Browbeating and threatening her weren't what he'd planned. But she hadn't given him much choice. If he let her go...he might never find her again. And he sure as hell wasn't going home and telling Tyler he'd failed.

Nope. Not an option.

"This is kidnapping!"

DJ paused, crossing his arms over his chest. "No, it's not." He waited, but she didn't say any more. "Let's consider it negotiating."

Her eyes flashed and DJ suddenly understood what it meant to see murder in someone's eyes.

The slamming of the bathroom door shook the walls of the entire place as she disappeared inside.

TAMMIE STARED AT her distorted reflection in the cheap motel room mirror. Her mother would say she looked like something the cat dragged in. She closed her eyes but the reflection remained imprinted on the back of her eyelids.

Her green eyes were flat and lifeless with no makeup to bring out anything. The shadows beneath her lashes betrayed her exhaustion.

Her hair, after the long hot shower, hung in dark locks to her shoulders. The light blond she'd had as a kid living on the beach was long gone. Opening her eyes, Tammie leaned closer to the glass, examining the crow's-feet she'd never noticed before.

She caught herself. What was she doing? She was in here to shower, to clean up. To escape *him*. Nothing more. She almost banged her head against the glass at her stupidity.

DJ's face flashed in her mind. First the angry, hard soldier who'd chased away Dom's buddy, and then the sweet man who'd stopped here and told her he'd take care of her. The contradiction intrigued and scared her.

Attraction was definitely not a part of this.

The man on the other side of that door was interested in her for one reason. Tyler. DJ didn't care about her. Didn't care about their past together or apart. And why should he?

She'd lied to him. She'd kept Tyler a secret. She hadn't even told him the truth when they had been together. Not about herself, her past, nothing. And now? Worn-out, desperate and tired, that's all she was.

Worthless, to him, to herself and, most important, to Tyler.

She was Tyler's mother…but from here on out, the title was all she had. She couldn't *be* that for him. It was too risky.

Disgusted with herself and the situation, Tammie turned away from the mirror and focused on doing the best she could with what she had to work with.

The warm water had washed off most of the dried blood from her knees and her hands, and she only had to pick out one piece of gravel. It stung like the devil when she put on the last of her antiseptic cream and a small bandage, but she'd live.

She yanked the blow-dryer from its hook on the wall and finished her hair. She stared at the few cosmetics in her pack that had survived her months on the run and scoffed at the idea of applying makeup. She simply pulled on a clean T-shirt and her sweatpants.

"This is as good as it gets," she said to the mirror

and pulled open the door. Standing in the doorway, she watched the last of the shower's steam swirl out into the cooler room before she faced him.

He wasn't even there. The room door stood wide-open. Panic returned.

DJ STOOD OUTSIDE the motel room, leaning on the wooden post that pretended to hold up the narrow overhang. He'd left the door open between them, partially to keep an eye on her, but also so she could find him.

The worn Western motif of the place hadn't been what had first brought him here. He'd been looking for someplace out of the way, somewhere no one would think to look for him. Tonight it was a place Tammie could sleep and feel safe.

Someplace he felt he could protect.

No one asked questions here. And if they did… there weren't any answers.

The main door and the large picture window overlooking the walk where he stood was the only way in. And the back of the room bumped against the rooms on the other side. No one would sneak up on him.

His bike was parked directly in front of their room. If someone did find them, the thundering v-twins could get them out of here in record time. Tammie only had her backpack and he had the duffel. He'd had less when he'd been on most missions.

The single white security light that remained in the parking lot cast eerie shadows over the bike and a couple of beat-up cars. The neon sign in the office window flickered a faded orange.

Nothing but the sign's light moved, and he liked it that way. His phone rang and he answered the distinctive ring. If only he had more answers for his son.

"YEAH, BUDDY. SHE'S HERE with me." DJ's voice was loud in the deserted night.

Tammie froze, hearing DJ's voice just outside the door. There was only one person he could be talking to. Tyler. The hard ache in her chest grew and she struggled to breathe.

"No, she can't talk right now. She's taking a shower."

He had to have heard her open the bathroom door. Just then he looked over his shoulder at her. She didn't move closer, and he didn't offer her the phone.

"I'll let her know you want to talk to her. Look, I gotta go." He listened intently, and in the silence, Tammie heard the soft echo of her son's voice coming through the phone.

Every cell in her body ached to grab the phone and listen forever to his sweet little voice. But she couldn't talk to Tyler, couldn't put him through it. And when it came time to say goodbye again, it would destroy her. She had to be strong, or this whole situation would do her in.

"Yeah, I'll tell her all about them. Don't worry, buddy." DJ paused. "We'll be home before you know it. 'Night."

He pocketed the phone a second later and turned around to face her. "Feel better?"

"Was that Tyler?" Her voice broke and she cleared her throat to make sure it didn't happen again.

"Yeah. He's anxious to talk to you." DJ smiled and she looked away, refusing to get sucked in. She looked like hell and he had the audacity to look little more than ruffled. The boy she remembered had grown into the handsome man she'd known he would be.

His gaze traveled up, then down, and she blushed under the intent stare.

"You okay?" he whispered.

DJ sounded so calm, so normal, as if he hadn't just been talking to the one person in the world Tammie ached to hold. "Yes. For a prisoner," she mumbled.

Holding her backpack, she went back inside and made her way to the nearest bed. She yanked back the blankets and settled between the sheets, turning her back on him.

She heard DJ rooting around in his own duffel bag on the farther bed. "You know you won't get far if you decide to take off."

"Uh...yeah." Her voice broke and she cleared it again as she looked over her shoulder at him. "I sort of noticed the miles of nothing we drove through."

His stare intensified, and for a long, painful minute, she forced herself to meet his gaze. The questions in his eyes were intense and many. He wasn't pushing her, but she could see he wanted to. Lord, he wanted to.

DJ stalked to the bathroom doorway, then stopped. "You even going to ask about him?" The scorn in his voice was thick.

She rolled over and stared at the "lovely" brown paneling. The silence stretched out and his words echoed around her. "I'm not going there with you."

"Where?"

"Wherever Tyler is." She knew he was with Wyatt but she'd refrained from learning the details. She didn't trust herself not to go get him.

"Why not?"

"I can't." She couldn't tell him more.

"You don't even want to see him?"

He waited, probably hoping she'd answer him. She couldn't lie about that.

"I'm not sure why, but he wants to see you," DJ finally said.

Why was he taunting her with Tyler? Teasing her with the reality of the horrible months that she'd missed in her baby's life? She swallowed hard and closed her eyes. "Don't assume you can guess what my reasons are or what I want." She turned to meet his glare, refusing to look away, and struggling.

Did he really think she'd leave her child, her baby, if she didn't have a solid, good reason? Did he really believe she was capable of just abandoning her son?

Despite the knowledge that she'd set it up to look exactly like that, his assumptions hurt.

She heard him take a step toward her. She braced for his touch. A physical connection she hadn't felt in years. She trembled, knowing it wouldn't take much, one kind word, one simple, earnest question from him and she'd crumble.

She couldn't afford that. She yanked the covers up to her chin and closed her eyes, putting up the barriers before she completely lost control.

"Yeah, I'm fine." The crunching sound of ice shifting was loud in the quiet. "Go back to bed, Tammie."

He sounded tired. Was he telling her the truth or was this some macho posturing? She wished she knew him better, wished she could read him.

"Fine," she whispered with a shrug. He could take care of himself. He obviously didn't need her. And she didn't need him.

She finished putting on her other shoe and grabbed her backpack. How many times had she done this? How many people did she have to leave behind? She was heartily sick of running, but Dom's thugs had finally found her at the diner. Time to move on—again.

"Going somewhere?" DJ's deep voice cut through her plans.

She froze, her hand curled around the doorknob. She could yank the door open and run. But being tackled in the middle of the asphalt parking lot held little appeal, and she knew he'd do it.

"It's morning." Her voice shook, and she slowly turned to face him. She leaned back against the door. "I was thinking I'd get us some breakfast."

"Liar." He'd pulled on a simple white T-shirt and black sweatpants. Her mind still saw the scars on his back, though the thin shirt clung to the well-defined muscles of his chest.

Sitting down slowly, he straightened his legs with a groan and a whispered curse.

"You couldn't lie worth a damn nine years ago.

You haven't changed that much." He slowly, carefully pulled on his socks.

"You don't know that."

He looked up and pinned her with one of those glares, the kind that had melted her so long ago. The kind that scared her to death now.

"I know more than you'll ever want me to tell you." He shoved to his feet, using his arms more than his legs. She realized that he hid his injuries well, until you knew what to notice, what to see, then nothing was hidden at all. He rummaged around in his own pack and pulled out one of those brown pharmacy bottles and gulped down two pills without any water. "I don't know about you, but I need some sleep."

She turned and yanked open the door. There, just outside the door, the huge Harley sat staring at her. She could swear it was actually standing guard. Tammie shook her head. All the fear and the uncertainty of the past few months had done a number on her. She'd lost what was left of her mind.

Strong arms wrapped around her from behind, pulling her back into the room and slamming the door before she could even think. She simply reacted, managing to knock him to the ground with one of the few self-defense moves she'd learned. In an instant, they were both flat on the floor. DJ cursed, loud and long.

She didn't care if it hurt him. Really, she didn't. She rolled away. "That'll teach you to grab me like that."

"Thanks for the lesson." Sarcasm filled the words. He used those strong arms to pull himself back up onto the edge of the bed, then faced her again. "Just to remind you—again—I'm here because you sent our son away." He faced her, anger filling his eyes. "And because someone is chasing you and, apparently, that someone has found you again. You think you're safer out there on your own?"

She looked at him, feeling the burn in her eyes. She missed Tyler desperately, and DJ's reminder was painful and unfair, but she didn't rail at DJ for it. She understood. He was right.

Slowly, with much more ease than he had, she moved away and sat down on the hard, wobbly chair by the table. She met his glare with one of her own. "No, I know I'm not safer out there." She swallowed. "But you are." She'd been a fool not to leave Austin as soon as Wyatt had picked up Tyler.

Those jerks back in the alley had come for her. Dom had sent them. She didn't want them to find her again, and she certainly didn't want them, or anyone related to Dom, anywhere near the people she cared about. Not Tyler. Not Cora. And not DJ.

She and DJ had spent a week together nine years ago, and he'd found her less than twenty-four hours ago. She didn't really know him, and she didn't trust any man, but something about him touched her. Made her *want* to trust. Made her wish—

He yanked back the covers on the far bed and

took his time arranging the limp pillows. "You know, Tyler was telling me you design jewelry."

Her head whipped up and she stared at him, dread ripping through her. No, he couldn't know about that. She hadn't told Tyler not to tell, but she hadn't thought he'd paid that much attention to what she did.

"What does that have to do with anything?"

"Everything. It shows me how little I know about you. That girl I met all those years ago? She had dreams. Sounds like she accomplished those dreams." He looked at her again. "I think someone stole them. And Tyler's paying for it. He loves you, Tammie."

"And I…" She swallowed the revelation. "What did he say about it, about my designing?"

DJ shrugged, not looking away. "Not much. He's pretty tight-lipped when it comes to you. Getting what information I did was nearly impossible. You trained the kid well."

"I didn't *train* him," she snapped.

"Could have fooled me." He grabbed a couple of things from his pack and returned to the bathroom. This time he didn't close the door. "So, do you want to enlighten me? I did save your pretty backside earlier. I think you owe me."

She got stuck on the word *pretty*, then chastised herself. She was being stupid again. "I don't owe you anything. Why are you doing this? Why don't you just let me leave?"

"I can't." He stepped back into the open doorway

and met her gaze. "For some reason, you're the most important thing in this whole world to my son. I won't have him look at me in five, or ten, or twenty, years and resent me because you couldn't be in his life. So *you*, not me, are going to explain to him why you left him."

That surprised her. She looked across the small room at the man she had once been so close to. The man who'd been out of her life for so long. He looked honest, he looked interested, but she'd seen that look before. When Dom was trying to convince her to trust him…

She closed her eyes, ignoring both of the images. She couldn't trust either of them, and she certainly didn't have faith in her own judgment. She'd made too many mistakes. She refused to make any more, not knowingly, anyway. Opening her eyes, she looked over at him. "No." She shook her head. "No. I can't." She wanted, really wanted, to trust him. But she just couldn't. And that disappointed her.

Without another word, she moved back to the bed and slid, fully dressed, beneath the covers. She turned her back to him.

"Guess that's the end of our conversation?" He leaned around the door frame.

Tammie didn't answer. She closed her eyes and prayed she'd fall asleep. Soon.

DESPITE HIS BEST EFFORTS, sleep eluded DJ. Again. Partially due to the dull ache in his back that never really went away, and partially because of the woman finally asleep in the other bed. But mostly because he couldn't stop wondering what Tammie was hiding.

He'd watched her as she slipped into unconsciousness. The frown slipped slowly from her brow. Her lips parted ever so slightly and her head lolled to the side just a little.

The few stray rays of sunshine falling through the worn blinds cast light and shadows over her face and glinted in the highlights in her hair. Blankets draped her curves from shoulder to hips, and clung to the flow of her legs. He hadn't expected to ever see her again. And here she was. Just as untouchable.

Last night, DJ hadn't pushed anymore. She'd been tired, though she'd refused to admit it. He'd wanted to question her as soon as they got here, but her exhaustion was painful to watch. She'd struggled to keep her eyes open. Even after the shower she'd looked beat.

She needed the sleep. That was part of why he'd brought her here. *Yeah, that's it.* He'd brought her out here to the middle of the boonies, where she had no means of escape, so she could nap. Who was he kidding?

He'd brought her here to do exactly as she'd accused—to trap her. To force her to answer his questions.

Somehow that plan had gone awry. All he'd managed to accomplish so far was to drive himself crazy.

What the hell had she meant when she said he'd be

safer without her? Safe. DJ laughed. He didn't live safe. Safe Special Forces was an oxymoron.

From across the room, DJ watched her wake slowly, quietly, shifting gently beneath the thin covers. His mind filled with memories of all the sounds she'd made in her sleep. She'd been sound asleep, dreaming. And crying.

Twice he'd tried to wake her. Both times she'd quieted, but barely minutes later, the despair in her dreams returned.

He sat in the hard chair he'd spent most of the night and day in, hoping it would distract him from the idea of crawling in beside her, to hold her and comfort her.

Tammie opened her eyes then, staring for an instant at the ceiling before turning her head and meeting his stare. She gasped as her memories returned. "I... How long have I been asleep?"

He didn't leave his spot, leaning his forearms on his knees, folding his hands together to keep from reaching for her. "Most of the day."

She sat up, shoved her hair out of her face and pulled the blankets up around her shoulders. She leaned back against the headboard. "Wow. I never sleep that long."

"You needed it. You were running on empty."

She didn't say anything more, simply sat there, half-awake, staring back at him.

"Looks like you've been up awhile. What have you been doing?"

"Watching you."

"Me? Why?" She blinked, obviously trying to focus and clear her mind. She didn't look as rested as he'd like—no wonder, considering her dreams.

DJ couldn't stand it any longer. He shot to his feet and paced. His back was stiff, and he'd pay for all the time he'd sat in the hard chair. His muscles protested and the scars across his ribs screamed in agony as he moved. But the more he moved, the better he felt. He breathed in slowly, in time with his stride.

Finally, he came back to face her, stopping at the end of the bed. "You need to tell me everything. *Everything*," he finished through clenched teeth. "And don't even think about leaving out a damned detail about Dom."

Her eyes widened as she gasped. "Wh-who?"

"I thought we already established that you're a lousy liar. I heard enough last night when you were talking in your sleep. I want the truth."

She stared at him like a scared rabbit from behind the bars of a trap. "Or what?" she dared to challenge.

"Or we're not going anywhere. I won't take you back to Austin. And we won't go to the ranch. Not now. Not ever. We'll just stay here until you tell me."

He leaned toward her menacingly. "There's a reason you sent Tyler to Wyatt, and it doesn't have a damned thing to do with not wanting him." He glared at her, as if his gaze could force her to give up all her secrets.

He watched her swallow, and despite the anger

simmering inside him, he wanted to back off, wanted to let her slip back into the denial she'd been living in. But he couldn't. Not with her agony echoing in his mind.

Nor could he take another day of knowing it was there, lurking in the darkness ahead. Or another night of listening to her pain. He needed answers.

"His name is Dominic Carlyle," she whispered, surprising him.

DJ didn't respond, just waited, hoping she'd say more.

After a minute she did. "I met him at a gem fair. I was there with my design business." She paused, waiting.

"The work Tyler told me about."

She nodded. "I was working my booth and Dom came over. We talked. Got to know each other a bit. It was fun." Her voice hitched, and DJ waited to see if she said more.

Finally, she started again. "He invited me to dinner that night. Over the week of the show, he wined and dined me." Anger crept into her voice. "I was so stupid. I fell for it hook, line and sinker."

"It's never stupid to trust someone's intent."

"Yeah, well, that's part of why this all ticks me off. I'm a mother. I have a child to protect. Tyler always came first until then."

Anger and indignation flared in DJ. "There's nothing wrong with having a life. After my dad died, Mom never dated. Looking back, I think she must have been lonely." Things looked so different from his adult perspective.

"Maybe." Tammie stared up at the ceiling instead of meeting his gaze. "But I have a responsibility to my son. My need for companionship doesn't trump his safety."

DJ let her words hang in the air for a minute. "Okay. So explain."

"He used Tyler to get me to do his dirty work."

"Dirty work?"

"A few weeks after the fair, he brought a dozen diamonds to my studio and wanted them reset. But I recognized them. They were stolen." She looked down at her clasped hands. "You might remember a story in the news about the Brighton family's collection. It was one of the largest jewel thefts in Florida history. It was an inside job and the stones are quite unique. Anyone who knows gems would recognize them. I did. But with new settings, most laypeople wouldn't have a clue what they were."

Tammie closed her eyes, but DJ saw the damp on her eyelashes. Finally, she nodded. "He threatened to hurt Tyler if I didn't do it. I gave in and reset them. I thought I was done and that he'd go away." She paused, her mind seeming to drift. DJ waited, struggling to stay put.

She took a deep, shuddering breath. Her voice sounded forlorn, but she seemed determined to finish the tale. "I came home one day and Dom was there. At my house. I'd left Tyler there with the neighbor but she was gone. Tyler came running out of the house. Dom had a belt and I could tell he'd hit him. He had more diamonds he wanted reset. I refused."

Her voice cracked on her pain. "He grabbed Tyler. Right in front of me. He broke his arm." Her sobs weren't held back now. DJ barely resisted the urge to move over to her. His arms ached to pull her close, to comfort her. He didn't dare or he might never get the details he needed. He didn't push her. Just simply waited.

"That asshole wouldn't let me take Tyler to the doctor until I finished the work." Her anger came to the rescue, and she dashed her tears away. "I did it to get rid of him, then once he left, I packed an overnight bag for each of us and headed to the ER. We never went back home."

"Never?"

She shook her head, her eyes distant. "I miss my little house. I worked hard for it. But I knew he'd never leave us alone."

DJ now understood a little more about Tyler. "Tammie, you should know, a couple of months ago Wyatt took Tyler to the ER. Tyler freaked out."

"Oh, God." All the color drained from her face. "Is he—"

"He's fine. He cut his hand and needed stitches. It's healed now. But he told Wyatt about how his mom's boyfriend, Dom, had hurt him. Wyatt was close to murder. He probably will kill Dom if he ever meets him."

Tammie leaned forward, her hands clenched. "Don't you see? That's what I'm afraid of. I don't want Dom to ever find Tyler again."

"Did you tell anyone about it? The theft? His attack?"

"In the ER they questioned me, and Tyler, like *I* had hurt him." He could see the pain in her eyes at the accusations. "When I told them what had happened, a cop came to the ER—a dirty cop, obviously. At first I thought he was going to arrest me for child abuse, but instead he came with a message. If I said anything, they'd make sure it came out that it was *my* designs that held the stolen gems. I'd be blamed as the thief."

"So you ran."

She didn't say anything, simply nodded. The silence grew long, and he knew she was far away in her mind—the horrors of her past with Dom too clear, too painful. "I didn't have any choice. I had no proof of anything.

"First I went to stay with a designer friend in New Orleans. I thought it would be far enough away. I figured he'd leave me alone. I didn't have any idea what else to do. I thought I'd figure something out eventually. But once we were settled in a temporary apartment, he found us again."

"If you don't have any proof, why is he still after you?"

"I...I don't know. I wish I did. Maybe just my knowing the truth is a threat."

DJ frowned. "What about your family? Couldn't they help?" Now that he thought back, he couldn't remember her talking about them before.

"I…don't really have anyone." She looked down, her features blanketed in something that looked like shame. "When I met you, I was living on the streets, the beach, actually. I ran away from home two months before that."

"What?"

"Not my greatest achievement. I've only seen my parents once since then. Tyler was just two at the time." Her gaze and her voice grew distant.

No wonder Wyatt hadn't been able to find them. "Siblings?"

"My sister still lives near them." She shrugged. "Her husband isn't any better than my dad."

DJ stared. None of this was what he'd expected.

Holy crap.

CHAPTER SEVEN

SEEING DJ, WHOLE and safe, on the other side of the room, helped chase away the last dregs of her nightmares. Still, Tammie's mind replayed the images as if they were real. Tyler and DJ together in the rubble of some strange building, blood covering them both, haunted her.

Logically, she knew it had been a dream—nightmare—but there was no shaking the fear it left behind. She bit back the sob threatening to break her.

Answering his questions was the least of her concerns.

DJ stared back at her, his eyes narrowed, a frown forming between his brows. She'd taken him by surprise by answering. More than surprise, she realized. She'd shocked him.

"Go ahead," she whispered. "Say it."

"What am I supposed to say?" he asked nearly as softly.

"I..." What was she expecting? Her shoulders slumped and she looked down at her hands, surprised to find them tightly clenched. She forced her fingers to uncurl.

She expected him to be angry. Expected him to laugh or berate her. To call her a fool. But silence was all she heard.

He slowly rose to his feet, pushing hard on the arm of the chair for leverage. Walking around to the side of the bed, DJ loomed over her. She didn't look up.

In her peripheral vision she saw his hand, saw him reach for her. Thin white scars she hadn't noticed before stood out against the thick, tanned skin of his knuckles. She waited, preparing herself for his touch.

His rough fingertips slid along her jaw before his palm cupped her cheek. Gently, he nudged her chin with his thumb.

"Look at me." His command was soft yet strong.

Slowly, Tammie lifted her eyes and met his gaze, foolishly defiant.

"You're strong. Tyler's lucky." The muscles of his throat moved as he swallowed.

"Oh." She shivered.

"Remember, I've spent the past few months with him. You raised him well. He'll be a good, strong man someday."

There was no anger in DJ's face. No censure. Instead, she saw something she barely recognized. She couldn't remember the last time someone had looked at her that way, that intensely, as if he wanted—

"I'm not afraid of you, DJ," she blurted to break the spell.

"I'm glad." His thumb moved slowly again, this time brushing over her lower lip. He shook his head. "Then maybe someday you'll trust me." This time the anger she expected surfaced.

She made herself stay where she was, though she

felt the wooden headboard dig a bit deeper into her shoulder blades. Surely he could feel her tremble. She wasn't used to praise or trust or any number of positive emotions. It made her uncomfortable.

With one last swipe of his finger over her skin, DJ turned away and headed to the door. The slam was loud and vibrated through the room as the glass in the window shivered with the impact of him leaving the room. Outside, the roar of the Harley shattered the quiet of the afternoon.

Tammie flung back the covers and raced to the window in time to see the cloud of dust that formed in the air behind him. The brake lights lit up, and then he was gone.

Several minutes passed and the deadly silence inflicted itself on her. Where was he going? Why had he left? And the worst, most frightening question of all: Was he coming back?

She panicked for an instant.

No one else was staying in the old, worn-down motel. Which was likely why he'd brought her here. And now he'd left her? She resisted the urge to stamp her foot. The rat.

The thought of hitchhiking scared the hell out of her. Maybe the old guy in the office would help her. She shook her head. None of her options were good. No, DJ *was* coming back.

Wasn't he? He'd better be, she decided. And when he did? She intended to give him a good piece of her mind...right before she killed him.

DJ NEEDED TO RIDE. To think and make some decisions—before he crawled into that bed with Tammie and pulled her into his arms. To protect. To comfort. To— He stopped his thoughts right there.

Opening the throttle on the bike, he let the tires eat up the pavement. For the first couple of miles he cursed and rehashed everything Tammie had told him. His admiration for her rose, as did the desire to strangle her.

She should have come to him. Should have trusted in *someone* to help her. But to live on the streets, build a business and raise a child—alone?

After ten miles, he pulled off the highway to the edge of a pasture and killed the engine.

DJ knew exactly where he was. Nowhere, Texas—about fifteen miles from Wyatt's ranch. Memories of another lifetime came rushing back.

Every inch of this piece of ground, save for the strip the state had appropriated for the highway, belonged to Pal Haymaker. Not someone DJ wanted to cross.

Lord, he'd been a wild child back in the day. He and his best buddy, Lane, had done a hell of a lot of damage to themselves *and* the scenery, with their horses, bikes and pranks. Pal hadn't liked them much then, and he wasn't one to make life easy for a Hawkins now. There was already trouble between he and Wyatt.

DJ couldn't help but wonder if Tyler would follow in his footsteps or Wyatt's.

DJ glanced to the west. He could head over to the ranch, but without Tammie along, he didn't dare. And he didn't really want to. Not yet. He agreed with Tammie. Wyatt, Tyler and this world had to be kept as far apart as possible. For now.

When he pulled out his phone and dialed, it wasn't Wyatt's number.

"Hey," a familiar voice came through the air. "Long time no hear." Colin sounded so blessedly normal. His face was the last one DJ remembered seeing before the explosion. Though Colin had miraculously escaped serious injury. Memories of his friend's voice in the shadows of the drug-induced coma they'd kept him in until he'd reached the United States came back to him now. But DJ didn't know if it was a dream or if Colin had actually been there with him. Didn't really matter.

Colin was as solid as they came and one of the best friends DJ had ever made. He trusted him completely. Colin was also one of the best trackers DJ knew. Not just on land, but in cyberspace. No one could hide from Colin.

"Yeah. It's been too long," DJ replied.

"So, when you gonna get your skinny ass back here?"

DJ didn't speak again for a minute, then, once he'd rearranged the lump in his throat, he said, "I'm not. They're medically discharging me."

Silence preceded the barrage of curse words. DJ smiled, appreciating his friend's loyalty.

"Damn fools. They need your skills."

"Maybe, but you guys *don't* need me as a liability. I can barely walk, much less run."

"You mean I can finally beat your ass in PT?" Colin's hoot of victory made DJ pull the phone from his ear.

"Yeah, yeah, you'd probably win."

"Probably? Man, that's cruel." For a long minute, the silence grew. Then a groan came over the line. "Ah, man. That means no more of your sister's cookies."

DJ laughed. He'd have to ask Addie to send some to Colin next time he deployed. DJ stared out over the pasture. The wind ruffled his hair and caressed the wild grasses hugging the hills. In the spring this hill would be covered in blue bonnets. He'd missed the sight this year.

"Where are you?" Colin finally asked.

"Just outside Nowhere, Texas. Hey, I need a favor."

"Sure."

DJ paused, then filled Colin in on what Tammie had told him. When he finally stopped talking, he heard Colin whistle softly. "Damn, man. What a mess. What can I do to help?"

DJ smiled. The adrenaline of a new mission coursed through him and he heard the same in Colin's voice. For the first time in months, DJ felt more like himself. "Get what info you can for me on this guy. And those diamonds."

"Can do. Anything else?"

"Not right now, but let's see what the intel gives us."

"I'll call you when I get things together."

DJ hesitated. He couldn't keep Tammie at the motel, and he couldn't take her back to the ranch. It was a short day trip to New Orleans, where Colin and the rest of the crew were stationed. "Okay. We'll be there tomorrow sometime. Let's connect then."

"Sounds good. We'll put a plan together. I'm anxious to meet your lady."

"She's not *my* lady."

Colin's laughter echoed over the prairie and in DJ's ear. "Uh-huh. I've traveled the world with you, buddy, remember? The correct response is 'not yet.'"

"See you tomorrow. We'll call when we hit the city." DJ disconnected the call as Colin continued to laugh.

For the first time since that bomb had ripped him apart, DJ felt as though he had a future. A purpose. Damn, he loved a good mission.

Now he had to make another call. This one wouldn't be as easy. With a deep breath, he thumbed the keypad again. Yesterday he'd told them he was on his way home with her. They deserved an update.

The phone on the other end rang three times before anyone picked up. That didn't surprise DJ. A glance at his watch told him it was the middle of dinner.

He'd be lucky if anyone even heard a phone ring in the craziness at the ranch during this time of day.

There was no hello. "About damned time. We thought you'd be here by now," Wyatt grumbled, but the relief was strong in his voice.

DJ heard another voice in the background. "Is that my dad?" That one he let wash over him. His son's sweet voice sounded so good.

"Yeah, well, I've been busy."

Silence reigned for a long minute. "You did find her, right?" Wyatt whispered.

"Yeah." DJ dragged out the word. "I found her."

"Where are they?" Tyler's high-pitched voice cut across the miles.

"Just a second, Ty." Wyatt's voice drifted as if he'd pulled the phone away. "Why don't you run up and get your backpack?" Wyatt said to the boy. "Get started on your homework."

"But, Uncle Wyatt—"

"Let me finish the business, and then you can have your dad all to yourself."

The promise must have worked. "Okay," Tyler whined, and DJ heard his footsteps recede.

"How's he doing?" DJ asked when Wyatt returned to the phone.

"Fine. He's worried about you guys, but school and the animals are helping distract him." Wyatt took a deep breath that traveled through the speaker. "You okay?"

DJ wasn't sure how or if he could answer. "There's been a change of plans," he said instead.

"What?"

DJ rubbed his eyes. Lord, he was tired. "I'd like you to keep a real close eye on Tyler for a while. We're not coming back right away."

Wyatt didn't say anything at first. "That's not a problem, you know that. We'll make sure he's okay. Safe. But why? What happened?'

"I— It's just not as simple as I thought. We gotta figure out some things. Just a few days, I think."

"Let me talk. Puleeese," Tyler's voice interrupted again.

"Okay," Wyatt said, and then there was a brief silence as Tyler took the phone. DJ's heart sank as he tried to figure out how to explain.

"Hey, buddy."

"Is Mama there?"

"Not with me right now. I'm just out for a motorcycle ride." He paused before continuing. "Hey, I just told Wyatt that it may be a few days before we actually get there."

The silence hurt to hear. "Why?" Tyler finally asked.

"We need to take care of some business first."

"Are you gonna go get Dom?" Tyler whispered. Was the kid psychic, or an eavesdropper?

"We aren't sure. You be good for Uncle Wyatt, okay?"

"Dad?"

"Yeah?"

"Hurry up, okay?"

DJ laughed. "I'll try."

THE SOUND OF an engine had Tammie peeking through the curtains. It wasn't DJ's motorcycle and her spirits dipped.

She hadn't heard from DJ since he'd called the motel room a couple of hours ago. The brief conversation hadn't told her anything except the fact that he'd be late.

She looked around. The parking lot was empty, except for a huge king cab, shiny fire-engine-red pickup truck. The streetlight gleamed off the chrome and…she stared. A suspiciously familiar motorcycle was secured in the bed. DJ's bike? What—

Pulling open the door, she stepped out, glanced right, then left.

"Ain't she pretty?" DJ asked from beside the door.

She spun around. "She?"

"Yeah." He pushed away from the wall where she hadn't seen him standing. "I know you don't like traveling on the bike, and with where we're going… I don't want to put the miles on it anyway."

She stared at him as her mouth hung open. She purposefully closed it. "Is that where you've been all this time? Buying a truck?"

He grinned and held up two fast-food bags. "I brought a peace offering."

"I'm not hungry." Her stomach made a liar out of her by grumbling just then.

He laughed and stepped inside the room. "Eat up. We've got work to do."

"Work?" He'd said they were going somewhere. "Where exactly are we going?" Did she really want to know?

"New Orleans to start," he said, in the same nonchalant voice he'd probably used to order their food.

"What? Oh, no, we're not." She'd expected him to say the ranch. What was happening here? "I'm not going anywhere with you." She tried to hold on to her earlier anger, but time and the relief that he'd actually come back made it difficult.

He laughed again and leaned in close. "You act like you have a choice."

She growled. She was so sick and tired of men telling her what to do. First her father, then Dom… and now…him. Uh-uh, no. She opened her mouth to speak, but before she could say a word, he continued.

"So, you weren't serious yesterday? When you said you wanted your life back?" He unloaded the food and spread the meal out on the tiny table by the window.

"I meant it."

"Then we need to get started."

"We?" Her head spun. "H-how? By having burgers?"

DJ was silent a long time, folding his arms over his chest and staring down at her the whole while.

She couldn't read his expression, much less his mind. It frustrated her that this man, who seemed to read her so well, hadn't shared much of himself with her. He'd given her a child, permeated her life, and in less than twenty-four hours, he'd turned everything upside down.

"You—" DJ strolled close "—need to learn how to hunt."

"Hunt? Hunt what? And why New Orleans?"

"The best tracker I know is there. Colin was in my unit, and if there's info out there to find someone, he's on it. He'll help us find him."

"Him?"

"Dom."

Dom's face, and all the months of pain and anger, filled her mind. She looked at DJ for a long minute, using time as an excuse to think. Was he crazy? Or was this the opportunity she'd been praying for? "I don't know..." But the longer she thought about it, the more she wanted it to be the solution.

Her decision must have shown on her face. DJ nodded and sat down at the table. "Oh, yeah. You're gonna do just fine, mama bear."

She fought the smile at his unintended compliment. She would do anything for Tyler, and she liked knowing that he knew it.

"What's this?" She indicated the table of food with a wave of her hand. "My last meal or fortification?"

"Definitely fortification. It'll do for now." He took a bite of the thick burger, and Tammie stared.

There was something different about him, something calmer, focused. Slowly, she sat down across from him.

"I remember you don't like onions," he said before stuffing a half-dozen fries into his mouth. "So I left them off."

A wisp of memory joined them. She didn't dislike onions. But she'd been on the beach with the cutest boy she'd ever met and was hoping he'd kiss her. Her face warmed.

She nodded, enjoying the greasy burger and the memory. Outside the window, beyond the behemoth truck and the ramshackle buildings, the sky sparkled with stars. So pretty.

They ate in silence for several long minutes. Tammie stared out the large window as she fiddled with her French fries. "So," she finally said. "Tell me… a-about him. How he's doing." She knew her voice sounded full of sadness and for the first time she didn't try to hide her emotions. They both knew who *he* was.

DJ didn't answer at first. He silently finished his burger. "He misses you. You taught him to wish on stars, didn't you?"

She looked down and nodded. What must he, the tough, strong marine, think of his son being caught up in fairy tales? "I…needed something that would connect us." She glanced out the window again. "The stars are always there."

Silence filled the room. Finally, she ventured a

look over at DJ. He was staring at her, his eyes filled with something she couldn't identify.

Their gazes met, clung, then suddenly, he stood, crumpling the paper wrapper in a noisy disruption. "Are you finished?"

"Uh, yeah." She hesitated, then reached out and put her hand on his arm. The thick muscles shifted beneath his tanned skin. "DJ?"

"Yeah?" He continued gathering up the unused napkins and empty ketchup packets, moving away from her touch.

"Are you? What I mean is—" She cleared her throat. "He's your son, too. I know you'd have taught him things differently." She grabbed her cup and took a deep swallow of the soda to keep from doing anything she'd regret. He stopped and met her stare.

"Last night I told you I was impressed with how you raised him."

"Yeah. But?" She could hear it in his voice.

"But, damn it, you stole eight years of my son's life from me. You put yourself and him at risk."

Tammie bit her tongue to keep from apologizing. More slowly than he had, she gathered up the remnants of her own meal and tossed them into the bag.

"Why the hell didn't you find me? Why didn't you at least try?" He walked across the room and tossed the crumpled bag into the trash with more force than was necessary. "Or was that the plan? If Dom hadn't come after you, would you have ever contacted me?"

The hurt filling his voice surprised her.

"I...I don't know," she admitted. "I'd like to say I would have, but I can't honestly say."

Tammie half expected him to leave her again, and this time not come back. She waited, holding her breath. He moved close, invading her personal space. "Tyler needs both of us." His voice was a deep growl. "I'm not giving him up. Don't ever try to keep me from him again."

She met his stare. "Agreed. But you can't keep him from me, either."

DJ's nod was swift and short. "Agreed."

The ping of DJ's phone surprised them both. He hesitated, then reached into his pocket and pulled it out. He smiled, a look that transformed his face. For an instant, she lost her breath.

"Speak of the devil." He looked at the phone's screen and laughed at what he read. "Tyler just texted."

"Texted?" Tyler knew how to text? She didn't even own a phone.

"Yeah, he's on Wyatt's phone." DJ laughed again. "It's about his 4-H project."

"His what?"

"His project for 4-H. It's an organization for kids. They do projects, learn about animals, farm life, that kind of stuff. It was Wyatt's idea when I left, to give Tyler something to focus on besides the people who aren't there."

"Oh." That hurt. She didn't want him lonely or

sad. Her hate for Dom grew a little more. "What's he doing?"

"I'm not sure I should tell you." He laughed, giving her a moment to wonder what he was hiding.

"Is it something dangerous?" Surely they weren't letting an eight-year-old raise a bull.

"Could be." He let her squirm just a bit. "Wyatt helped him buy those two baby pigs in the picture I gave you. He's going to raise them for market."

She stood and walked over to her pack. The picture was already safely stashed inside her book. Carefully, her back to DJ, she pulled it out and returned the book to its spot.

Tyler's smile was so wide. He must have been laughing. She could almost hear it. Her eyes burned.

"He just texted to let me know what he's named them." DJ hit the keypad and scrolled down on the screen before handing her the phone. She read the words, trying to hear Tyler's voice in her thoughts. She ignored the faint tone of it. "Hamlet and Pork Chop?" She wiped her eyes, unsure if her tears were from joy or pain. Probably a little of both. "Wyatt let him name them that?"

"Why not? Sounds appropriate to me."

He loved Tyler, she realized. She saw the pride in his eyes, saw the likeness again that he shared with her son.

"Thank you." She looked at DJ as she handed the phone back. "He hasn't changed. He's still my Tyler."

"Yes, he is."

With a prayer of thanks, she vowed she'd be with him again. Soon.

They each held an end of the phone. "So, what do I—*we*—do now, DJ? How do we hunt?"

CHAPTER EIGHT

ENDLESS STRETCHES OF highway normally gave DJ a sense of freedom. Usually, though, he was on a bike, in the open air. Not sitting in a closed truck cab with a woman—a woman he vividly remembered spending the night with on a faraway beach.

For the first fifty miles, Tammie sat staring out the side window, barely speaking, leaning against the door, as if she wanted to be as far away from him as possible.

He glanced at her every once in a while. The circles under her eyes this morning were proof that, despite her recent sleep, she was still near exhaustion.

"You can rest," he said softly, not looking directly at her.

"I'm fine."

"No, you're not. But do whatever you want." He focused on the road ahead. Glancing at the dash clock, he mentally calculated how much longer they would be on the road. It took eight hours to get from Austin to New Orleans. They were three hours in. He nearly groaned.

Another twenty miles and Tammie's head was leaning against the glass, her eyes closed. He took the luxury of looking, really looking at her.

He definitely saw Tyler in her face. Their son

looked a lot like he had at that age, but the eyes, the point of his chin…those were pure Tammie. For the moment, she looked relaxed and more like the girl he remembered. With a sigh, he settled deeper into the seat and sat back for the long haul.

"Tell me something," she whispered.

"I thought you were asleep."

"Almost," she admitted, not moving, not opening her eyes. "Back at the motel, when you were talking to Tyler, you said something about the ranch. That's where he's staying?"

"Yeah. At Wyatt's place. It used to be our granddad's."

"Tell me about him."

The silence grew long. "Who? Wyatt?"

She nodded with a faint smile on her lips.

DJ started slowly. "He's a good man. Tough. Solid. Perfect older-brother material." DJ paused as if thinking how to word what he said next. "He's eight years older than me, and remembers Dad and Granddad better than I do. Maybe that's why I don't have the attachment to the ranch that Wyatt does." He paused, seeing his brother in his mind. "I think Wyatt must have ridden the range in a former life, back in the Old West."

"What do you remember about your dad?"

"Not much. Snatches, mostly."

"I know you probably told me, but how old were you when he died?"

"Six. I'd just started first grade." DJ recalled the

sadness of Dad's funeral, vaguely, from a distant child's point of view. He remembered his grandfather's funeral a few years later more clearly. Maybe because DJ had been old enough to understand what was happening. Maybe because Wyatt had been so deeply affected.

Or maybe because it had been the last true connection to that side of the family. He wasn't sure.

Family. DJ hadn't thought much about it until lately. Until Mom had passed away last year. Until he'd come face-to-face with the reality of being a dad himself.

Until Tyler.

"You talked about hunting. Who taught you how to hunt?" she whispered, half-asleep.

"None of them." He wanted to laugh. "That was the military."

DJ stared out the brand-new, filthy windshield at the two-lane highway. A soft sigh came from Tammie, and he glanced sideways again.

"So, why exactly do we have to go to New Orleans?"

DJ frowned. "It's the old kill-two-birds-with-one-stone idea. Colin's researching Dom as we speak. He'll have plenty of info for us by the time we get there."

"Why not just talk over the phone?"

DJ shrugged. "It's easier to work together in person. Besides, I think you're right."

"Right about what?" She perked up as if he'd paid her a compliment.

"That this needs to stay as far away from Tyler, and my family, as possible. I'm banking on Dom following you."

Tammie nodded. "What if he doesn't?"

"He will." At least, DJ hoped he would. Otherwise, he wasn't sure where they'd go from here.

A few more miles passed before he looked at her again. This time she was asleep, her head lolled on the lovely new leather bucket seat. The crown of her head rested against the windowpane.

What was she dreaming about? Every few minutes she mumbled something or frowned. He wished he could slip into her mind and see what she saw. Hear what she heard. Fix what was obviously bothering her.

She'd given him some information—enough to convince him that she needed a champion. She didn't think she did, and while he wasn't the white knight riding in on his trusty steed—his gaze flicked back to the bike anchored in the bed of the truck—he *was* here to help her.

No one should battle alone. Independence was one thing—alone was a totally different equation. And DJ didn't believe in alone. As one of six children, he understood mob mentality. Which might partially explain why he'd joined the military straight out of high school instead of going to college to pursue his own career.

Everyone needed someone at their back.

And he would watch Tammie's—whether she liked it or not. He settled deeper in his seat, the reassurance of making a decision keeping him company over the next four hundred miles.

TAMMIE STARED OUT the truck window as they approached the outskirts of New Orleans. Her heart sank just a little as she saw the familiar skyline. It didn't look all that different from when she'd left here just a few months ago.

It had been nighttime then, not late afternoon with slanting sunlight like now. She remembered that second time she'd run, with nothing more than the few things in her backpack and Tyler.

She'd naively hoped that by leaving in the middle of the night, they'd elude Dom. Memories tightened her throat. She'd never felt so alone and lost as she had that night. The first time, when she'd left Florida, she'd had her anger to keep her going. Desperation wasn't nearly as good a companion.

"What're you thinking about with that frown?" DJ's voice startled her. He hadn't said much for the past few miles, likely focusing on the drive and his own thoughts.

Tammie shook her head. "I don't know," she whispered.

"We're doing this together, remember? You're not on your own anymore."

She looked over at him. The setting sun painted his

tanned skin and blond hair a rich gold. His gaze met hers, and for an instant, that old connection returned. She looked away first. "Where are we staying?" She didn't care, but she needed the conversation.

He laughed. "Don't get your hopes up." He signaled and headed to the next off-ramp. "It's about the same star rating as the last place." He stopped at the light along a deserted cross street. There were several buildings to the right—one was a truck-stop motel. She sighed. It would do.

She had less than a hundred dollars to her name. She'd have to take what she could. And besides, he was footing the bill.

She hadn't asked him about his funds—maybe she should have. She knew he was supporting Tyler, though she supposed Wyatt was helping out with that.

"Sorry, it's not what I'd like, either." He pulled up in front of the office. "For now, this is the best place." He reached for the door and turned back to face her once he stood on the pavement. "You coming?"

She appreciated that this time he asked her. But the reality was that once again, they were out on the edge of nowhere. She wasn't going anywhere, and they both knew it. "I'll wait here while you check us in." He nodded, and the resounding slam of the heavy metal door seemed so final.

She watched through the dirty window. He was limping again. She knew he'd deny it. The closer he got to the door, the smoother his gait became. She needed to stretch, too. Slowly, she opened the truck door and jumped to the pavement. The landing jarred her bones, and, as she walked back and forth along the length of the truck, everything ached. Thank goodness they'd stopped for the day.

The row of faded red doors caught her attention. She froze. *Gulp.* She hadn't thought about their sleeping arrangements before. She'd been too angry that he'd trapped her. She'd been exhausted, frightened, upset. Now? Now she was wide-awake and aware.

The glass door of the office opened then, and DJ stepped out. Their eyes met. Her breath hitched and time stood still. He wasn't limping now, though his steps were slow. As he moved closer, she tried, but failed, to pull her gaze away.

Sharing a room last night had been necessary, a simple solution. Tonight? She swallowed. She'd never get any sleep, not with him in the same room.

"You okay?" He stopped at the front of the truck, frowning at her.

"Uh, yeah. Just stiff from sitting so long." *Lame, really lame.*

He seemed satisfied with her answer. "We're right here." He nodded toward the first door beyond the truck. "Seemed easy."

"Works for me."

DJ walked over to the pale red door with an old brass number seven in the center and unlocked it. The darkened room beyond didn't look even remotely inviting. Her heart sank further.

Shaking her head to dispel the melancholia, she turned to grab her pack. DJ reached over the side of the truck bed and grabbed his duffel. He turned and a grimace flashed over his face. The whispered curse seemed loud in the quiet afternoon, but he didn't say anything more, ignoring her and disappearing into the shadows of the room.

She wanted to ask him if he was okay, to make sure his back wasn't hurting. But she knew he'd deny it even if he was in misery.

Slowly, her pack hitched up on her shoulder, Tammie followed him inside. The ancient hotel room was cramped, just like the last one. Two double beds with a wall-mounted nightstand between them. The pictures on the wall were definitely mass-produced… something. *And* bolted down.

DJ's phone rang then, startling her. She looked over as he pulled it out of his pocket and answered. He'd gotten two calls today. One from the friend they'd come here to meet. He hadn't mentioned who the second caller was, but she knew. Based on the way his body language softened and how the smile grew on his face—if it hadn't been Tyler himself, the call was definitely in relation to him.

She was glad they'd developed a bond, cared about each other. Yes, she was glad about that. She flopped back on the bed and stared at the ceiling, trying not to think about the sound of DJ's voice, or the information that might come from the conversation he was having.

It was hopeless. His voice, deep and smooth, washed over her. If he weren't a marine, he could easily make a living on the radio. Late-night radio where it was quiet and dark… She popped her eyes open again, trying to ignore the image of DJ behind her eyelids.

"That was Colin." He tapped her leg as if he thought she'd actually gone to sleep.

"Okay." What else could she say?

"He'll meet us in about an hour, once he's off duty. That work for you?"

He'd already ended the call, why was he even asking? "Sure." She closed her eyes again, glad when he stopped talking, so she didn't have to deal with how his voice sounded and felt.

The silence grew thick. The bed dipped from his weight. She opened one eye just enough to see that he was sitting there, staring at her.

"What?" she asked.

He frowned and shook his head. Slowly, he rose to his feet, and she realized he must be in pain. The hours sitting had exhausted her. What had they done to him? She didn't know the full extent of his injuries. It obviously hadn't been that long ago that he'd been hurt. She rose up to lean on her elbows. "DJ? You okay?"

"Yeah. I'm used to it." He dug around in his duffel bag, tossing shirts on the bed. She watched him pull out the amber pharmacy bottle.

"DJ?" she repeated.

He stopped and looked back over his shoulder at her. "I'm fine." He went into the minuscule bathroom and filled the cheap glass beside the sink with water and downed the pills and several swallows of water. A couple of deep breaths later, he turned around and came out to face her. The lines of pain etched into his face.

"You should have said something. We could have stopped earlier."

"I said I was fine."

"Oh, great." She flopped back on the bed. "Typical stubborn man," she mumbled.

"What?"

"It's true. Rather than admit you're in pain, you suffer and just keep driving." She really needed something to do—something to distract herself from actually worrying about him.

"I've been through worse."

She knew that. She'd seen the scars on his back.

"I know." Slowly, she turned her head and met his stare. He looked better already—the medication was helping. "What happened to your back?"

DJ's eyes widened and two flags of color appeared on his cheeks. "It's not important."

"Not important?" He'd obviously suffered. It had changed him—of course it was important.

"Yeah, not important." He glanced at his watch and moved away. "We're meeting Colin in an hour. We can leave in fifteen minutes and be there in plenty of time."

"Tyler tries that, too."

"Tries what?"

"To change the subject when he doesn't want to talk to me about what's going on."

"You're comparing me to an eight-year-old?"

"Yep." She tried to lighten the mood. "An eight-year-old who *is* related to you." Maybe DJ would share if he didn't feel threatened.

"Not going to work." He grinned, with little humor in his face. "Besides, behavior isn't inherited. Ask Colin about what happened if you're so danged interested in old news. He loves to gossip." DJ headed back to the bathroom. "I'm gonna take a quick shower."

Exasperated, Tammie let him off the hook. She took the opportunity to freshen up, too, and soon they were headed back to the truck. She dreaded more driving, but it wasn't far, and there was a purpose to the trip. To put an end to the nightmare she'd been living for the past year. She hoped.

Neither spoke as they drove through the streets of New Orleans. Sights grew familiar as they passed older buildings and houses, some still storm-battered. The sun vanished and the daylight gave way to neon and the thumping beat of music. DJ pulled into the parking lot of a club at the edge of the French Quarter and killed the engine. She not only heard, but felt the music wrap around them.

She'd already climbed out when DJ rounded the front of the truck. She watched him, looking for signs of his pain. His face was irritatingly blank. Offering her a hand, he waited for her to slip hers into his. She didn't say anything, simply lifted a brow in question. He didn't say anything, either, just stared back.

As they walked toward the club, he curled his fingers around hers. Possessive, warm, solid. She should resent it, but for some odd reason she didn't. It felt good. Right.

"Stay close," he said in her ear, the heat of his breath sending shivers over the skin of her neck and the exposed ridge of her collarbone. She resisted, barely, the urge to lean into him and complete the illusion that they were a couple simply going out for the evening.

But that's all it was—an illusion. Why did that realization steal her energy, filling her with a disappointment she didn't recognize? Or maybe she did recognize it. She just didn't want to admit that he was getting to her. Mentally, she cursed and forced herself to ease her hand out of his warm grasp when they reached the bar's door. She put space between them, and he let her.

Her disappointment grew. Life sucked.

Thank goodness the sudden blare of music shifted her attention to the insanity of the club.

NEW ORLEANS AT NIGHT. The lights. The music. The clubs. DJ watched the flashes of red and gold light play across Tammie's face as she stared in wonder at all the sights around them. Colin was already here—

he'd texted from inside the bar. Colin had insisted they meet away from the base and their commanding officer's all-too-observant eyes.

Neon lights bathed the front section of the club. DJ remembered another trip here a few years back. Not a good memory. They'd ended up in a bar fight that resulted in two months' restrictions. They'd have gotten away with it if Colin had ducked instead of taking the full force of his opponent's punch. The shiner he'd sported for weeks afterward was all the evidence their commanding officer needed.

"Do you see him?" Tammie stopped and looked around the crowded club.

"Not yet." He took her arm. What was Colin thinking? How were they going to have a conversation here? Shaking his head, he wove through the crowd of gyrating bodies.

They finally found him at the back, in one of the wooden booths that lined the far wall. Colin lifted a beer in salute as he met DJ's eye.

"Is that him?" Tammie asked.

DJ nodded and considered turning around. He didn't, though. Usually, he enjoyed Colin's company and they certainly knew how to paint a town red. Every shade of red.

But introducing him to Tammie was a whole new thing.

Tammie scooted into the booth, leaning back against the wall and smiling across at his friend. Colin smiled back and waved the waitress over. From the number of empties on the wood surface, it looked as if Colin had been here awhile, and the waitress's smile indicated she'd been here, too.

Surprisingly, the high wooden walls muffled the cacophony of music in the club. After they'd ordered drinks, DJ looked over at Colin. "What the heck are we doing *here*?"

"We needed to talk and I need sustenance." He lifted the beer and took a swallow as he glanced over at Tammie. "Plus, no one will hear us here." His smile broadened. "This must be Tammie."

Colin was over six feet tall, broad shouldered with a warm, if reserved, smile. He attracted his own brand of trouble, but DJ wouldn't want anyone else at his back. He'd entrusted this man with his life countless times.

"Colin, right?" Tammie asked. "Thanks for meeting us."

"Always nice to share a drink with a pretty lady."

Tammie blushed. DJ stared. What the hell was with her, anyway?

When he'd stepped out of the motel bathroom from his shower this afternoon, she'd transformed from the worn-out late-night-diner waitress into the ethereal girl he'd met all those years ago. She'd done her hair so that the long curls wound around themselves to just past her shoulders, and she'd slipped on a white shirt and formfitting jeans.

This was supposed to be a business meeting, not a frickin' party. He cursed and ordered another beer.

"Are we going to discuss anything here tonight, or just drink?" DJ finally snapped, finishing his beer.

"Maybe." Colin tilted his head, considering them both. "You two look like you could use a little break. Maybe dance or something." He took a swig of his beer. "Cut the tension."

DJ growled. The idea of holding Tammie, dancing, not a good idea. At all.

"You're right. We are a bit tense." She took a deep breath. "Seems like ages since I could relax." She actually looked at the dance floor…wistfully? Longingly?

"Not my fault." DJ glared at her. Maybe if she'd told him about Tyler. Maybe if she'd told *someone*, and let them share in the caregiving, she might have had a chance to enjoy life. Maybe…

"Excuse me?" Tammie shot to her feet, glaring down at him. "I'll be back." She headed toward the ladies' room, her back straight, her chin high.

He let her go without a word, since he could see the door from here.

"Brilliant move." Colin took a drink of his beer. "You *trying* to piss her off, or is that simply one of your many talents?"

"Shut up." DJ regretted the outburst. He'd apologize later. He shifted in the seat, putting his bad mood off to the dull ache in his back, not his reaction to the way Tammie seemed immediately comfortable with Colin.

"How are you doing these days, DJ?" Colin leaned

back, his eyes serious, intense. He wasn't saying much yet, but he didn't have to. DJ knew him too well, knew what he was really asking. He appreciated his friend's concern, but now wasn't the time. Besides, he was healed. As good as he was going to get.

DJ shrugged. "Fine. For an unemployed, unskilled marine." Before he could let any more of his own uncertainties surface, he shut off the conversation. "You know why we're here." DJ looked directly at Colin.

"Yeah."

"Well? Are you going to help us?"

"Depends. You going to keep treating me like I'm moving in on your territory?" One eyebrow lifted, but otherwise, there was no indication of emotion, which only ticked DJ off more. That look reminded DJ way too much of his older brother Wyatt.

"You're imagining things."

Colin leaned forward, his forearms on the worn table. "Am I?"

DJ wanted to deck him, but didn't think that would help their cause. He and Tammie needed Colin's help. He had access to some of the country's most crucial intel—intel that might tell them where the hell Dom was.

Tammie returned then, taking her seat and sipping her beer without a word.

DJ looked over at her. She glared at him, but he couldn't read her. Maybe he didn't want to. "Okay," DJ relented. "We're all on the same team here. I guess the question really should be, *can* you help us?"

CHAPTER NINE

THE NOW-FAMILIAR RINGTONE of DJ's phone shattered the night. Tammie stared into the darkness, her heart pounding. Where was she? Slowly, memories returned. Of the motel. Of meeting Colin at the club earlier. Of the silent trip back in the truck with DJ.

The ringing continued, accompanied by a soft thump. DJ's curses stopped only when the screen lit up after he found the phone on the floor. "Hello," he answered.

"Dad?"

It was so quiet, Tammie could hear Tyler's voice echo across the room.

"What's wrong?" Tammie whispered, suddenly wide-awake and perched on the edge of the mattress. "Is he okay?"

"Are you awake?" Tyler whispered.

DJ's deep chuckle dispelled some of her fear. "Uh, I am now. You okay?"

"Yep. I need to talk to you. 'Simportant."

"It better be, considering it's nearly two a.m. Shouldn't you be asleep?"

"Yeeeeah." He stretched the word out. "I don't have school tomorrow. And I was out in the tree thinkin'. And I…I can't wait too long."

"Can't wait for what?"

"To tell you and Mama stuff. I'm 'fraid I'll forget 'fore you and Mama get home."

The silence in the room thickened. The phone looked minuscule in DJ's big hand, and though it was against his ear, faint light from the screen outlined his features. His eyes were closed, but the hint of his smile teased the corners of his lips. "Okay, what's so important?"

"I wanna tell Mama, too. Is…is she really there with you?"

"I think she's sleeping, buddy."

Tammie had made it clear she wasn't up to talking with Tyler on the phone. The fear of breaking down and not being able to say goodbye was too strong. She appreciated DJ remembering that.

"Are you sure? Maybe you should check."

"Hold on a second."

DJ turned on his side, levering up on an elbow. For a brief instant, she saw the rest of him illuminated in the phone's light. His chest was bare, the blankets pulled up to his waist. Tearing her gaze from its wandering path, she forced herself to look at his face. Only his face. Then regretted that, as well. His hair was sleep-mussed and she could even smell him—he smelled like heaven. Man and aftershave.

He shoved the phone under a pillow, plunging them both into darkness. "I know you're awake."

"Yeah. Loud enough ring?"

He laughed. "Does the job. You ready to talk to him yet?"

She'd known this moment would come. Known she couldn't avoid it forever. Knew she had to shore up her weaknesses. She closed her eyes for a long minute and took a deep breath. "Yes. I can do this," she said as much to herself as him.

DJ pulled the phone out from under the pillow and hit a button. With a soft little beep, the call went to speaker. She moved closer to the phone as he waved her nearer. She perched on the very edge of his bed.

"Okay, kiddo. We're here. What's so important?" DJ asked.

Suddenly in DJ's space, with his body-warmed bed beneath her, she realized this was a mistake. Just as she could see him, surely he could see her in her thin blue T-shirt and short shorts.

"Mama? Are you really there?" Tyler's voice was a breathy whisper that made her tear her gaze from DJ. She ached to reach through the phone and hold her son.

"Yeah, baby. It's me." She struggled to keep her voice even.

"I miss you, Mama. When are you and Dad comin' home?"

"We talked about that, remember?" DJ saved her from having to speak. "We have some business to take care of for your mom, and then we'll head back to Texas. We'll let you know."

"I— Okay." He didn't sound happy.

Tammie found her voice. "It's late. What do you need to tell us, baby?"

"Uncle Wyatt said I had to ask *you*, Dad."

"Oh, Lord," DJ whispered and looked at her. Their eyes met. He didn't look away. "What'd he tell you to ask me?"

"It's 'bout Pork Chop. She got an infected tooth."

"Pork Chop?"

"The pig," Tammie reminded him with a whisper.

"Oh, right," he whispered back.

"Uncle Wyatt said it's a tusk," Tyler continued as if there hadn't been any interruption. "She was chewin' on the fence and got a splinter stuck in her mouth."

DJ's scent wrapped around her, and even here, in the dim light, Tammie saw the glint in DJ's eyes, the rough stubble along his strong jaw, the broad muscles of his shoulders and chest.

DJ cleared his throat. "What'd Wyatt do?"

The silence on the line vibrated through the room. Tammie tried to focus on her son, but the man so close, staring at her so intently, disrupted all her coherent thoughts.

"Tyler?" DJ asked without looking away.

"Well, the vet was s'posed to come take the tusk out next week, but Pork Chop was really unhappy and Uncle Wyatt said she was in pain. So we bought a twelve-pack of beer for her."

That broke through the haze in Tammie's brain. She turned to stare at the phone still nestled in DJ's hand. "You what?"

"Yeah, Mama. That's how you save on a vet bill. We got her drunk and then she let Chet pull her tooth. We pulled that tooth out real quick and easy. Uncle Wyatt and Walt—he's worked on the ranch forever—held on to Pork Chop after she fell asleep. Just in case."

"Um—" Tammie was speechless, and not just from the image of a drunk pig. DJ's breath fanning over the bare skin of her arm and neck made her shiver, and not with cold.

"Pork Chop wasn't very happy today."

"I'll bet not." DJ laughed the same instant he reached over and looped a stray curl falling across Tammie's eyes behind her ear.

"I heard Uncle Wyatt and Chet sayin' she had a hangover. What's that?" Tyler's voice seemed suddenly loud in the room.

Tammie looked over at DJ. She wasn't explaining, and she couldn't wait to see how he handled the question. He met her gaze with one of those cocky grins she'd come to know so well. "It means she had too much to drink and it didn't agree with her tummy."

Tammie rolled her eyes, and finally gave in to the laughter bubbling inside.

"Oh. Maybe we should give her some Pepto-Bismol. Chet has some. I'll ask him."

DJ lost it then. "Yeah," he croaked out. "You tell Chet I'll pay to see those pictures."

Tammie laughed then, too. She reached over to playfully smack DJ for being no help. "Stop encouraging him." But as soon as her hand touched bare skin, her laughter died and she froze. The room fell silent again as DJ's laughter dissolved.

Slowly, oh-so-slowly, DJ leaned toward her. The warmth of him reached out and touched her an instant before he slid his hand beneath her hair and around to the nape of her neck. Gently, he anchored her there as he moved in to kiss her.

His lips were warm, soft, yet solid. Just like the man whose chest muscles flexed beneath her palm.

"Mama? Dad? You still there?"

"Uh, yeah." DJ recovered first, pulling back slowly. "Was that what you were supposed to ask me?"

"No. I wanted to know what a tusk is worth if the tooth fairy came."

DJ couldn't answer. He was laughing too hard.

Tammie glared at him and took the opportunity to scamper back to her bed. "It's late, Tyler," she said from across the room. "Your dad will have to think about that. You need to get to bed, sweetie." She hoped neither Tyler nor his father heard the tremor in her voice.

"I know." The sad, pitiful note in Tyler's voice tore at her heart.

"We'll be there soon. Promise. Now, get some sleep."

"Okay. Love you, Mama."

"Love you, too, sweetheart." Her voice shook only a little this time.

"'Night, Dad."

Once the call ended, the room fell dark and silent again. Tammie tried to quietly take several deep breaths, putting off the pounding of her heart to the suddenness of the late-night call.

"I'm not apologizing." DJ's disembodied voice startled her.

"I…I didn't ask you to." She nearly told him it didn't matter but decided to remain silent since he wouldn't like her flippant answer. Besides, she'd be lying.

The silence stretched. "Good night, Tammie." She heard the rustle of blankets and then the quiet of no one stirring. Why was she disappointed? She rolled over and spent the next hour trying to force herself to fall asleep.

"YOU'RE TAKING ME SHOPPING?" Tammie stared at DJ in the mirror as she combed her hair the next morning. He'd surely lost his mind. "I don't need anything. I'm fine," she lied.

"Uh, yeah." He smirked. "You keep telling yourself that. Come on." He headed to the door and held it open for her. With a mock bow, he waved her through and out into the midday sun.

The big red truck gleamed in the bright light. She'd spent so much time in it the past couple days that she was starting to feel as if it was as much home as any of the apartments she'd lived in over the past year. Her heart hitched as she thought of her house, gone. Long gone. She missed it. Missed that sense of coming home. Of feeling completely safe and comfortable in something she'd worked so hard for.

Anger threatened to overcome her good mood. Her anger at Dom never really went away, but right now, she didn't have the time or energy for it.

She didn't ask where they were going. It didn't matter. They could look, but she wasn't buying anything. Her measly hundred dollars was for bare necessities. That was it. Dread threatened to suck her in. Looking at all the things she couldn't have wouldn't make for a good day. Her heart sank. "We aren't going to look for something for Tyler, are we?" His birthday loomed on the horizon and she couldn't bear thinking about being away from him for it. She'd never been away from him on that day—it was their special day.

"Nope." DJ turned into the parking lot of an upscale mall. "But if you see something you think he'd like, let me know. I'm still trying to figure out what to get him for his birthday. He sure as hell isn't getting what he asked for."

Another dagger to the heart. Not knowing what he wanted was a new and unpleasant feeling. "What… what did he ask for?" she whispered, struggling to get the words out.

"A dirt bike."

"You're right. You're not getting that for him." She turned in the seat as much as the seat belt would allow her. "And you certainly aren't ever going to teach him how to ride one." The way DJ had spun the bike the other night came to mind and she shivered.

DJ laughed. "I may be new at this parenting thing, but I'm not *that* stupid." He parked and climbed out. He pocketed the keys and waited for her to follow.

Despite it being the middle of the week, in the middle of the day, the parking lot was already busy. Dozens of cars lined up in neat rows, all gleaming in the hot sun. The air-conditioning inside the mall felt good.

DJ led her to a women's store not far from the entrance. Beheaded mannequins wore stylish outfits complete with jewelry, scarves and purses to match. One display wore an outfit similar to one she'd left behind in Florida. That pang of missing her house, her stuff, her life, came back.

"See anything you like?" DJ sidled up next to her. "I like this." He pointed at the outfit she'd been eyeing.

"It's nice."

"You don't like it?"

"It's fine."

DJ watched her for a long minute—long enough to make her feel uncomfortable. "What?" she finally asked.

"Get it. It's my treat."

"No."

He kept staring. His gaze took her in and she wondered what he was thinking. He didn't say anything, simply turned around and waved at the saleslady.

"Come on." He grabbed Tammie's hand and pulled her behind him.

"DJ, stop."

He did, two racks away. "Okay, here's the deal." He made sure she was looking at him, listening. "You and I are going on a hunt, right? Colin is getting us all the information he can about the *who.* Now we need to set the trap. Consider this your part of our hunt."

"That's ridiculous."

"No, it's not."

As he led her to the counter, DJ pulled out his wallet, and once they'd reached the saleslady, he tossed out a couple hundred-dollar bills. There were more in his wallet. "Get her that outfit in the window. And a couple others. Please. This should get us started."

The girl's eyes lit up. "Do you have anything else in mind?" She looked at DJ, not Tammie.

"Don't ask me." He frowned. "She's the one buying and wearing it."

"Sure." The girl reluctantly faced Tammie. "Let's see what we can come up with."

Two hours and a zillion outfits later, DJ led Tammie out of the shop with three bags and a feeling of shell shock. "I… Thank you," she whispered.

He didn't respond immediately, but then stopped and turned to face her. "I wish I could convince you how much you deserve this." He waved at the array of bags. "Here, let me take those."

"I've got it." She pulled back, thinking of his

"You're killing me," he murmured as he gathered up the trash and strode to the trash can nearby. "Before I do or say something stupid, let's go." His voice came out gruff.

Silently, Tammie followed him out of the food court and back into the flow of traffic moving down the aisle. They didn't speak. She had no idea where they were going or what to say.

A jewelry store, and the glimmer of gold in a bright spotlight, caught her eye. She looked up, seeing a familiar name. The store chain had carried her work before. She turned her head, and then as if in slow motion, she stopped and stared at the display.

Her design. Her unique blend of gold and gems, twisted and wired together, the necklace laid there on the white velvet bed. She couldn't breathe. She couldn't move. How had it gotten here? Who—

"What's the matter?" DJ stood at her elbow.

Again in slow motion, she turned to look at him. "Mine," was all she could manage to say.

"Really?"

She nodded.

"Your property, or your design?"

"I…I made that." Her throat closed up and the burning in the back of her eyes hurt. "He made me—" She couldn't speak.

DJ didn't say anything, just stalked into the store. "We want to see that display piece."

"Yes, sir." The young man with a key ring walked

up to the window, and Tammie watched him open the locked door.

"Tammie?" DJ called, his voice breaking through the spell that had enveloped her. She followed DJ into the store. Without the velvet display behind it, the necklace looked even more like the piece she remembered.

Slowly, she reached out, running a finger over the smooth gold. Touching it, feeling the curves and edges, shook her out of the stupor. She lifted it—it was the correct weight in the palm of her hand. She tilted it in the light. Checking. Examining. Confirming. "Do you have a loupe?" she asked the clerk and he quickly produced one from under the counter.

Putting the loupe to her eye, she could see the work and jewels clearly. "Yeah, it's mine." The jewels were different, though. Not the stolen ones. She swallowed hard. She'd made a dozen pieces. Where were the others?

"Excuse me." The salesman took an offended stance. "This is the property of the store."

"No, not my property," she hastily corrected before he called the mall security. "My design."

"I don't think so." The young man looked genuinely puzzled. "This is the work of a man. *He's* a hot new designer. That's why the work is on display in the window."

"Who?" Something resembling anger, mixed with fear, raced through her.

"I have a brochure." He walked to the back of the

store and reached beneath the counter. "Here." He handed her a glossy tri-fold with beautiful pictures of several all-too-familiar designs.

Tammie turned it over and could barely see the designer's picture through the bright angry red haze. It was Dom, from several years ago, and he was using a different name. "I'm gonna kill him. I'm seriously going to kill him. The picture's old and has been digitally altered, but that's him."

She looked over at DJ and shivered. The fun-loving man she'd just shared a sweet snack with was gone. The soldier was back. She might have *vocalized* that Dom was going to die, but the look in DJ's eyes suggested he had a good idea of how it could happen.

The salesclerk took a step back, his eyes wide.

"We'll take it," DJ growled.

"No, you can't afford it," she protested. Even if he were paying for it at her cost, it was too much.

DJ glared at her, then whipped out his wallet and tossed a platinum card onto the glass counter. "Wrap it up." DJ glanced back at her. "Please," he said through clenched teeth as if he were only being polite because she was there. She could envision him grabbing the necklace and pulling the clerk across the counter with one hand.

"And throw in one of those brochures," he called to the clerk as he returned to the register. "So I can cram it—" he whispered before she stopped him.

"DJ, please." How could she tell him she didn't want the necklace, that it was tainted now? That she couldn't ever look at that design, any of the designs Dom had made her do, without remembering, without hurting? Without feeling the urge to maim and cry at the same time?

DJ signed the credit card slip and took the small package. Instead of handing it to her, as he had all the other packages, this one he shoved into the pocket of his jacket.

"What are you going to do with that?" she asked as he stalked toward the shop's exit. She followed behind, trying not to drop any of the bags.

At the truck, he hit the key fob, startling her with the beep it made unlocking the doors. Silently, DJ helped her put the bags in the backseat and climb up into the cab. Finally, once he was settled behind the wheel, he turned and faced her.

"To think—" He stared at her for a long silent minute. "That you made that. It…it's amazing. And he—" DJ's fists curled around the steering wheel in a stranglehold. "He took it, and thinks he can get away with this?"

Tammie stared at DJ in shock. No one had ever taken her side like that before, with such passion. Her vision blurred, and she looked down at her hands clasped in her lap. "Thank you," she whispered.

"What for?" His confusion showed in her eyes.

"For—" She couldn't put it into words. Instead, she leaned across the console and gently kissed his cheek. "For believing me."

DJ let go of the steering wheel. His hands settled

along her jaw, holding her face to his as his lips found hers. Tasting, kissing, devouring.

The silence stretched out, punctuated only by ragged breaths as his lips returned to hers—again and again and again.

He leaned forward to pull her into his arms, then cursed. "Damned bucket seats."

DJ's cell phone rang just then, and he cursed a little more. Tammie laughed and settled back with a smile.

"It's Colin."

"You'd better answer it," she said, wishing the world hadn't come back so quickly.

"Hello." DJ started the truck, and when they reached the exit of the mall, and he'd finished his conversation with Colin, he turned left, toward the military base, instead of right, toward the motel.

Tammie stared out the window and ignored her disappointment.

CHAPTER TEN

DJ PRETENDED THE KISS wasn't anything special. *Like hell.* It shook him. Shook him hard. On autopilot, he drove toward the base. *Focus on something else. Anything else.* The necklace. He was grasping at straws, but he really did want to show Colin the necklace. Hopefully the pamphlet would help him dig up more on this guy.

Besides, returning to the motel right now would be a mistake. A *big* mistake. DJ tried not to think about later.

Colin had agreed to meet them at the Exchange. Lunch in a very open, very public place with plenty of audience might help DJ resist the urge to grab Tammie and finish what he'd started.

Getting on base wasn't difficult as his ID was still active. Neither was navigating the streets, even though he hadn't been here for a couple of years.

Which was a good thing since his brain was misfiring. At every intersection, he imagined pulling a fast U-turn and racing back to the motel room… He forced his thoughts to stop there—before he mentally ripped off Tammie's clothes.

Finally, he pulled the truck into the parking lot.

Colin stood at the entrance, looking more familiar in uniform than he had last night at the bar.

Colin grinned at them. "Don't you look lovely today."

"Why, thank you." DJ smirked.

"Not you, dork. Her."

All three laughed as they walked and joined the lunch crowd filling the building. Once seated in the molded plastic benches, DJ reached into his jacket pocket and pulled out the jeweler's package. He didn't open it, simply handed it to Colin, who peered inside.

"Holy—" He broke off and stared at Tammie. "That's amazing. DJ said you made this."

Tammie nodded, her cheeks bright red as if she were self-conscious. "It was one of my favorite designs."

DJ watched her closely, noting the past tense in that statement. Hurt and loss flashed across her face before she shut both down. The urge to reach over and grab her hand was strong, but he didn't. Something told him she wouldn't like it. He felt her pulling back. "What's wrong?" he finally asked.

"Nothing." The jeweler's bag sat in the middle of the table, and made a crinkling sound as she fingered the edge. As if suddenly realizing what she was doing, she yanked her hand away. She looked up, pinning him with a stare. "Why did you buy it?"

"Good question," Colin chimed in.

DJ shrugged. "It's yours."

"No, it's not." She bit out the words. "It's tainted and ugly now. He stole it. He stole everything." She focused on her meal, and DJ didn't push her.

"Captain Hawkins!" a young voice broke through the crowd.

DJ turned to see a teenager headed toward them. About fifteen, Caleb Walker was the son of the first sergeant in his unit. "Caleb, how are you?"

"I should be askin' you that. Nice to see you up and about." DJ knew all the kids of the men he served with. They were like his family. Suddenly, he realized none of them knew about Tyler, and Tyler would miss out on knowing them.

He'd always thought he'd be career military and his family, if he had one, would be a part of the military life.

A parade of familiar faces over the next few minutes helped distract him from the disappointment that threatened to swamp him.

When they'd finally finished eating, Tammie stood and gathered the remnants of their meal.

"You don't have to do that." DJ picked up his own trash and put it on the tray.

"I don't mind." She didn't look at either of them.

DJ's gaze followed Tammie as she wove through the tables and crowd.

"You better watch it, buddy." Colin's voice broke into DJ's thoughts.

"Watch what?"

one else. As they'd eaten and talked at lunch, several people had come up to DJ and greeted him. Smiling. Expressing well wishes.

She hadn't been able to read his reactions. He'd been polite, cordial and professional. She wondered what he really thought and felt.

The tall, steel-haired man facing them now, Major Dixon, was clearly someone DJ knew and respected. His polite facade remained in place, though.

"What are you doing here, sir?" DJ asked.

"Sergeant Walker said you were here. I wanted to see for myself if what he said was true."

"What did he say?"

"That you're doing well. Looks like he was telling the truth."

DJ nodded with a forced smile. "Still not good enough, though, sir."

The major shook his head. "I was real sorry to hear about your discharge. Damned shame."

The silence stretched out. "If you have time, stop in and see the men—I think they'd like that." He looked over at one of the office buildings behind the one they'd just left. "You know where they'll be this time of day."

"Yeah, that I do."

"If you want to go, I'll keep Ms. Easton company."

"Oh, I'm fine." Tammie found her voice. There was something strained about the men's interaction that intrigued her. "I can wait here on my own."

"Nonsense." The major laughed. "My father would

roll over in his grave if he knew I'd abandoned a lady to this heat. Go see the men, Captain. We'll be fine."

Tammie could tell DJ was torn. He clearly wanted to see his friends, but felt obligated to stay with her. He probably hadn't seen them since he'd been hurt.

"Go ahead," she urged him with a tight smile. Once he was gone, she'd beg off and let the major get back to his work. There was a lovely shaded grassy area just outside the food court where she could wait until DJ returned.

She felt safe here. She *was* safe here. Dom wasn't going to find her on a military base. And if he did, there were plenty of people around with the skills and know-how to stop him.

"I won't be gone long." DJ looked at her for a long minute before he turned and headed down the walk.

"The men will appreciate seeing him," Major Dixon said softly, watching DJ walk away. "It's good for them to see he's back on his feet. Last time they saw him, he looked half-dead."

The silence, and a thick cloud of sadness, settled over the man. After a minute, he shook his head and turned to face her with a smile. "Why don't you walk with me, Ms. Easton? I'll show you around our humble place here."

The major guided her down a path that circled the big stone building. *So much for sitting in the shade, alone, relaxing.* Without being rude, she couldn't escape him.

He explained the history of the base. Of the build-

"We found those when we located Captain Hawkins after the explosion," Major Dixon whispered.

Tammie looked up. She had seen DJ's injuries, but he hadn't told her how it had happened—and she didn't think he would. She didn't interrupt the major, knowing this might be her only opportunity to learn the truth.

"If they'd been in his pack when that bomb went off, they'd be gone. Instead, they were in the front pocket of his uniform."

Where he could get to them, quickly and easily.

Tammie's eyes burned as she looked up at the older man. "Wh-why didn't you give these back to DJ?"

Major Dixon stared at her. One of those stares she was sure he reserved for his stupidest recruits. She bit her tongue, barely refraining from reminding him she was *not* in the military. But she knew DJ would be the one who paid the price if she said anything, so she waited.

The warm welcome had vanished from his eyes. "I recognized you from these."

"And?" She didn't want to hear what he was going to say, but she knew he intended to make sure she did. She now realized that's why he'd encouraged DJ to leave, why he'd brought her over here, away from the crowds.

"Captain Hawkins was one of my best men. Those pictures, your situation, proved to be too much distraction for him."

She stared at him. "You're saying it's my fault DJ was hurt?"

He didn't say anything, but the look on his face told her she'd hit the nail on the head. She shot to her feet, shocked when his hand clamped down on her arm.

"One little distraction is all it takes to get people killed." He pushed to his feet and glared down at her. "Ms. Easton." He continued to use the formal address—an intimidation tactic. "In addition to Captain Hawkins being injured, two good men died that day."

Guilt and outrage warred within her—she didn't know which to accept. Indignation won. Tammie's free hand curled tightly around the envelope. "I'm not responsible for that explosion."

"It's my job to look out for my men. When the threat back home is as strong, or stronger, than the threat on the battlefield, I step in."

"I'm not one of your soldiers." She glared at him.

"You're right. No one under my command would be so careless."

Tammie yanked her arm from his grasp and hurried away, barely holding back from hitting a flat-out run. At the corner of the food court, she realized she still had the envelope clutched in her hand.

She headed to the metal garbage can and threw it all inside. A few pictures spilled out on top of the trash. Tyler's face stared up at her amid the ashes and crumpled paper. Tears burned her eyes. She couldn't do it. She couldn't give up the thin connection she had to her son. Despite the state of the pictures, Tyler's face, smiling and sweet, still shone bright. "Oh, baby," she whispered.

Her chest hurt and her heart pounded. She missed him *so* badly. But she couldn't let anything happen to him. She'd never survive that. Her resolve grew.

Reaching in, she gathered the pictures and shoved them back into the envelope.

She couldn't deny the fact that Major Dixon was partially right. Her actions, Dom's actions, had contributed to DJ's injuries. He probably *had* been distracted. But knowing that, then or now, wouldn't have stopped that explosion.

She knew all about unintended consequences. As a kid, she'd grown up dirt-poor, living in the hills and hollows of the Ozarks. She'd run away and gotten herself out of there. On her own as a single mom, she'd supported herself and Tyler working waitress jobs. Even when her design studio began making enough money to support them, she'd kept a side waitress job. Just in case.

Just In Case was her motto for everything.

But she'd been blindsided by Dom and the events of the past year. She was running out of energy. She didn't know what to do now—she didn't have a "just in case." And that scared her.

Her shoulders shook. Hugging the envelope tight, she slipped back into the restaurant and headed to the ladies' room at the back. Inside the stall, she finally let go. A year of pent-up hurt, fear and pain engulfed her. She let it. She deserved it.

BEING BACK ON BASE was nice—and strange. Comfortable in its familiarity, and yet, DJ felt different, not really a part of this world anymore.

The conference room sat at the end of the hall. He'd walked these halls too many times to count. He knew Major Dixon wouldn't have sent him in here if they were in the middle of a debrief or getting info about their next mission. No, this was a training session. Nothing secret or sensitive. Or interesting.

DJ pulled open the door and slipped in, grabbing a seat in back. The speaker had his back to the room. Everyone looked forward, but these men were soldiers, elite soldiers who never really relaxed or let down their guard. They knew immediately when their environment shifted. Walker noticed first. "Hey, Captain's back."

Easily a dozen men, the roughest, toughest soldiers in the world—Colin included—grinned and slapped DJ on the back. Shoulder bumps stood in for hugs. DJ ignored the lump in his throat. He'd spent the past five years with these men—most of them, anyway. He looked around. Only two new faces in the crowd looked out of place. Replacing Kauffman and Reed… His heart hitched. He'd been in a coma when the flag-draped coffins of his comrades had come home. When they'd arrived at Arlington.

"Don't think about it," Colin said before slipping back into the crowd.

Easy for him to say. He came out of that inferno with his life, with his job. No injuries that altered everything.

"When you coming back for good, Captain?" Sergeant Hayes asked.

DJ cringed. How many people would ask that question? DJ figured he could get through about a dozen of them now. "I'm not." He explained the medical discharge and while he stood there, he watched the change among the group. He'd just stepped outside the box. He'd moved into the civilian realm.

And…he realized he was okay with that, which surprised him. "You need to get back to work," he finally said, getting slowly to his feet, hoping the men didn't notice his stiffness. "And I've got a lady waiting on me."

"Why didn't you bring her? We'd like to meet her," Hayes said.

"Dixon is keeping her company."

Several sets of eyes glanced at each other. DJ didn't like the looks passing between his men. "What's going on?"

"Oh, nothing," Walker hedged.

"Don't give me that crap." He pinned the man with an intense glare—the glare they'd all dreaded out in the field. "Explain."

A few more glances passed between them. "Dixon

hasn't been the same since the attack. He thinks it could have been prevented."

"How?" DJ's mind returned to that night, to the events before. "We were guarding the munitions. It was rigged. How could the explosion have been prevented?"

No one answered. Understanding dawned. He looked at Walker, then at Colin. A chill washed over him. And he'd left Tammie alone with him? DJ hurried from the room, cursing his damaged legs and the slick tiles of the floor. He needed to get out of here, get to Tammie before Dixon said or did something that would upset her.

He knew how Dixon thought. They'd spent too much time together not to. Too much intensity had passed between them. Hot, thick air outside slammed into him. He'd forgotten how muggy it could be here. As he hit the sidewalk, his phone went off. He pulled it out, thinking maybe it was Tammie. He reminded himself she didn't have a phone. He needed to get her one. She'd probably never agree to let him pay for it.

Wyatt's number appeared on the screen. DJ cursed. "Yeah," he answered.

"Dad!" Tyler's voice ripped through the air. "I need you." DJ's heart sank.

"What's the matter?"

"Pork Chop ran away from home."

DJ was proud of himself. He didn't trip and fall on his face. "What?"

"She's gone. And Hamlet's going crazy. He doesn't

know what to do. Dad?" Panic filled Tyler's voice. "I don't know how to find a pig."

DJ would have laughed, if the panic wasn't so thick coming through the line. He crested the hill and saw the truck still parked where he'd left it. The sun glinted off the chrome. Where was Tammie?

"Tyler, I can't get home to help you just yet. Where's Wyatt?"

"I don't know. Pork Chop ate Juanita's flowers. She chased her with the frying pan and said… She said she was gonna turn Pork Chop into bacon!" The last came out in a painful wail.

Reaching the truck just then, DJ looked around, hoping to see Dixon or Tammie nearby. Nothing.

"Dad. I don't know what to do."

"Buddy, you gotta call Wyatt. He can definitely find one pig." Torn between soothing his son and finding Tammie, DJ had no idea what the right choice was.

There, in the doorway of the food court, he saw her. Relief washed over him. He'd reached the truck and leaned back against the fender, trying to catch his breath. She was headed this way, slowly, her arms wrapped tight around her backpack.

He watched her, his eyes narrowing. Something was different. He cursed. What had that jerk said to her?

"Dad?"

DJ heard the hiccup in his son's voice. Crap. He was screwing everything up. Knowing Tammie was okay and headed this way, he closed his mind off to the events going on around him and focused on the voice on the phone.

Tyler was distraught. The little-boy tears were killing DJ, and he couldn't do a thing about it—Tyler was over five hundred miles away. Where the hell was Wyatt?

DJ heard Tammie's footsteps. As if in slow motion, he turned his head and watched her reach for the door handle. "Here." He handed her the phone.

Startled, she nearly dropped the backpack and he caught it, shocked at its weight. "It's Tyler," he hastily explained. "I haven't a clue what to do."

"Sweetie?" She took the phone, the backpack forgotten, DJ gone from her attention. "What's the matter?"

DJ heard the squeal of Tyler's voice through the phone as he repeated the tale of the missing pig. He watched Tammie's whole demeanor shift. To the mom. To the responsible adult who could handle the boy's fears. "It's okay, Ty. She'll be fine… I know… she's just a little pig, but Wyatt will help you." Silence grated over DJ's nerves. Hadn't he just said the same thing?

"Yes, you do that. Don't worry. Take a breath… There you go. Okay. I'll call you later and double-check…Love you, too."

She smiled, though it was a sad smile, as she hung up the phone and handed it back to DJ. She climbed into the truck without a glance back at him.

"How did you do that?"

"Practice. Don't worry, you'll get it." She slammed the door and sat waiting.

DJ stood there for a long minute, not sure what exactly had just happened. This whole parenting thing was tough. Finally, shaking himself out of his stupor, he tossed the pack over the seat. Climbing in behind the wheel, he roared out of the parking lot.

What a joke. He'd looked forward to coming back here, returning to his work, to the world he knew. Now he couldn't wait to get out of there.

They'd just reached the gates when the rain began. Great big drops splashed on the windshield. He flipped on the lights and waved at the sentry as they left the gates behind. The streets shone with the wet, reflecting the myriad headlights coming at him.

Tammie was silent, her hands twined together in her lap, staring unseeing at the rain in front of them. DJ's heart had slowed slightly, and his brain escaped the panic. Finally able to focus, he glanced at Tammie again. Something was up.

"What did he say to you?"

"Who? Tyler?" Her voice was a shadow, monotone and flat. "Pork Chop is missing."

"Yeah, I got that. No, Dixon. What happened?"

If she could sink in on herself any more, she did it then. "Nothing. Just a conversation."

"Uh-huh." He focused on the road, collecting his thoughts. He knew Tammie was dodging him, but pushing her could backfire on him. "Let me guess.

He told you about the explosion. Did he say *why* he thinks the explosion was preventable?" He saw the men's glances again.

She turned her head and looked at him, surprised.

"The guys told me he'd probably say as much. Dixon wasn't there, Tammie. I was. Believe me. There was no way to guess that magazine was set to blow like that. We did everything we could." He swallowed hard, suddenly remembering, too clearly, the minutes before the blast. He had been distracted, he'd had to admit that to himself a dozen times while laying in that hospital bed. He'd rehashed it all. But nothing would have stopped the explosion.

"Are…are you sure?"

He heard the tears in her voice. With a flick of his glance he looked at her. Her eyes were dry. Distraught, but dry.

"I'm sure."

Her only response was a nod as she stared out the window again. She barely seemed to breathe.

In silence, they drove back to the motel, the rain intensifying with each mile. Thunder roared overhead, the reverb shaking the truck. A stoplight ahead turned bright red, streams of the color reaching toward them through the water on the pavement. Cringing, DJ pulled to a stop and waited for the question. It wasn't long.

"If…I hadn't sent that letter…distracting you… would those men still be alive?"

CHAPTER ELEVEN

DJ'S SINGLE-WORD CURSE exploded like a gunshot in the truck's cab. Tammie jumped, smacking her elbow hard on the door handle.

Outside, raindrops beat on the metal frame of the truck, blurring the view of the road ahead. She expected DJ to pull over. He didn't.

Instead, he plowed through the puddles at full speed, sending waves of water up on both sides of the street. No wonder the major had made the accusations to her, instead of DJ. Any sane person would think twice about talking to him right now.

When they reached the motel, they found the parking lot full. The weather had travelers stopping to wait it out, as the thick, dark clouds overhead testified to the long rainy night ahead.

DJ parked and turned in the seat to face her. "Dixon is a fool."

She let his words linger unanswered for a long minute. She shrugged. "Maybe." Fidgeting, she ran her finger along the edge of the door handle. "I realize an explosion in a war zone isn't my fault. But if you hadn't been distracted—"

"No." DJ reached over and gently turned her face toward his. "It wouldn't have mattered. I couldn't have done anything different." He paused. "Believe me, I've had plenty of time to second-guess myself." He took a deep breath. "What if I'd been more focused? Maybe I would have been right there with them."

Them? The men who'd died, he meant.

Tammie stared back at him. So many thoughts and horrific images spun through her mind. She shook her head. Was he telling the truth? Did he really know that or was he just rationalizing? Her heart hitched and she closed her eyes. So many what-ifs… Too much to take in.

She felt the panic rising.

"Hey." DJ's finger swept over her lips, slow, soft, startling her out of the downward spiral her thoughts were taking. "That's a very real part of what I do, or rather, used to do." A sad shadow flitted through his eyes.

"He said you were discharged."

DJ nodded. "Medically. I'm as good as I'll get." Settling back in his seat, he put distance between them, staring out the windshield at the rain. "I don't think it's gonna let up," he said, abandoning the subject neither of them wanted to face right now. "Do you want to sit here and wait, or make a run for it?" Their room was clear around the other side of the building—all the closer parking spots were taken.

"We'll—" She cleared the emotion out of her throat. "We'll be soaked before we even get out."

"You do have new clothes to wear." The shadow of a smile flitted over his lips and the darkness in his eyes had faded. Tammie relaxed, letting the mood shift.

She couldn't help but smile back at him. "I guess I won't melt."

He stared at her for a long minute. "You should do that more often."

"What?"

"Smile."

Their eyes met and warmth rose in her cheeks. The air shifted and time stretched between them as the specter of their earlier kiss whispered around them.

"Let's go." Breaking the spell, Tammie turned to lean over the seat and grab the plastic shopping bags. She couldn't reach her backpack, which he'd tossed in on his side.

"I'll get it." DJ twisted, then moaned. He managed to snag the pack, but quickly sat back down with a thud. He leaned his head against the headrest, his eyes closed, and took several deep breaths.

"Are you okay?"

"Yeah." His voice was thready and thin. "I forget sometimes what I can't do. Add that to the list."

"What can I do?"

"Nothing. It's a muscle spasm. It'll pass. Eventually."

Tammie sat waiting, feeling so helpless. She had to do something. She doubted he could run through the rain. "Can you drive back over by the door?"

He shook his head. Long minutes passed. Finally, he opened one eye. "I think I need to stretch it out.

Got everything?" He looked pale, his lips thin, his jaw clenched.

"Yeah."

DJ shoved the door open, allowing the water to fall in and soak the leather seat. Carefully, he planted his feet on the ground and gripped the door frame. He sighed. "That's better." He looked over his shoulder at her. "Let's go."

Tammie scrambled out her side and hustled around to him. "Let's get under the overhang as much as possible," she called over the storm's roar. He followed, not hurrying, probably because he couldn't. He didn't really seem to care if he got soaked. Looking down at her own soaked clothing, she realized it was too late anyway. "Come on."

Moving seemed to help him, and by the time they reached the red door of room number seven, DJ looked closer to normal and moved more easily. He opened the door and reached to help her with the cumbersome bags.

Not wanting a repeat of his earlier agony, Tammie shoved past him, tossing the soaked bags onto the nearest bed instead. With the door closed, the only sound was of water dripping from their clothes. She didn't dare look at him, with his T-shirt all wet and clingy…

"You should get changed," she said instead. "Do you need ice or anything?" She'd get it for him. "I know you used it the other night. I'll get some."

"Stop." DJ's hand shot out and stopped her before

she headed back out into the storm. "I'm fine now. That's how it works most of the time. Bad for a minute, and then it's fine. Sorry."

"Oh." He stood close. Too close. Not close enough. "I didn't know."

"That's okay." DJ tried to smile. Slowly, he lifted his hand and cupped her chin. He took a step closer. "You need to get out of those wet clothes, too."

For an instant, she leaned into his warm palm, her eyes closed. Reality returned as she remembered his grimace of pain. She stepped back. "Just be careful, okay? I'll get you a towel."

She headed to the towel rack on the wall by the sink. Guilt washed over her. He'd been in pain, and she couldn't stop thinking about doing things with him that had nothing to do with healing.

"I'm sorry," she caught herself saying.

"What the hell for?" DJ cut the distance between them. "Look at me. Don't tell me you still buy into the crap Dixon said." He looked closer. "Hell. You do!"

"No..." she hastily went to reassure him. "You're hurt—"

"This—" DJ ripped the sopping-wet white T-shirt over his head and presented his scarred back to her "—doesn't make me any less of a man. It doesn't define me."

He turned around, searching her face. Was he looking for her horror? Her desire? She didn't know which she even felt.

"I know." She slowly met his glare. "But you can't be a soldier, can't keep your job." What else couldn't he do because of her stupidity?

"I have a new job, remember? You gave it to me. I'm a damned good father, Tammie." A flash of hurt showed briefly in his eyes. He stepped closer and glared down at her. "There's more to life than work."

Then, as if something new crossed his mind. "Or do the scars bother you?" He moved away. "Sorry. I didn't think—" He backed away and walked to his duffel. He rummaged through his dry shirts.

Tammie gasped at the cruelty he imagined. Where had he gotten that idea?

"Of course not!" Tammie slowly followed him. At close range, she could feel his warmth, hear the whisper of his in-and-out breath, taste her own anticipation.

"This—" She reached out, and with a trembling hand, gently touched the ridge of scars running down his back. The muscles beneath her fingers, beneath the scars, flinched. She didn't know how much he could feel, how much it hurt, so she moved carefully. "This shows me you're a strong man, and soldier. You survived." Her voice hitched as his earlier words of how swiftly the pain could come and go returned to scare her. She didn't want to hurt him. She didn't stop herself from leaning in and putting her lips against the bright red skin.

"I know you're a good father. Tyler adores you. I hear it in his voice. And I can see you love him."

So close. Alone in this small room, they could be the only people in the world. Tammie took a step. No longer able to resist the promise from their earlier kiss, she trailed a finger along the waistband of his jeans, across his back, around the warm, tanned skin of his side and back to his flat belly.

Facing him again, she stared at the finely honed muscles of his chest. "As far as the other—" She slid her fingers to the fly of his jeans and pushed the metal button through the opening. "My memory is a bit rusty. You might have to remind me."

DJ sucked in a hard breath, unwittingly giving her fingers easier access. She lowered the thick metal zipper before his big hand captured her fingers to stop her.

She looked up at him. The heat in his eyes washed over her, pooling low in her belly. "Don't tell me to stop," she whispered.

"I don't do pity."

She looked him directly in the eye, making sure he knew this wasn't about anything but her wanting him, and him wanting her. "Me, either."

"Be sure. Be very, very sure."

Tammie smiled. He was giving her an out. *How sweet.* Even though he was obviously ready, willing and oh-so-very-able.

Unable to speak, she tilted her head and rose on her tiptoes. She found his lips the same instant her hand slid lower.

The sound in DJ's throat was nothing short of a

growl. Deep and rich. He pulled her into his arms, nearly engulfing her with his embrace.

He tasted of rain, heat and pure, sweet DJ. She drank him in, winding her arms around his neck as he briefly knelt and lifted her up. Wrapping her legs around his waist, he took the few steps to the bed. "Too many clothes," he mumbled against her lips as he laid her down.

"Yes," she whispered. While he straightened, she reached for the buttons on her shirt.

"Allow me." DJ shooed her hands away and quickly opened the sopping-wet fabric. The lacy bra beneath barely covered anything, even less, wet. She arched into his hand as he gently, reverently cupped her breast.

Slowly, he lowered his head, replacing his fingers with the heat of his mouth. "DJ!" she cried. Lacing her fingers through his hair, she held him there, never wanting it to end.

He slid his hands down her rib cage to the waist of her jeans and unzipped them just as she had his, only much more slowly. His big hand slipped inside, finding her damp heat. She moaned and pushed back against his touch. So good. It felt so good.

Heat washed over her. Inside and out. She lost herself in sensation.

Somehow, he slipped her jeans off. She didn't know or care how. She simply wanted his skin against hers. His jeans already hung low on his hips and quickly followed hers to the floor.

"Blue lace. Nice." DJ's voice was deep and thick with passion while he traced the top edge of her panties with a rough finger. Then, as if his patience had snapped, he shoved them down and his hand took their intimate place, teasing and stroking until she cried for relief.

DJ stretched out beside her and pulled her close. Tammie opened her eyes and looked up at him. She saw the stubble along his jaw, several faded scars and a deep intensity in his eyes as he looked back. She reached up and traced a tiny scar that arched over his eye.

"That one's old." He reached out and brought her hand to his lips, kissing the finger that had touched the scar. "My first motorcycle."

Tammie caressed the one below his eye, knowing it was newer. "Shrapnel," he confirmed, kissing that finger, also. This time, he guided her finger to the scar on his chin. It was more recent, too. "Yes, the explosion." Instead of kissing her finger, he slowly ran the tip of his tongue along it.

Mesmerized, Tammie watched him close his eyes as he kissed her fingers, her hand. And then as he moved over her, he kissed up her arm, along her collarbone until he found the column of her neck.

His hot tongue returned to touch and taste her skin. She shivered in anticipation. He didn't disappoint. Finding her lips seconds later, he claimed her with a long, slow kiss.

He'd left the lace of her bra in place, and now, with

his weight and skin pressing against her, she gasped at the sweet friction. While he kissed her again, his fingers slid back to the curve of her breast. Her sigh of contentment wrapped around them and she gave in, taking and accepting every sensation.

She wanted him. More of him. All of him.

DJ lifted his head and waited until she looked at him again. "Protection?" A flash of agony lit his eyes.

She smiled, glad he hadn't planned for this when they'd left Austin. "I learned my lesson with Tyler. We're covered."

"Good." He sighed. "I'm okay, too. Hospital checked everything—"

Impatient, Tammie reached up and pulled his lips back to hers. "Please don't stop."

And he didn't. Shifting, DJ's hips aligned perfectly with hers. Hot and heavy, he paused, not hesitating, but savoring, teasing.

Impatient, Tammie wrapped her legs around his waist, intending to urge him faster, closer, deeper. Her now-bare skin touched the scar across his back and she gasped. Her eyes flew open, and they both froze. "I don't want to hurt you."

He laughed, his breath fanning across her skin. "Then don't stop. Stopping might just kill me." Slowly, oh-so-slowly, DJ moved, pushing gently inside her, rocking her in his arms as he rocked her world.

They moved together, and the tension built inside

her. So close, so sweet, she never wanted it to end. He was here, with her, alive and strong. Unable to hold back any longer, she let go, throwing her head back and crying out his name as tears trickled from her eyes.

DJ stiffened and she heard his whispered groan join her cries. His arms tightened around her, as if he was afraid she'd slip away. She wasn't going anywhere.

Minutes passed and Tammie held on as tight as he did. Finally catching his breath, DJ raised his head and smiled down at her. "That was—"

"Yeah," she whispered.

With his thumbs, DJ wiped the damp from the corners of her eyes. "You okay?" He frowned at her.

"Fine. Just…a bit overwhelmed. I haven't— I don't—"

DJ rolled over, taking her with him, snuggling her against his side. She fit perfectly; it felt so natural to be here with him.

DJ planted a kiss on her hair and settled back against the rumpled bed. He closed his eyes, gently running his hand up and down her back, soothing. "We can't forget to call Tyler later to see if he found the pig," she said.

His laughter, rich and warm, washed over her. She could get used to this. DJ grinned and her heart swelled. If he kept this up, she could fall for him all over again.

She froze…realization dawning. She already had.

Lying there, listening to his breathing, Tammie let the stunned silence settle over her.

"Relax," DJ commanded and nuzzled her neck. "Or not..." He slid his hand up over her bare skin, and the thin bra quickly joined the other scattered pieces of clothing on the floor.

DJ WATCHED TAMMIE try to resist the lure of sleep. It was almost funny. If she didn't need the rest so badly, he'd have laughed and teased her.

So he stayed where he was, holding her, while figuring out their next move. He'd be happy staying here and whiling away the week between the sheets, but that wouldn't solve their dilemma. It wouldn't help in the long haul.

And something about the long haul appealed to him suddenly.

Tammie snuggled against his shoulder, her hair fanned out across his chest, her breath warming his skin. He closed his eyes, savoring the moment. Tammie, naked and in his arms, was as close to heaven as he could remember.

His phone buzzed on the nightstand. Slowly, carefully, he grabbed it and thumbed the screen. A text from Colin.

"Who is it?" Tammie mumbled.

DJ read the text and frowned. "Colin says this is the address Dom has listed online for his design studio. You recognize it?" He turned the screen toward her.

Tammie squinted. "Yeah. It's my house. Was." She closed her eyes and a few seconds later her even breathing told him she'd finally fallen asleep, her exhaustion finally too much.

House? She had a house? He glanced at the screen again. In Tallahassee? Interesting.

Questions mounted in DJ's mind as he tried to think of a plan that would work. Dom was elusive and dangerous from what DJ had seen in Austin. Everything Colin unearthed confirmed that.

The text alert went off again. *He's using credit cards in Tal. We going after him?*

That was the plan. DJ responded, *We?*

Yeah. No one goes out alone. Got leave. Later.

The reminder of the unit motto reassured DJ—and reminded him that he had work to do. Slowly, he pulled away from Tammie, reluctant, but hoping this was only the beginning.

He was still hoping for that when his phone rang an hour later while he stood in the checkout line at the nearby big-box store. Two suitcases filled the cart. Smiling, he pulled out the phone. He'd left Tammie a note, but she probably didn't appreciate him leaving her alone. Or going shopping without her.

But it wasn't Tammie. His sister Mandy's number glowed on the screen. "Hey, little mama." She was the sister nearest to him in age and the one he was closest to. And no matter how adamant she was that he call her by her proper name, for some reason he couldn't call her Amanda, her full name. So he'd started with the goofy nicknames. This one looked as though it might stick.

"You haven't seen me lately, soldier boy," she grumbled. "I'm not that little anymore."

"And I'm not a soldier, so we're even." He laughed with her. "What's up? You okay?" Seven months pregnant, she was probably miserable. Not that he would know, but he'd heard the guys in the unit complain when their wives were almost due.

He'd missed that experience with Tammie. He wasn't sure how he felt about that.

"I'm fine. Little one's impatient these days. Just checking to see what's going on. We thought you'd be home by now."

So had he, but he'd had no idea about Tammie's situation when he'd set out to find her. The silence stretched out over the air.

"Do you really think this is a good idea?" Mandy asked.

How could he explain? No, it wasn't a good idea. There were too many unknowns—and too much risk—going after an enemy as unpredictable as Dominic Carlyle. But leaving Tammie to deal with him on her own wasn't even an option. And neither was taking this mess back to his family. "Yeah. I have to."

Mandy was thinking; he could almost hear her doing so. He waited patiently for her to put her thoughts together into words.

shocked him. Carefully, putting the book down beside the pictures, he reached in. The leather casing was exactly what he thought it was.

A gun? Why the hell did Tammie have a gun?

SHOWERED, DRESSED, AND primped and polished, as much as a person with limited, cheap cosmetics could be, Tammie stepped into the room—and froze.

At the end of the bed, neatly lined up, sat her backpack, the envelope of pictures from the major—and the gun she'd bought. DJ's big, boot-clad feet were next to it all as he stretched out across the bed, waiting.

She met his gaze—anger and darkness swirled there. That dark glare had returned. Every inch of him was taut and ready. Angry.

"Care to explain?" he asked through clenched teeth.

"As soon as you explain why you were going through my things."

He moved so fast, she jumped when he was suddenly beside her. "I wasn't. It was there, open when I got back. And to my surprise, I saw an envelope with my name on it there."

"I didn't leave it for you."

He stepped away. "I know that." If anything, his anger intensified. "Were you even going to tell me about the pictures? Dixon gave them to you yesterday, didn't he?"

She nodded, not sure what to say or do. Anger was

the easiest emotion, but there was more under the surface she didn't want to explore right now. Besides, she'd been so sweetly distracted last night. Tearing her thoughts from that cliff, she focused on the here and now.

"What upsets you more? The fact that I didn't tell you about the pictures? Or the gun?"

"I'm not sure." He grabbed the few things he'd scattered around the motel room and shoved them into a new suitcase, open on the other bed. Finally, some of his anger spent, his hands stilled in fists, he faced her.

His voice was deceptively soft. "Next time you're carrying a weapon, tell me. Especially if we're on the bike."

"It's not loaded."

"I know that. I already checked."

"Don't treat me like I'm stupid," she shouted. "I know better than that."

"Really? Do you even know how to shoot it?"

She hesitated. "Sort of."

DJ rolled his eyes and bent to grab the gun. "Until you do, it's going in the truck. Locked up."

"But—"

"But what? You think you'll need it?"

"No." Truth be told, she'd nearly forgotten she'd bought it. She felt safe around DJ.

"And these?" He picked up the manila envelope. The anger in his eyes was different now. Painful.

"I wasn't trying to hide anything." She extended a

“Tallahassee.”

“What? Why?”

“That’s where Dom is. Colin’s been tracking his credit cards.” DJ crossed his arms over his chest and glared down at her. “Well? What’ll it be?”

Silently, not sure what to say or how to say it, she grabbed her suitcase. Struggling with the weight, she threw it into the truck bed. Then stomping around the side, she yanked open the passenger door and climbed in.

CHAPTER TWELVE

TAMMIE WASN'T SPEAKING to him, which was just fine with DJ.

The suitcases were stowed in the back of the truck, next to the bike, under a brand-new tarp. He'd purchased it when he'd bought the suitcases—he thought it a smart thing to have after yesterday's deluge. Its bright blue color was an interesting contrast to the red truck and the midnight-black motorcycle.

Halfway to the base, he broke the silence. "Tyler's birthday is in two weeks."

Tammie flinched and turned her head to stare out the side window.

"I have orders to be home by then."

She didn't speak, which disappointed him. He'd hoped the reminder of Tyler would shake her up. Instead, it only seemed to make her curl in on herself more.

"Look, I'm sorry. I shouldn't have lost my temper." That was all he was going to give. But another ten miles passed and she was still silent, and she remained that way until they reached the base.

They cruised past the sentry and headed toward the barracks. Colin had said he'd have more info for them when they got there. Maybe it was a good thing Colin was going with them, to break this god-awful tension. Or maybe, knowing their luck, he'd just make it worse.

DJ pulled to the curb, and as he helped Colin load his gear, Tammie restlessly moved around inside the cab.

"What's with her?" Colin asked, tilting his head toward the cab.

DJ shrugged. He wasn't in the mood to explain. "Just a disagreement." What an understatement.

"Great." Colin's sarcasm was hard to miss.

"Watch it. There's a lot of empty space between here and Tallahassee."

"You threatening to throw me out?"

DJ laughed. "Hell, no. Can't make any promises for Tammie, though."

Tammie had settled in the rear seat, putting an obvious barrier between them, and a less obvious one when she refused to look at or speak to him.

Colin simply lifted his brow. DJ shrugged. The next four hours of driving stretched out long and empty in front of them as DJ headed out of town.

TAMMIE PRETENDED THE ANGER between her and DJ didn't bother her. Thankfully, Colin had plenty to say—all of which she needed to hear.

Armed with his laptop, he filled them in on Dominic Carlyle.

"That picture from the brochure?" Colin tapped the touch screen and Dom's face filled the view. "That was one of his high school graduation pictures."

Tammie leaned forward to look over the seat. "How in the world did you find that out?"

Colin laughed. "I'd love to say I'm a great detective, but it came up on one of those reunion sites. Too easy. You should see the rest of the dorks he hung out with back in the day."

Picturing him as a nerdy teenager took the edge off Tammie's fear of the man—momentarily.

"Don't let that pretty-boy face fool you." Colin seemed to read her mind. He flipped through a couple more screens. "By the time he was eighteen, he had a juvenile record."

"What for?" DJ didn't look away from the road, but the intensity was clear in his voice. He was paying close attention to everything Colin said.

"Don't know. It's sealed, but the fact that it exists says a lot."

DJ simply grumbled low in his throat, like an animal thwarted. Colin barely looked up, as if the response was normal. Tammie looked back and forth between them, overwhelmed by the intensity.

"Dom's adult record is pretty impressive, if size impresses you." He laughed at his own joke, not seeming to care if anyone joined him. "Breaking and entering. Theft. Impersonating an officer."

"What?" Tammie almost couldn't believe it.

"Multiple charges, same heist." Colin tapped a few more keys and brought up another record. "He broke into a jewelry store with the story that he was a cop checking on a call." Colin laughed. "Gotta give the guy points for creativity." The silence was broken only by a few more taps of Colin's fingers on the keys. "But most of that was small-time. This gig?" Colin pointed at the article Tammie remembered from the paper about the jewel thefts in Florida. "This was his first deal with the big guys. My guess, he's as scared of them as you are of him."

"Why?" Did she really want to know?

"Because somehow he must have screwed up and double-crossed them or something. None of that's online, just in the intel chatter I heard and from the contacts I called."

"What contacts?"

DJ nodded, as if he knew all this. Maybe he expected it.

"I have lots. That's my job." He looked up at her, seemingly surprised she didn't know. "You didn't fill her in?" he asked DJ.

DJ shrugged. "We've been busy."

Colin laughed, swallowing the sound as DJ turned his gaze from the road and glared at him. "Grumpy today, are we?" Colin teased. He turned in the seat to face Tammie. "One of the projects our crew works on is interface with the local authorities—police, fire, most first responders. Bases in or near cities have to work with the locals when big events happen. Good and bad."

She glanced over at DJ, seeing another piece of him. And Colin.

"Over the past couple years, we've worked with

several agencies and I've gotten to know the guys pretty well."

"Is that why you beat them at poker every chance you get?" DJ asked.

"Gotta keep them in line, show them who's in charge." Colin laughed and settled back in the seat. "Anyway, when DJ contacted me about Dom, I called up a guy I know on an FBI task force, and a couple other guys I know from the Tallahassee police force."

Tammie could only stare. "And?" A shiver shot up her spine. "What did they say?"

"Not enough. We'll touch base with them once we arrive." He sounded all business. "What neither they nor I can figure out, though, is what do *you* have that Dom wants so badly?"

"Nothing." That's what she'd been trying to tell everyone. That's why she was so surprised he kept coming after her.

"Your threat to tell someone about his involvement in the theft wouldn't have carried much weight when you ran after his guys paid you a visit." He seemed to be thinking out loud, not really asking her questions. "And he could more easily prove *you* committed the crime than you seem to be able to prove that *he* did."

"That's what I thought, too."

Colin was silent a long while, his brow covered in a frown as he stared at the computer's screen. "There has to be something. Ideas, DJ?"

DJ's jaw was set, his gaze focused on the road. The intensity between the two men increased. She could only marvel at them. Was this what they were like when they'd been deployed? Hunting the enemy? She was glad they were on her side.

"Think, Tammie," DJ spoke, surprising her by catching her eye in the rearview mirror. "I know you don't have much—you left it all behind. But is there anything, anything at all—in your backpack, or in your book—that he might want?"

"No. I don't know what it could possibly be." Her heart sank. "Maybe he thinks I could testify against him or something."

Colin shook his head. "No. He'd have to think he'd get caught, and I don't get the impression he believes that'll happen." Colin powered off the laptop and stowed it at his feet. "Besides, that crime family could put him away for the theft, if they want to—or worse. No. Something's just not adding up."

The road stretched out, the big truck's tires whining on the asphalt. No one spoke as they were each engulfed in their own thoughts.

Was there something? She'd never thought about it this way. But what?

She grabbed her backpack from the floor and settled it on the seat beside her. Her fingers shook as she opened it. It seemed empty now, with her new things in the suitcase in the back and the gun locked in the glove box.

She pulled out the book, slowly going through every page where she'd stashed some piece of paper. Money. Photos of Tyler. She looked closely at each picture. They'd all been taken before she'd met Dom, so there wasn't any evidence in them. The envelope of photos was the same—pictures taken before she'd met Dom.

Carefully, she laid everything out beside her on the seat. Slowly, methodically examining every single item, over and over.

Her toiletries and cosmetics were in the suitcase, but the two necklaces she'd had in the pack before she'd gone on the run were still at the bottom. The fragile gold chains were tangled and twisted together. She pulled them out, looking at them for the first time in ages. She'd nearly forgotten about them. Her fingers itched for her tools as she looked at the scratches on the once-polished surfaces—

"Oh God, oh God, oh God." She dropped the necklaces. They hit the carpet with a muffled thud.

"What the—" DJ slammed on the brakes, pulling the truck to the side of the road with a squeal of tires. The guys piled out and DJ yanked the seat forward as she scrambled to retrieve the jewelry from the floor. Finally, her fingers grasped the tangled chains and she straightened. She handed the mess to DJ. "I'm so stupid," she wailed.

"I don't understand, Tammie," he said as he stared down at the handful of mangled chains.

"Those are my display pieces. I kept them in this backpack for shows. I didn't purposefully pack them—I just forgot they were there. Because they were for display only, I had put fake stones in them, but these are real. These are the stolen diamonds."

"What?" Colin rounded the hood of the truck. "Are you sure?"

"Positive." She crawled out of the truck. "See those gouges. I didn't do that. And I can tell even without my loupe that these are real stones. See that gold cast?" She pointed to one of the bigger stones. "That's the signature of the stolen ones."

Colin yipped loudly and reached out to grab her and spin her around. "You, girl, just gave us the upper hand."

"What do you mean?" She looked at DJ, who wasn't nearly as exuberant as his friend.

"He means now we have a bargaining chip and the missing piece of the puzzle." DJ kept turning the jewelry in the light, looking closer. "Now we have our bait." He looked up at her. "We just have to figure out how best to use it."

DJ NEEDED TO THINK. Staring down at stolen diamonds was a bit to take in.

DJ turned and walked away. Not far, just enough to get away from the insanity.

He was surprised when, moments later, Tammie's voice called after him. Turning around, he saw her standing there in the afternoon heat, the sun glinting in her hair, but resistant to touching the shadows of her face.

Colin was behind her, still leaning against the side

of the truck, staring in the other direction. Hell of a team.

She slowly walked toward DJ, her shoes crunching in the stray gravel. He didn't move, curious about what she had to say.

Nothing at first. She didn't have to. He saw the hope flicker on her face before she snuffed it out. Her agony was nearly more than he could stand. He knew better than to give in, though. Tammie was the one who had to reach out. He waited.

"I'm…" She swallowed hard, looking down at the dirt at their feet. "I'm scared, DJ."

It took everything he had not to pull her close. He clenched his hands into fists, each muscle in his body tight from holding back. She tested everything in him. Every instinct to protect and save.

"I've lost everything," she said. "It's all gone. I can't lose any more."

"What's left to lose?"

She looked up then, and he realized her eyes sparkled with unshed tears. "You. You and Tyler are all I have left." She sniffled and looked away. "He's just a voice on the phone right now."

"What am I?" Colin called from the truck. "Chopped liver?"

"Shut up, Colin," DJ yelled back, leading her a few feet farther away. He stopped and faced her again. "I know you've been on your own for a long time, but everyone needs someone." He shoved his hands into the pockets of his jeans to keep from touching her.

"Let me do what I do best. I'm a soldier even without the uniform. I can protect both of us. I can do this."

"But—"

Carefully, DJ tilted her chin up to face him. "You're *not* a soldier, thank God." The very idea of her being in harm's way on a battlefield— He couldn't even go there. "Part of why I do what I do is to preserve and protect *this*." Without any hesitation, the anger no longer standing between them, he kissed her. Long and sweet. Hoping it communicated what he couldn't say.

She leaned into him, wrapping her arms around his neck and holding on tight. He felt her tremble. With everything she'd been through, he was surprised she'd held up this long.

TWO HOURS LATER, Tammie stared out the wall of windows in their hotel room. The two-bedroom suite was top-of-the-line. Did DJ trust her now? Or was this his nod to respectability for Colin's sake? Or a last hurrah in a fancy resort before he ended this relationship…with a jewel thief?

She shut down her negative thoughts. The view from the window was stunning. In the distance, Tallahassee, Florida, lay like a rim of gems on the far horizon. She'd lived in this area for nearly ten years and she'd never seen it from this point of view. It was beautiful, which only made her realize how much she missed her life.

She'd lived here most of her adult life, first as a

runaway on the streets, and later on just outside the town where the land met the sea. She glanced briefly in that direction, imagining her tiny bungalow as she'd last seen it. Sadness engulfed her. Every other place they'd stayed had been a motel, a cheap motel along the highway. This was a hotel, a high-class hotel. With a doorman, bellhops and a restaurant that took reservations. She'd eyed the diners with a definite dose of jealousy as they'd walked by.

"How come we're here?" she'd whispered to DJ as they'd stepped into the elevator.

He'd leaned in, slipping an arm around her waist, and had whispered close in her ear, "Just follow my lead, okay?" His hand had slid lower, distracting her. "For once, stop asking questions."

At the time she'd been so befuddled by the place, his touch and proximity to even think. Now, though, staring at the view and having had a few minutes to adjust, her mind filled with questions.

"You still haven't answered my question," she reminded him as he slung his suitcase on the end of one of the beds.

"Which one?" He grinned at her, and she knew full well that he knew exactly what she meant.

"The one I asked in the elevator."

"Ah, that one." He pulled out his expertly packed shirts and hung up the bundle on the bar in the closet. How did he do that?

"Yes, that one." She tore her gaze from him and returned it to the view.

She saw his reflection in the glass, his form mixed with the glittery city beyond. He stood still for several seconds. "We're here to lure Dom out. And I want him to know I mean business as far as you're concerned. As far as this whole situation goes—I want him to know I have the upper hand."

She frowned and their gazes met in the glass. "Why *this* place?"

"He's used his credit card at this resort twice in the last week."

She saw DJ's reflection move to stand behind her. He followed her gaze to the lights below. "What are you looking at?"

She waited, formulating an answer. "Home. Or what used to be home." Even she cringed at the sadness in her voice.

DJ's hands, warm and strong, settled on her shoulders. "Dom lives a playboy high-end life. We're going to play his game…and win."

The edge in DJ's voice surprised Tammie. She'd never seen this side of him. She almost turned to look over her shoulder at him, then stopped herself. His reflection was intense enough.

This was the man who'd gone to Afghanistan. The soldier she'd never met. And that glint in his eyes? That wasn't laughter or joy or anything remotely good. She shivered, knowing she was safe, but afraid anyway. Very, very afraid.

A KNOCK AT the door surprised Tammie, but DJ didn't even react—obviously he wasn't surprised. He answered the door and Colin stood in the hall.

"What'd you find?" DJ asked him.

"Oh, you're gonna love this." The room was quiet for an instant after he closed the door. "What's with you two?" He looked back and forth between them.

"Nothin'," DJ snapped. "Tell us what you've got."

Colin looked at Tammie. "The house is fine. Apparently, just as you left it."

"That…that's impossible." She stepped into the middle of the room. "I haven't paid the mortgage in almost a year. No one's lived there. Surely the bank foreclosed on and sold it."

Colin shrugged and opened the minifridge.

"You're payin' for that," DJ reminded him as he took a swallow of the freshly opened beer. Colin just laughed.

"What else?" Tammie asked.

"I tried to find some of your neighbors to talk to, but no one was home. I only went to a couple of houses, though." He took another swig of beer.

"And?"

"Well, one old guy out walking his dog said a lawn company comes every other week, but otherwise no one's been there since you left."

"No one?"

"Nope."

She stared at him. Shocked. "Would…would Dom

actually take care of my house? He's the only one who knows I'm gone." Did he own it now? Panic shot through her. Would he use it against her now, too?

Everything felt strange. She sat down on the end of the bed, before the kaleidoscope of colors sent her to the floor. Was this what fainting felt like?

"She's losing it."

"What the—"

DJ's strong arms caught her before she tumbled to the floor. "Hey," he said softly.

Somehow, his stable presence wiped away the fear and panic. The look on his face almost made her believe. She met his gaze and nearly leaned into him.

"He's taken everything," she whispered. "Everything."

The room fell silent. She tried to hold back the tears gathering in her eyes. But failed.

"We're going to get it back. I promise," DJ said.

"How can you say that?" Something inside her snapped, like on the night the kid had tried to steal her backpack, the night she'd bought the gun. Anger and pain all welled up inside her.

She shoved against the strong chest she'd just moments ago wanted to lean into. "You can't promise that." When Colin opened his mouth to speak, she glared at him. "Neither can you."

She spun on her heel, wanting, needing to escape, but finding nothing but the hall or bathroom as choices. Neither would do. She gazed out at the city again, knowing that out there the beach was wide and open. She wanted to go there.

Yanking open the door, she stared at the long hallway. Pretty. Fancy.

Empty.

"Tammie," DJ's voice, soft and strong, called from behind her. "Wait."

"I need time and space." She stared at the fancy, empty hall some more.

"No. You need to win." The anger was a passion in his voice.

She looked over her shoulder at him. "Win?"

"Yeah. You need to win." He stepped closer, carefully as if afraid to spook her. "We will win." His conviction was real and she almost believed him.

"When Colin and I were up in those hills near the desert," he whispered, "I hated that place. Hated being stuck in that god-awful hole. I sat there all day and half the night, trapped, staring at that endless sea of nothing."

She wasn't able to speak. DJ's face was distant. Full of pain.

"But you know what?" He shook off the daze. "When we were attacked and we won, that was better than running away would have felt. And that's what you need."

"I don't know how—"

"I know. We know."

DJ reached out a calloused hand, palm up, toward her. “Trust me,” he said with a smile. “I will get it back. All of it. Your house. Your job.” He paused. “Tyler.”

CHAPTER THIRTEEN

"WHAT ARE WE doing here?" Tammie kept her voice as even as she could manage while DJ parked the truck across the street from what used to be her house. She noticed Colin stayed quiet in the backseat. "What if Dom's here?"

"Then we confront him." DJ glanced at the mirror, and Colin looked up, meeting his gaze. What did that look mean? What were they thinking?

"What would you do if you did find Dom?" she whispered. Maybe she should have asked that question earlier.

"I doubt he's here, but he isn't the first hostile we've dealt with." DJ faced her once the engine was quiet. "But we're mainly here to talk to some of your neighbors. See what they saw, or remember."

Tammie tried, but couldn't keep her gaze from wandering to the house. The sun was low in the water beyond, bathing the white-and-blue bungalow with its sweet dying rays. The stretch of white sand glowed in shades of red and gold just a few yards away. She'd always loved this time of day here.

"It looks the same," she whispered. A wave of homesickness nearly made her double over. The yard had been kept up—the lawn was trimmed, the bushes full and the flowers she'd planted under the front window were blooming as pretty as she'd expected. A lump lodged in her chest. No longer hers.

Her eyes burned, and she hastily blinked away the betrayal.

Someone knocked on the truck window beside her and Tammie jumped, surprised. She turned to see her old neighbor Mrs. Houston standing there, frowning.

Her brow cleared when she saw Tammie's face, and she smiled. Tammie opened the door and climbed out.

"Oh, it's you, dear." Lila Houston nodded her scarf-covered head. A long-time fan of old movies, Lila never went out in the sun or wind without a scarf wrapped around her heavily doused-with-hairspray, silver curls. "I thought someone was camping out here again."

Tammie frowned at the same time DJ got out of the truck. He joined them on the sidewalk. "These are my—uh—friends DJ Hawkins and Colin McCray. My neighbor Lila Houston."

Mrs. Houston blushed. "Military men, I see. Mighty nice to meet you, gentlemen." Then she turned and winked at Tammie. "If this is why you've been so scarce, I don't blame you one little bit."

"No—" Tammie didn't know how to explain.

"You said someone has been hanging out here?" DJ broke in as he stared at the house across the street.

"Yeah. Every couple of months, a black car sits here for a couple of nights. Makes us all uncomfortable. I decided last time that I'd see who they were."

"You shouldn't confront these people, Mrs. Houston. Call the police." DJ stood with his hands on his hips and a frown on his brow.

"Oh, I've tried all that. They say it's not illegal to park on a public street."

"They have a point," DJ said. "So, do you see anyone else come to the house?"

Mrs. Houston looked back and forth between them, finally landing on Tammie. "I…I thought you must have been keeping it up for a while there, though I never saw you. But no one else has been there for months, except that pretty little friend of yours, Robyn? Isn't that her name? She comes by every once in a while."

"Robyn?" Tammie looked over at DJ, confused and not sure how to answer the questions she saw in his eyes.

"So, it hasn't gone up for sale, Mrs. Houston?" Colin asked.

"No. Not that I know of. No signs, anyway. Are you moving, dear?"

"I don't know."

"Who's Robyn?" DJ asked.

"She's—" Tammie stared at her house. Was it even possible? "A friend. We met when we were kids working at the ice cream shop." She couldn't help smiling. Robyn was her best friend, if she had one of those. "Now she works at the bank where I got my mortgage."

DJ nodded but didn't comment. She wasn't even sure what to think, much less say or do.

"You got your keys?" DJ asked.

Of course she did. They were always in her backpack. She reached into the cab and found them.

"Wait here, Tammie," DJ said softly. "Come on, Colin." He took the keys from her and the men strode across the street. If Mrs. Houston thought it was strange, she didn't say anything.

Tammie hurried after them. "Not likely." DJ was getting entirely too good at this macho crap, she decided. Besides, no way was she staying out here like the proverbial sitting duck.

DJ shot her a warning glance. "Fine, but keep up." He headed toward one corner of the house while Colin went across the front. She hustled to follow.

"Why are we going in the back?"

"We're not. We're checking it out. Making sure no one's inside." He spoke softly as he led her across the back, peering in windows, then around to the front, where Colin sat on the front porch.

Fascinated, she watched DJ transform. She had no idea how to check out a potentially dangerous place, but she'd seen enough on TV to recognize that they did. Their movements were in sync, and they used hand signals like a second language. She was impressed and felt an odd sense of pride in DJ.

There were no lights on in the house, and it was dark enough now that they'd be necessary to anyone inside. If someone was in there, they were hiding in the shadows. Colin gave his report. "I didn't see anything. Looks empty."

DJ stopped at the front door and glanced back at her. "You ready?"

She had no clue, but she nodded anyway.

"Stay against the wall and keep low. Stick close to me, and don't get all full of attitude. Just trust me."

"Okay." The harsh expression on his face deterred her from replying more honestly. And then he was on the move and she plastered herself to his shadow. Out in the open like this, anyone could see them. Dom, or his thugs, could be watching them go inside. She swallowed the fear bubbling in her throat and moved with DJ.

He fit the keys into the lock. Entering a potentially dangerous room, waiting, looking, expecting to be attacked, they moved like a choreographed machine. She felt the tension—not fear, but readiness—that radiated off DJ. Colin looked the same. It bolstered her courage.

As soon as she stepped inside, a sense of familiarity reached out for her. She almost gave in to it, but something was missing. Tyler—and that feeling of safety, of comfort that came with coming home.

It was gone. The house felt hollow, no longer her home. She wanted to scream at Dom for taking that away from her.

DJ found the light switch, but when he flipped it, nothing happened.

"It's going to be totally dark soon. We'll need a light."

"It looks clear." Colin kept peering into closets and behind large pieces of furniture.

"I've got a flashlight in the truck." DJ left to get it.

On her own while Colin continued his search, Tammie slowly walked around, looking, cataloging. Everything was here. Just as she'd left it.

Until she reached her studio. At the end of the hall, the third bedroom had the most natural light with big, west-facing windows. She'd converted it into her work space as soon as they'd moved in. Situated next to Tyler's room, she'd been able to work and still watch over him. She cautiously pushed open the door and stepped inside.

She didn't need the flashlight to see it was a mess. And she hadn't left it that way. She stood gaping at her things. Her heart ached.

"He's been here," DJ said behind her as the flashlight's beam illuminated the destruction. "Or someone nasty has."

She resisted the urge to say "Duh." She didn't think he'd appreciate it. Besides, her heart was sinking too quickly. All her tools, her work—ruined. She didn't think anything was left intact.

Slowly, with leaden feet, she walked over to the drafting table she'd loved so much. Handmade, it had belonged to one of the early architects of the city. Its mahogany finish was scratched and destroyed.

Her heart broke as she reached out a shaking hand to touch it.

"Robyn and I found it at an estate sale." She'd fallen in love at first sight and paid too much money for it. "It was the first thing I bought to start my business." Her first investment. She'd drawn most of her best designs on it.

"Damn," DJ said behind her. "There's not much here to salvage." DJ carefully waded into the mess of the room, looking around, his gaze intent as if looking for a clue. "Can you even tell if anything is missing?"

"Not so much missing as ruined." Her voice cracked.

"What do you think they were looking for?" DJ turned slowly, inspecting everything. "The jewels?"

She shrugged. "If I'd known back then, I'd have given them to him." She rubbed a hand over the table's ruined surface and tried not to cry. However, she did cry out when she saw her shattered computer.

Colin stepped into the doorway just then. "I'll see if I can retrieve the data from the hard drive." He walked over and bent down to it. "Looks promising."

DJ walked over to her. "I know it's tough, but think about what was here. Was there anything that could lead him to Tyler now? Or you? Anything that could tell us how he found you so easily?" DJ said it softly, the intensity in his voice sending shivers up her spine.

"I..." Tammie couldn't think of anything. Then,

turning on her heel, she hurried to the kitchen. DJ and his light beam followed. The room looked clean and neat…not at all as she'd left it. Hadn't there been dirty dishes in the sink? Why would Dom clean up? Had Robyn?

Suddenly, she shivered. Robyn wouldn't realize the risk. What if she'd walked in when Dom was here?

Focus, she reminded herself.

What were the odds it was still here? She yanked open a drawer and dug through the inevitable junk. At least this mess was hers. Her fingers finally hit something hard and she nearly sank to her knees in relief. The address book was the only thing that connected her to DJ, her family and her friends.

She had no way of knowing if Dom had seen it, but at least he hadn't taken it.

She hugged the book. How many times had she wished she'd taken it with her? Her eyes burned. "My address book. It's still here," she whispered. "It has everyone's info in it."

An old-fashioned habit, one she'd clung to after too many computer crashes. The pale blue cover of the address book was familiar and soothing.

She couldn't seem to move. The book clutched to her chest, she fought the tears filling her eyes. She had to rebuild her life, but how? Where? Time vanished. Hours, minutes later a strong, warm hand touched her shoulder. She nearly leaped away. She spun around to find DJ beside her.

"Hey," he said softly, and she realized the harshness had faded from his face. "You okay?"

"Uh, yeah." She stared at DJ and saw in him their son's face. She was so glad Tyler wasn't here now.

"The room next to your studio? Tyler's?"

Oh, God, what had Dom found there? "How bad is it?"

"No, it's fine." DJ settled his hands on her shoulders and she didn't resist when he pulled her close. "I just thought we should take what he might want or need."

Tammie pulled back, trying to find answers in his face. Take Tyler's stuff away? As if he wasn't coming back to her? But then again, what would he come back to?

She heard the frequently used curse word that DJ favored echo in her head. She'd been around him too long.

"He's probably outgrown all the clothes…" She couldn't remember what was in there. She didn't want to.

Turning to follow him, she saw a note stuck on the board beside the phone and gasped. *Tammie when you get home, call me!* The "call me" was underlined three times. Robyn's single *R* signature and her home phone number were below it.

Tammie pulled the phone off the wall before realizing that if there were no utilities, there wasn't any phone, either. The silent line was too damning and painful. *Please, please let Robyn be okay.*

"Can you call her?" Tammie pulled the note from the board and handed it to DJ. He nodded and dialed his cell, putting it on speaker. The sound of Robyn's familiar, recorded voice telling them to leave a message was heartbreakingly familiar.

"Pack all his stuff," Tammie whispered to DJ. "I don't want him to ever come back here. Not ever."

THIS WAS A MISSION, DJ reminded himself. Just like during every other mission, DJ needed to focus. Letting Tammie's fears and emotions get in the way was not acceptable. He'd been doing fine keeping to that line, until he stood in the doorway of Tyler's room.

Mission be damned. This was his family. And too damned close to home. Anger had him clenching his fists at his sides. Ready to pummel something—or someone.

No one had to tell him this was his son's room—a little-boy bed shaped like a race car, shelves of dinosaurs and animals, blue walls and bright red curtains. He pictured Tyler here, playing, sleeping and running a hundred miles an hour.

DJ walked through the doorway, looking around with hungry eyes for clues to the years before he'd met his son.

He'd told himself that he couldn't get back those past years. Told himself there was no sense in dwelling on it. But standing there, in the room his son had slept in and lived in, all those thoughts vanished.

DJ was ticked.

Turning to see Tammie standing in the doorway was bad timing. Very bad.

"Did you need something?" He stepped back from the emotions threatening to overwhelm him.

"No." She walked into the room. Sitting down on the bed, she grabbed the pillow and hugged it. "Still smells like him." Her voice cracked and DJ resisted the urge to move toward her. "He was a good baby, mostly. So happy and sweet," she whispered.

DJ hadn't moved, watching her, trying to envision her holding Tyler as a baby. He couldn't see what he'd never witnessed. The hunger to know more was too strong. "Tell me about him." His voice was harsh. He couldn't help it.

"He was only sick a couple of times." She held her breath for a long minute, and slowly let it out. "He had pneumonia when he was two. I spent hours rocking him." She glanced over her shoulder at DJ.

Her eyes shimmered even in the dim light. "His first word was *hi* and he said it to everyone. He walked, or rather, ran, at nine months."

DJ clenched his hands into fists, as much to keep from grabbing her and comforting her, as from his anger. "Did you ever think you could ask for help? Did it ever cross your mind that I might want to be there for my son? Because I would have been there, Tammie—for Tyler and for you."

She put the pillow down, patting it softly, smoothing it with a mother's hand. She walked over to face DJ. "I never meant to hurt you. And, yes, I felt so alone those nights. But I'm also proud that I did it on my own."

"I don't want to take that pride from you. I just need to understand it."

Their eyes met, the eerie glow of the flashlight beam bouncing around the room. "Why?" She stepped closer. "We knew each other a week. We made a baby, but why would I have trusted you any more than anyone else?"

She turned away from him then and left the room. DJ cursed. This was getting them nowhere.

Stalking to the closet, he threw open the doors. She was right. Most of the clothes there would be too small. Hell, Tyler had already outgrown half the things Wyatt had bought for him in the past two months.

He'd grabbed a garbage bag from the kitchen and he threw a bunch of the animal toys inside. Turning, DJ found himself staring at a small child's chair and desk, with papers sticking haphazardly out of one of the drawers.

Carefully, he pulled open the drawer and smiled at the crayon-drawn pictures. A dinosaur, a tabby cat and—DJ laughed—a couple of pigs. Prophetic or Tyler's talent at dropping hints? DJ folded the pictures and slipped them into his pocket.

DJ turned to leave, knowing neither he nor Tyler would ever come back here again. The small wooden chair at the desk caught his eye again, reminding him of the chairs he and his siblings had brought home from Mom's house after her funeral. Every time he sat in his, he thought of her, thought of home. He wanted Tyler to have that same feeling. He snagged the chair and threw it over his shoulder.

Tyler was his son. Texas was his home now.

But DJ acknowledged that there'd always be a piece of this place in Tyler. He couldn't give it back to him, but he could preserve some of the security that used to be here.

CHAPTER FOURTEEN

DJ WATCHED TAMMIE through the hotel's sliding glass door. The shadows blanketed her, but he could see her outline in the reflection of the glow of the security lights from the grounds below.

She was curled up in one of the wicker chairs on the balcony, her feet under her and her arms wrapped around a book she'd brought with her from Tyler's room. She'd been sitting like that for over an hour. Not moving, simply holding the book, staring out over the water.

He couldn't see her features, but her worry wafted in with the salty breeze. Robyn hadn't answered the half-dozen calls they'd made, and she had yet to return their messages. Colin had left half an hour ago to check out the address listed for Robyn in Tammie's address book.

There wasn't any word from him, either.

DJ had taken the time to check in with most of his siblings. Not because he felt accountable to any of them, but because he needed to give Tammie—and himself—some space.

DJ leaned against the door frame, briefly closing his eyes. His head pounded. He was more than ready to head home.

The trip to Tammie's house had been hard for both

of them. He just hadn't quite figured out who was more disturbed.

He'd been surprised at the house itself. The mid-century bungalow with the beach in its backyard and well-kept yard was beautiful. And expensive. Very expensive. And the necklace he'd bought at the mall in New Orleans had cost him a pretty penny.

She made a good living. A danged good living.

Or she had.

His phone rang just then. Not Robyn. Not Colin. His sister Mandy.

"Wyatt says you're still running around the world for her?" Mandy seldom started a call with hello, so why should this be any different? DJ didn't have to ask who "her" was. Of all his sisters, Mandy was the most straightforward. And the hardest to ignore.

"Not quite the world, but yeah."

Tonight each of his siblings had offered him plenty of advice. He didn't want it, nor did he plan to take any of it. But he knew better than to completely ignore them or they'd descend for one of their family "interventions."

"This better be worth it," Mandy said.

He took a deep breath. "It has to be." He looked over at Tammie, wishing he knew how to solve all this. If they could just find— His phone buzzed in his ear. "I gotta go. I'm getting another call. I'll keep you posted, sis."

"No, you won't. But that's okay. I'm used to it."

"Are all pregnant women as grouchy as you?"

"Yes. So don't do anything stupid. If you know what I mean."

Every one of DJ's siblings had a trick to get info out of him. She was fishing, wanting to know what was going on between him and Tammie. No surprise. "Not going there with you, Mandy. Bye." Colin's number appeared on the screen and DJ switched calls before she could yell at him. "Tell me something good, buddy."

"Robyn moved out two months ago," Colin said, sounding as tired as DJ felt. "I talked to a couple of neighbors. I'll fill you in when I get back."

"Good or bad?"

"Not sure. If Tammie can fill in some blanks, we'll know better."

"Take your time." DJ moved into the doorway as he ended the call. He wasn't in any hurry to share her.

THE FAMILIAR SCENT of wet sand, leftover sunshine and the sea wafted over the balcony's edge. Tammie sat in the cushioned wicker chair on the balcony, looking toward the darkness that cloaked the sea. She didn't need daylight to know it was there. She heard its crash, felt the pull of the water as it called to her. Closing her eyes, she let the damp breeze caress her skin and the scents wrap around her.

Wrapping her arms around the book she'd found in Tyler's room, she let its sharp edges dig into her arms. His favorite bedtime story. How could she have possibly forgotten to pack it for him? What kind of mother forgot one of her son's favorite things? What kind of person put her son at risk like this?

DJ was still inside, for which she was thankful. She couldn't face him or anyone right now. In the distance, she heard his voice. An occasional burst of laughter punctuated the stretches of quiet and his deep-voiced responses. Earlier, he'd been talking to Tyler, but he'd made a couple of other calls, too. His brother Wyatt. His sister Mandy.

She'd known he came from a big family. When they'd met nine years ago, they'd spent the first few days getting to know each other. He'd been honest, telling her about his family, about his dreams to join the Special Forces—sharing with her the details of so much of his life back home.

And she'd lied to him. Oh, not outright, but by omission. She hadn't shared anything real with him. Looking back, she wondered why in the world he'd even been attracted to her. She ignored the simple fact that he'd been eighteen and a guy—and she'd been a girl the same age in a bikini…

Shaking her head, she tried to block the lurking loneliness. It wasn't working.

The breeze picked up, cool now that the sun had gone down, and she pulled her sweater tighter. She could go inside. But she didn't want to.

She wasn't sure how long she sat there before the sound of the screen door opening told her DJ had come outside. He stopped, resting his forearms on the rail.

"It's beautiful out tonight," he said softly.

"Yeah." Too pretty almost. "Everything okay at home?" She didn't want to be envious of his family, she really didn't. But wanting and doing were two different things.

"Tyler's taking the pigs to his 4-H meeting tomorrow."

"As show-and-tell or as guests?"

He laughed and the warmth of it washed over her. "So they can start working on what his presentation will be at the fair."

"Fair?"

"Yeah, the county fair is mid-August. He wants to enter. He has dreams of making it to state."

Tammie had no idea how 4-H worked. "Is that possible?"

"Yep. Wyatt says Tyler has good potential to place. He's got some good stock. He's excited."

"That's the important part." She refrained from reminding him that Tyler got excited about most everything. At eight he had no idea how to *not* be excited.

"That's the goal," DJ said.

The conversation died, the breeze and the crash of the waves the only sounds. Time ticked by. Finally, DJ turned to face her, leaning back on the rail. "Walk with me on the beach."

"I—" She loved to walk on the beach. At her house, she'd done so nearly every night. She'd often waded into the simple waves, remembering a night so long ago that had been a dream, a night that had given her Tyler. A night that she had to admit was safer in her memory than reality.

"Come on." He laughed. "It'll be nice. You need to burn off some of this tension."

"I'm not tense."

"Oh, not at all." His sarcasm was thick. "If you're not stressed, I'm worried about you."

"Why?"

DJ sighed, and she watched in the dim light from the doorway of the suite as he shoved his hand through his hair. The gold curls were growing out, and she wondered if he'd let it grow as long as it had been when he was eighteen, or if he'd keep it short. She liked it shorter.

He pinned her with a dark, intense glare. "I don't know why you shut yourself off—from me, from the world, from your son—but damn it, you're going to end up alone."

Wasn't that what she was already? Her throat tightened. She'd never meant it to be this way. But she'd been alone—on her own—for longer than she'd been a part of anything. "I don't know how to be any different."

DJ stepped away from the rail and faced her. He extended his hand. "Let me show you."

Tammie stared at him—at the strong, scarred hand reaching toward her. She wanted to take it, wanted to grab him and wrap her arms around him and hold on tight. She knew he'd let her. And that's exactly why she couldn't give in.

Finally, he let his arm fall back to his side.

She didn't have the nerve to meet his eyes. She stood, turning toward the sliding glass doors. In the dim light, she stumbled at the raised threshold. The book clattered to the wood and, as smoothly as if he'd choreographed it, he caught her. She didn't move away. She didn't want to. She looked up.

He was close. So close. Gentle, golden light fell through the doorway and across his face, reflecting warmth in his eyes. For the first time all day, she felt safe. But she didn't have the luxury of believing this could possibly last.

She pulled away. Bending to pick up the book, she cradled it tight again and looked back at DJ. He stood there, a shadow in the night. "Thank you for your help today."

"You're welcome, but I didn't do it for you." His voice wasn't angry, which surprised her, considering she'd refused his offer. He was so different from the other men she'd known.

She tried to read his expression and failed. The moon had come over the ridge, a bright white half orb that shone bright over him and on the distant water.

Slowly, DJ moved toward her, never breaking eye contact. "Remember on the beach that last night?" He was closer, leaving the shadows outside. "You said that someday you were going to do more than dream. You were going to be a success. You were going to conquer the world."

"Vaguely," she whispered, remembering all too clearly that conversation. She'd been so full of herself—an eighteen-year-old's arrogance. She'd been a fool.

"That's who I'm doing this for." He reached up and gently plucked the book from her arms, then carefully set it on the table. Oh-so-gently, he cupped her chin, making sure she couldn't look away. "*She* deserves to have her dreams. *She* doesn't deserve to have some jerk steal them away."

"Look where that dreaming got me," Tammie whispered, because her only other option was to scream with frustration.

He took that final step, and his next words came with a whisper across her lips. "I *am* looking. I like what I see."

Tammie closed her eyes, for a moment letting that girl rise to the surface, just to catch a glimpse of what could have been.

DJ's kiss was warm compared to the cool evening, soft compared to the solid arms that wrapped around her and pulled her against him.

Her defenses low, Tammie leaned into him, shut off her brain and let her body simply feel. It felt so good.

DJ was the first to pull back, but not far. He leaned his forehead on hers, not allowing any other space between them. "Colin will be back any minute. I'm not up to sharing you just yet. Let's escape to the beach for a while?"

She couldn't help but smile and nod.

Their room was on the third floor. Tension of a totally different kind than earlier tugged at her as they walked down the hallway and rode the elevator to the lobby.

"Come on." DJ's fingers curled around hers and he tugged her across the patio to the beach stretched beyond the walls.

The evening-cooled sand sifted up between her toes. Savoring the feeling, Tammie walked slowly, keeping to DJ's pace. He tried to hide the difficulty he had walking on the shifting sand. She wasn't going to point it out, and no way would he admit it. She had to smile because she also wasn't going to admit that she was glad he'd convinced her to come out here tonight. She liked his persuasive techniques.

The tide was low, leaving a thick stretch of damp, compacted sand just beyond where they were now. She headed toward it. Not only would it be easier for him to walk on, but the crystal waters beckoned to her.

She'd missed this, missed the sand, the sea and the freedom, and hadn't realized how much until now.

Her heart hitched as she thought of home, of her damaged house.

"Stop thinking," DJ said behind her. "Just relax and enjoy tonight. Tomorrow we'll deal with the real world."

She hadn't realized how close he'd come. Stopping to stare at the moon's bright face, she felt his heat reaching out to engulf her. She resisted the urge to turn and answer his silent call.

The power of the ocean washed over her and she soaked it in. She didn't know how long she could hold out. DJ was too much temptation. If she leaned on him too much, if she let him or anyone else take over...what happened to her? What became of her hard-won independence? Until she knew the answer, she couldn't do it, she just couldn't.

He had no such qualms. His arms slipped around her waist, pulling her against his chest. It felt so good, so right. Her fragmented thoughts barely connected. Memories of their last trip to the beach were suddenly fresh in her mind. She needed to distract him, and herself.

"Where is Colin tonight?" she whispered.

"I don't know and I don't much care."

She could tell he was lying. She turned then, glad for the chance to pull away from him. Why was the cool night air so disappointing? "Yes, you do. He didn't come with us for a vacation."

"And right now we're not worrying about Colin. Or Tyler, since I know he's your next excuse. Just relax and enjoy."

The moon washed over his features, but the night stole the color and clarity from his eyes. What was he thinking? She had no clue.

Maybe that was a good thing. He stepped away, slowly, carefully, letting the waves reach and splash over his toes. He shoved his hands into the pockets of his jeans. The fabric of his T-shirt stretched across his broad shoulders. Why couldn't they just pretend this was a new beginning? Why couldn't they erase the past?

The silence was heavy and dark. She waited, looking up at the sky, where the stars were scattered and bright.

"He's at Robyn's apartment." DJ spoke to the sea, and she had to focus on hearing his words over the ocean's cry. "Or where she used to live. She moved."

She'd asked for his honesty. She'd put the question out there. So why didn't she want to hear any more? Slowly, she sank down and sat on the sand. Just above the wave's reach, the sand was still warm.

"I guess it's stupid to think the world, life, didn't go on while I've been gone. She could have moved across the world for all I know."

DJ settled beside Tammie, a sigh of relief escaping him. "Damn, that feels good." He leaned back on his elbows. "Add walking on the beach to that list of things to avoid." The neutrality in his tone told her more than anything that he didn't like that realization.

They sat for a long time, watching the rise and fall of the breakers. "How well do you know Robyn?" DJ broke the silence.

"Very." She frowned at him. "Don't be so suspicious."

"I am suspicious. You trust her?"

"Completely. If she moved away, it was for legitimate reasons."

For several long, tense moments, DJ looked at her. She didn't look away. "Good enough."

Sifting sand between her fingers, she watched it fall back to earth. "I'm sorry," she whispered. She jumped when his hand shot out and he grabbed her chin.

"Don't even go there, Tammie. We've had this conversation before. None of this is your fault. And I'm sure as hell not going to let you keep that burden."

His touch, rough and warm, was her downfall. They were right back where they were up in the room. "DJ," she whispered and let him push her back onto the sand.

"I like the way you say my name," he breathed across the skin of her neck. Trailing his lips to her jaw, he teased and tasted her.

Tired of waiting, she felt her blood race through her veins and heat the air between them. Tammie captured his jaw in her palms and brought his lips to her. *Yes.* This was what she wanted. What she needed. Desperately.

"Love me, DJ. Help me forget," she whispered.

He didn't need any more invitation. His lips came down on hers, urging and seeking. Leaning on his elbow, he moved closer, aligning his body along hers, hot and hard. So right.

Her sigh of pleasure was loud in the night. She wrapped her arms around his neck, urging him closer. Turning, DJ used his weight to push her deeper against the sand. Angling his body atop hers, his leg slid between her knees, nudging her thighs apart.

Then his groan, not of pleasure but of agony, broke the spell. DJ cursed and hastily pulled back. Lying flat on the sand, he stared at the stars, his jaw clenched.

He'd looked just like this that day in the rain, when his muscles had tightened in a painful spasm. Guilt and worry washed over her. "What can I do?"

"Just wait. It'll pass. I swear."

"What if it doesn't?"

"It will." His angry glare made her pull back. Wasn't there anything she could do right anymore?

"WOMAN, YOU WILL be the death of me yet." DJ stared up at the sky, taking careful, measured breaths. The walk on the beach had seemed like a good idea. Heck, the last time they'd spent the night on the beach…

He hadn't expected the uneven sand to play such havoc with his back. The muscle spasms were fewer and farther apart these days, but when they came, it was like a truck ramming into him.

"DJ." She leaned over him. "I'm sorry."

"For what?" he said through gritted teeth. "And if you say for the damned explosion, I'm going to throw you into those waves."

"Not likely," she mumbled. "Give me your phone."

"Why?" The muscles were already starting to release. Another few minutes and he'd be fine—or as fine as he got.

"Colin's up in the room. He can come help you." She was staring back at the hotel, panic all over her face. He followed her gaze. They'd left the lights on, and sure enough, he was moving around.

"He can stay there. I'll be fine."

She glared at him. "No. Let him help you."

DJ cursed as she palmed the phone and started to dial. She might be down in the dumps these days, but when she took charge she was just *too* happy. He sighed. What would she be like in twenty years?

That gave him pause. Where had that thought come from? Twenty years? Looking at her, with the moonlight painting itself over her features, and glinting off her long curls, he realized he'd always thought of her as a forever kind of girl. The mother of his child, and the only person, outside of his family, who he'd want in his life all the time.

"What do you mean, what kind of beer does he want you to get?" Tammie's voice put a halt to his disturbing thoughts.

DJ reached over, grabbed the phone and yelled into it. "Where the hell are you?"

"The grocery store. Why?" Colin answered.

"Then who the hell is in our room?" The maid had already come and gone and, while this was a nice place, they didn't turn down the beds.

DJ didn't wait for an answer. He tossed the phone to Tammie and forced his damaged legs to stand.

His head spun with the sudden shift. But he'd been in worse shape before and he'd fought through it then. Angry pain clawed at his spine, but he swore and ignored it.

He had no intention of giving in now.

He headed across the sand, trying to run, wishing for the days when he could run miles with a fifty-pound pack on his back. He cursed and fought to cross the beach.

"DJ," Tammie screamed after him. He heard her voice but not the rest of her words. She was telling Colin, he was sure of it. His friend wouldn't be able to help.

The even surface of the patio around the hotel made movement easier, though he still struggled against the spasm that was, thankfully, letting go. He'd pay for this later, but damned if he'd let anyone invade his territory.

He barreled down the musty-scented hall and pounded the elevator button. Tammie hopped into the elevator right behind him. Once at their suite, he shoved open the door, hoping to find the bastard still there and planning how he'd beat the crap out of him.

But the room was empty. Except for the mess the intruder had left behind.

DJ cursed. Again and again. He paced, moving from one side of the room to the other. Tyler's book lay on the floor, thankfully undamaged, but still violated. DJ reached down and picked it up before Tammie saw it.

"Is it okay?" She stood in the doorway, her face pale, her hair a scattered cloud around her face from her race after him. She fought to catch her breath as she moved toward him. "I called security. Colin's coming back." She looked around. Her eyes widening first, then glowing with tears. Watching her heart break almost destroyed him.

"How do they keep doing this?" Her voice shattered with tears and anger. He couldn't answer her. Someone must have seen them at the house and followed them. But who, damn it? Dom? Someone he'd hired?

Carefully, DJ set Tyler's book on the side table and walked toward her. Adrenaline kept the pain away for now, but he felt it looming.

Yes, they'd come here to get Dom's attention. But this was not what DJ wanted.

"Oh, God, no." Tammie stood in the doorway of the bedroom. The room was dark, but the look on her face told him she could see just fine.

He moved to stand beside her. No destruction, except for her backpack. It was on the bed, its contents dumped onto the previously smooth bedspread.

The valuable book, its goodies, pictures, money and mementos were scattered on the fabric. The pictures spilled out over the floor. Tiny clumps of ash had fallen to the carpet.

DJ flipped on the lights and strode into the room. Thankfully, the gun she'd had was safely locked in the truck.

The thug had gone through all of Tammie's personal belongings. This only confirmed that Dom was after those two display necklaces.

"Anything missing?" DJ yanked open the closet door. The room safe was still there, still closed. He quickly worked the combination. Nothing was missing. The necklace he'd bought and the two mock-ups Tammie had found in her pack were still there. He breathed a sigh of relief, fairly certain they'd be gone if he hadn't locked them up.

Tammie simply stared. "I think everything's here..." she whispered. Moving woodenly, she dug into the pack. "Except—" She dumped the remaining contents of the backpack. "The address book." She kept flinging things around, looking. "It's gone."

He started searching, too. And gathering things, trying to bring order to the chaos.

A knock at the door had them both looking up.

An older man in a security guard uniform stood in the open doorway. Colin was behind him, a six-pack of beer in one hand and an angry stare on his face. DJ had seen that look before.

Just before they'd left for a mission. Before they'd headed into battle together. And in the mirror.

This was frustrating. But it also told him more than the intruder meant to communicate. "Well, we got what we wanted," DJ said.

"What?" Tammie stared at him.

"Yeah, we did." Colin stepped into the room. "Dom knows we're here."

DJ nodded, trying to put everything into perspective and failing. Anger, hot and evil, had him fisting his hands and wishing…

For the first time he couldn't cool the anger he felt.

For the first time since returning to civilian life, he missed something he hadn't even realized he'd lost.

The ability to kill the enemy legally.

CHAPTER FIFTEEN

TAMMIE HAD BEEN questioned and interviewed by a couple of different officers and the hotel security to the point where she couldn't even keep her eyes open. Once the police had taken their statements, and after gathering all their things, they moved to a different room in the hotel.

DJ looked as tired as she felt, though he kept pacing around the room, prowling, actually. Colin was perched on the couch, his feet crossed atop the flimsy hotel coffee table.

The last of the blue uniforms disappeared out the door. Only one man remained. He was tall, early thirties, burly and wore a suit instead of a uniform. As she looked at him, she frowned. She hadn't talked to him yet and she dreaded more questions. With a sigh she flopped down on the end of the bed. Maybe he'd take a hint and decide to just get notes from the other guys.

The silence grew. Finally, DJ went over to the door, and after a quick glance outside, he closed it. What was he doing?

The stranger pulled up his jacket sleeve and glanced at a big silver watch on his wrist. "Give 'em another couple minutes," he said to no one in particular.

"Stalling won't help." Colin grinned. "I still get the better hand."

"Like hell." The man smiled back. "Your ass is mine next time we play." He pointed at Colin and they both laughed.

She was definitely missing something and her brain was too fried to follow the bumpy road. "Someone tell me what's going on before I fall asleep," she said, lying down and grabbing a pillow to snuggle. Ah, that was *so* much better.

The bedspread was made of that slick, fake fabric stuff, but Tammie didn't care. She'd sleep on a hard floor at this point. Voices hummed around her and she tried to focus on what they were saying.

"Carlyle's a known player." The stranger's voice broke through the fog of her mind. He knew Dom. Her eyes popped open, and she forced herself to sit up and focus on him.

"Hey, sleepyhead." DJ looked over at her. "I thought you were asleep."

"I wanted to be," she admitted. She looked at the man. "Hi. I'm Tammie Easton."

"This is Sam. Agent Sam Watson. He's one of those contacts I was mentioning earlier," Colin explained as the big man nodded. "He's not officially here."

"Ah."

"But if I need to be official, I can do that." The agent seemed to want to reassure her. "Colin called a couple days ago, and I've been taking mental notes while you told the boys in blue about the break-in." He pinned her with a direct stare. "So, now I'd like to hear the rest of your story. The part that involves Dominic Carlyle."

Tammie swallowed, surprised at first that he knew she'd held back information. But then she realized this was one of the guys both Colin and DJ had been talking about, encouraging her to trust. She knew they were right. But why did it feel too much as if she was hanging on the edge of a cliff by just her fingernails?

The detective cleared his throat and met her gaze. "I know you don't fully trust my colleagues, and to be honest, I'm not sure I always do. But I can't help you if I don't know everything." Hadn't DJ said the same thing? She looked at him now and saw encouragement in his stare.

Slowly, she stood and walked over to her backpack. It had been dumped, the precious contents scattered on the worn carpeting of the room. She'd tried to put it all back together, but it was too fresh and even now, two hours later, she couldn't face it.

She did however find the mangled piece of paper that was the copy of the police report she'd filed all those months ago. Being a carbon copy, it was hard to read now. Still, she handed it to him. "This was the beginning."

He nodded, pulling a smartphone out of his jacket pocket. The modern version of the little notebook cops used in the movies? He typed in some info from the report and handed the paper back to her. "Keep that. I've got the particulars. I'll dig up the original."

He faced them all a few seconds later. "Here's the situation as I see it." He paused, and Tammie could see his active brain behind his eyes reordering itself. "I know you think Carlyle has the power to lay the blame at your feet. And even though he's a small-time crook…honestly, he can make life miserable for you."

"So, what else is new?" Her shoulders sagged. This didn't sound like much help.

He smiled then and she relaxed just a little, which was really strange.

"I know you've already been over this, probably a dozen times, but tell me everything from the beginning."

Tammie sighed, not wanting to do this, and yet knowing that this time someone was actually listening to her. And so she began. Telling him about the trade show, about the necklaces, about the night he'd hurt Tyler and she'd run. Everything up to tonight's break-in. "And now? You're here." Even she heard the doubt in her voice.

"He's here to help," DJ softly reminded her.

"How?" She turned her frustrated glare on DJ. "I don't see how talking about it to everyone is going to help. It hasn't done a bit of good yet."

All three men looked at her. Agent Watson leaned forward. "Let us help you. These two lunkheads have the skills to find and take this guy out. What they don't have is the authority to do so." He looked pointedly at both Colin and DJ. "But I do."

Tammie shivered at the intensity in their eyes and the tension in the room. She wouldn't want to be in Dom's shoes when these guys found him.

BY 2:00 A.M., DJ was wired and exhausted. Once everyone had left, DJ couldn't sit, couldn't relax. Tammie, on the other hand, looked beat. Her eyelids were at half-mast and her shoulders drooped. "Get some sleep," he told her.

"What about you?"

The smaller room didn't give them the separation that the suite had. Here, the beds were in the same room, side by side—close.

"I won't be sleeping anytime soon." He wasn't about to tell her how he felt. On edge, on guard and more than a little disturbed by his urge to maim and kill.

Too many guys came home from the war zones damaged, with, and without, obvious injuries. He'd been counseled about post-traumatic stress disorder, on what signs to watch for. He tried to be self-aware. But was he even able to do that?

Or was he too far gone?

"Does your back hurt? I'll get you some ice if you want."

"I'm fine."

"Then let's get some sleep."

Sleeping was the last thing DJ wanted to do with

her. “Just go to bed, Tammie.” He walked over to the window and stared out at the ocean to where the moon was now high in the sky and covered everything with its pale, colorless light.

“Do you need any pain meds?”

DJ froze. Curling his hands into fists at his sides, DJ didn’t trust himself not to touch her. “Go to bed,” he repeated, more tersely.

“Why?” He sensed her standing behind him. “So you can play the tough soldier and be on guard duty all night?”

“Don’t push me, Tammie.”

“Why not?” Her temper flared and before he could react, she was in front of him, glaring. “You’ve pushed me for days. ‘Get on this motorcycle.’” She mimicked his voice with an angry sneer. “Let’s go to this motel in the middle of nowhere. How about we stop in New Orleans, where my CO can insult you.” She poked his chest with her finger, punctuating her words.

He grabbed her hand and yanked hard so she had to lean against him or fall over.

They stared at each other, both of them breathing hard. “Just go to bed, Tammie. Leave it be.” His voice was hard, but he couldn’t soften the edges. Exhaustion was creeping in.

“What do you want from me?” she whispered.

“What do *I* want? I want you to be safe. I want Tyler and you to have a safe, happy life. I want—” DJ slipped his hand to the nape of her neck, his fingers winding through the silky strands of her hair. "I want this." He pulled her close and let himself get lost in her lips, in her taste, in the heat that erupted inside him and begged to have her.

Tammie didn't back away, or turn away from the monster DJ feared he'd become.

He should tell her to run, but then he'd have to let her go. And that wasn't happening. Not now. Maybe never.

DJ backed her against the wall. All those soft, sweet curves leaned against him, driving him crazy.

She gave as good as she got. Her fingers dug into his shoulders, urging him closer.

This wouldn't be the sweet, slow kind of loving. He wanted it, needed it, fast and intense. Her whimper was not one of pain when he pushed her legs apart with his knee, but a plea for more.

"Please," she whispered, reaching down to grasp the hem of her T-shirt. She wanted it off and he was glad to oblige. Her bare skin against his palm felt smooth and soft—and hot. Oh-so-blessedly hot. Unclasping her bra, he tugged it off, tossing it aside, where it quickly joined her shirt on the floor.

Sweet heaven, she was beautiful. He ached to taste and touch every inch of her and started with the soft ridge of her chin and made his way down.

The column of her neck led to the rise of her breasts, where his tongue sought a taut peak. Her full breasts filled his palms and teased his fingers. She leaned into his touch, seeking more.

"DJ," she said. "Bed. Now." She didn't wait for him to move, but tore away from him and grabbed his hand. Dragging him to the bed, she pushed against the center of his chest until he sat, then tumbled back onto the spread.

He extended his arms to grab her and bring her with him, but she dodged him with a peal of laughter. He'd almost decided to sit up, and go after her, when he saw what she was doing. Facing him, she stepped into the space between his knees.

Slowly, holding his gaze with her hot stare, she lowered the zipper on her jeans. Then with a flash of pink pantie, she dropped the rest of her clothes to the carpet.

DJ was still fully dressed in the gray T-shirt and camo pants he'd grown accustomed to wearing, while she was there before him—beautiful and naked. Just for him. All his.

Unhurriedly, Tammie moved onto the bed and straddled him, her palms on his chest and the heat between her legs pressed against the erection trapped behind his fly.

He groaned in painful pleasure. "Darlin', we aren't going to have near as much fun this way."

"Maybe you aren't." She leaned forward, brushing her firm breasts against the thin fabric of his shirt. "I like unwrapping packages." Reaching down, Tammie grabbed a handful of his shirt, pulling it up to expose his abs, then the solid ridges of his chest, and finally yanking it over his head. She tossed it over her shoulder toward the pile of her clothes.

"Mmm." Tammie took her time exploring him with her fingers and mouth.

Unable to take any more, DJ grabbed her hips and flipped her over, trapping her beneath him. Her screech of surprise flowed into a moan of pleasure as he leaned down and took one distended nipple deep into his mouth.

She arched into him, her hands fisting in his hair as she held him there.

Pleasuring her soon became torture for him. DJ needed to be inside her, needed to take her with him into completion. Pulling away, he finished undressing then wrapped his arms around her, molding her soft curves all along his body. He left no space between them. None.

With a single hard thrust, DJ entered the sweetest place he'd ever known. As he moved back to do it again, he looked down at her and momentarily froze.

Beautiful. Tammie's face, flushed with desire, her eyes closed, her bottom lip caught between her teeth in anticipation, had never looked so perfect.

Suddenly, the urgency evaporated. Not the passion by any means, but instead of rushing to the finish, DJ moved slowly, gently, prolonging the perfection of the moment. He didn't want it to ever end.

He watched her as he moved, marveled at the intensity on her face, listened to the uneven gasps of her breath as he drove her nearer the edge.

She felt so good. So right, surrounding him completely.

"DJ."

The sound of his name on her lips was a caress, and he moved in to capture it. Kissing her thoroughly and sweetly as her cries melted into him.

He couldn't hold back. He let himself fall—into the release and into love.

THE FIRST RAYS of dawn reaching across the bed woke Tammie. DJ's arm, heavy and warm, wrapped around her waist as he lay curled against her back. Closing her eyes, she savored the moment, wishing it could go on forever. If only she could just fall back to sleep and pretend this was reality.

But her mind was filled to nearly overflowing. She should be exhausted and sound asleep. They'd been up half the night... But her brain wouldn't shut off. The events of the past year, of yesterday, of last night, raced round and round.

After the furious sex, something changed. She wasn't exactly sure when, or why, but DJ had grown tender. At one point, he'd pulled her to his side and kissed the top of her head as he settled her in his arms. She'd found comfort listening to the pounding of his heart.

She felt safe with him.

Carefully, she turned to look at him now. His arm

fell away, and he mumbled something unintelligible before settling back to sleep. His bare chest rose gently, and he looked relaxed and carefree, making, the resemblance to Tyler even stronger.

Last night— Dear Lord, she'd never imagined she could feel so close to someone. No one had ever made her feel so alive, so wanted, so sensual.

Sliding from the bed, Tammie stood there, watching him, and lost track of time. Wrapping her arms around herself, she fought the shiver. Not of cold, but fear.

She wasn't afraid of his actions. It was his words. He wanted her safe. Wanted her and Tyler safe. He'd never get his wish.

Her eyes burned as she drank in his image. The soldier in him had come out full force last night as he'd raced from the beach. And she'd slept with that soldier.

A soldier who would die for her.

She reached for the suitcase and started to pack. She couldn't let that happen. DJ was right; she needed to stop running. But otherwise they disagreed. *She* needed to take care of her own problems.

DJ WAS SURPRISED when he awoke and instinct told him he was alone. The hotel room was silent, too silent. No sound of the shower. No breeze wafting through the room from the open door where Tammie sat on the balcony. Nothing.

Panic and anger warred within him as he jumped

up and raced to the bathroom, looking for her, praying he was wrong. The clear counter ratcheted up his panic.

He cursed. He was going to strangle her.

Returning to the bedroom, he froze. The spot where her backpack had sat was empty. The only thing there at the end of the bed was the suitcase he'd bought her. He threw it up on the bed and popped it open.

Tyler's book, which she'd cradled so preciously last night, sat on top. The denim jacket and jeans she'd worn were neatly folded on top of the other clothes they'd bought at the mall in New Orleans.

His heart pounded and sank into his gut. She was gone. Why? Last night had been amazing. Looking out the window to the blue sky with its wispy clouds and sunshine, he groaned aloud.

She was out there on her own. In this town, where Dom knew her, where Dom was at home. Where she was vulnerable and at risk.

He cursed and dug around for his phone, finally locating it underneath the nightstand, where it had bounced last night. One bar and only 3 percent battery. He cursed again, using the last of the power to dial Colin. His buddy's sleepy hello was not reassuring. She hadn't called him to go with her.

"She's gone." Was that raspy voice his?

"Who? Tammie? For good?" Colin was wide-awake now.

"I don't know. I think so. She's out there—on her own."

Colin's curses were loud and colorful. "You got any ideas where?"

"Unfortunately, yeah."

"I'm on my way."

DJ didn't bother hanging up. The damned phone was dead.

TAMMIE STOOD OUTSIDE the bank for a long time, waiting for it to open. It seemed like ages since she'd been here, and looking back, she realized it had been nearly a year. Lord. "Time flies…" The rest of the old quip about having fun vanished, not at all fitting her situation.

Finishing the coffee she'd grabbed at the hotel, she tossed the paper cup into the trash and squared her shoulders. She was ready. Pushing the brass-and-glass door open, she stepped into the cool marble interior. It was at once familiar and intimidating. She'd always liked it in a strange way.

The teller windows looked the same, though most of the faces were different. She would ask one of them if they knew where Robyn had gone. Maybe she'd gotten some big promotion and had a cushy job and fancy house in another city. Robyn had always been ambitious. It was one of the traits Tammie admired most about her friend.

"Tammie?" a woman's voice came from the right,

and Tammie spun around. Shocked, she stared at the very person she'd hoped to find.

They'd met as girls working in an ice cream shop; Tammie to feed herself, Robyn to get through college. Robyn had been the one to help Tammie navigate the myriad forms and processes to get a small business loan. Over time, they'd shared drinks, dinners, tears and a half-dozen broken relationships between them.

Robyn was more aunt to Tyler than Tammie's biological sister. And here she was, safe and looking great. A dark blue suit and her dark auburn hair pulled into a smooth chignon stamped her as the successful banker she'd struggled to become.

Tammie hadn't expected to find Robyn so easily, but seeing her cheerful face touched Tammie's heart. She'd missed her friend and was relieved she was safe.

The door whooshed open behind Tammie, and the growing heat of the street swept across the back of her legs. Customers were arriving. She knew DJ and Colin would follow her. She needed to make this as quick as possible. She didn't want to be found.

Robyn came over and wrapped Tammie in a warm hug. "Where have you been?"

"I've been trying to get hold of you since yesterday." Tammie returned the hug, ignoring the complicated question. "I was worried."

"*You* were worried?" Robyn stepped back and

stared into Tammie's face. "You scared me half to death."

"I'm sorry." Tammie didn't want to talk in public, and the lump in her throat kept her from saying anything more.

"Come back to my office." Robyn tilted her head to a glassed-in cubicle behind them.

Tammie frowned, glancing around at all the people coming and going. No hulking marines. Not yet, anyway. Maybe he was still asleep. She could only hope.

Tammie followed Robyn to the office, and while the glass door wasn't solid in design, it closed tightly and Tammie knew what she said would be contained in the room.

"It's so good to see you." Robyn's voice shook, and she took a drink from the mug beside her computer monitor. "I'm glad you're okay. You are okay, right?" Her eyes darted back and forth to the lobby.

Tammie forced herself to smile. Robyn knew her too well. "Yeah, I'm okay. I just got back to town and I have some questions."

"Sure. Hey, where's the little guy?"

Tammie swallowed. She missed her son and any reminder hurt. "He's with his dad's family." She didn't want to go there. Not now. Maybe later, another day, with a few margaritas under their belts, she'd spill her guts to Robyn.

"I'm sorry I can't explain everything now. I don't

have time. I promise I will when I can. But…I need some answers."

"Anything. What do you need?"

"I know I left suddenly last year. I should have called. But I didn't have a chance." Tammie curled her fingers tight around the strap of her backpack. "I expected the house to be sold by now, or at least under foreclosure. I…I haven't been able to make the mortgage payments." Her failure hurt—hurt more admitting it aloud.

Robyn looked around, at the tellers who weren't looking at them, to the lobby of customers. Tammie frowned. Who was she looking for? Maybe coming here wasn't such a good idea.

"Robyn, I need to know if Dom— You remember him? Did he pay the mortgage?" She didn't want to be indebted to him, and she certainly didn't want him to own her home. It was hers, damn it. He'd taken everything else. She couldn't bear the idea that he'd taken that, too.

"I…" Robyn looked around again, and Tammie resisted the urge to get up and run. Something wasn't right.

"I was hoping you'd come back. And that you'd come see me," Robyn whispered.

"What…what's the matter?" Dread ripped through Tammie.

Robyn took a deep breath as if she was on a high dive ready to plunge over the edge. "When you'd been gone a month, I got worried. I went to your house and saw your studio. I knew something had happened. I…I'm sorry, but I went through your file here. I know it was a violation of company policy, but you're my friend."

Another furtive glance to the lobby only added to Tammie's fears. "That's okay." Tammie was confused. "But I don't understand."

Just then, one of the tellers knocked on the glass door and pushed it open on its silent hinges. "Robyn, the team's here. Shall I put them in the conference room?"

"Sure, Linda. I'll be right there." Robyn smiled at the teller, then turned to face Tammie with a frown on her face. "Look, we can't talk as much as I'd like. Can you meet me after work?"

"I don't have much time." Tammie glanced at the lobby, still not sure why Robyn was so nervous. "Can't you just tell me now?"

Robyn took a deep breath. "I found your parents' information in the file."

"My parents?"

"I…I called their number and your mom answered." Robyn's gaze finally met Tammie's again. "She's worried, too. She's a sweetheart, you know." Robyn stood and rearranged her already-organized desk.

"I don't understand." Tears burned in Tammie's eyes. Her mother had never been the problem. No, that honor belonged to her father.

"She's been sending money to me every month. I

make the mortgage payment. Look, I can't talk any more now. An audit team is coming in today. That's who's here. Otherwise, we could leave now."

Tammie shook her head, trying to clear the surprise so she could focus. Robyn and her mother had saved her house? They'd taken care of her? Suddenly, Tammie couldn't see the objects on Robyn's desk as they blurred into watery blobs. She was shocked when the damp trickled down her cheeks. She'd never, ever expected this.

Another sharp knock on the glass door made them both jump. Tammie watched the color drain from Robyn's face as she turned around to see two very stern, very handsome marines standing there. With their arms identically crossed over their chests, she wasn't sure whose glare was worse.

Tammie shivered. This was not going to go well.

"Um, Robyn, that's DJ. He's Tyler's dad."

"I can see the resemblance." Robyn continued to stare. "Who's the other one?"

"Colin. They're Special Forces. They're helping me."

That got Robyn's attention. She turned to stare at Tammie this time. "Helping you? With what?"

"I'll explain. Later, over dinner." Tammie stood, hustling to the door, not because she was intimidated. No. She just didn't want to watch them dismantle the entire building, which was what DJ's stare told her he had in mind.

"How does The Thirsty Parrot sound, Robyn?"

Not waiting for an answer, Tammie pulled open the door. "I don't want to hear it," she said to DJ as she exited the office. She stalked across the lobby, not looking back, but knowing from the looks the other customers threw her way that both men were following her.

Any other day, having two hunky men on her tail might be a good thing. Now she just wanted to get outside before the inquisition began.

How far could she run before they caught her? She discarded that idea as soon as it appeared, remembering DJ's sprint across the beach despite his injuries.

And Colin was in perfect health—so those odds were even worse.

At the corner of the building, she stopped and spun around. It might have been funny that DJ nearly tripped over her, except for the fact it gave him a better opportunity to grab her.

"Okay, get it over with," Tammie snapped.

"Get what over with?" DJ didn't move away or let her go.

"The tongue-lashing, or the reaming, or whatever you intend to say."

"Why do you always assume the worst of me?"

"I— What? I don't."

His left eyebrow shot up. "Yes, you do. Why did you sneak out?"

She wasn't going to tell him that.

"Especially after last night."

Glancing at Colin, and seeing his overly interested stare, Tammie blushed, remembering all the sweet, hot things that she and DJ had shared. With a chuckle, Colin stepped back a few paces, turning away as if to give them privacy. Unfortunately, he could still hear every word. "Exactly." She'd left *because* of last night, because of what she'd learned about herself.

Because she'd fallen in love with him. And she couldn't let him do what came so naturally to him. Sacrificing himself—for her.

Pulling her arm from his grasp and turning on her heel, she saw the truck parked down the block. She headed for it. "I need breakfast. And judging from how quickly you two got here, so do you."

She waited beside the truck until DJ unlocked the door. Climbing in, she settled in the passenger seat and waited.

Even with the door closed, she could hear the men as they walked around the truck.

"How does she do that?" DJ asked.

"Do what?"

"Get us to do what she wants and not tell us a thing."

"I don't know, but damn, man, you're in trouble." Colin's laughter was infectious, and Tammie decided to take it as a compliment.

CHAPTER SIXTEEN

BY LATE AFTERNOON, Tammie was anxious to talk with Robyn. DJ's hand curled around her elbow as he and Colin walked with her to the Mexican restaurant she and Robyn used to frequent, The Thirsty Parrot. Was it because he didn't trust her after she'd sneaked out of the hotel this morning? Or was he making a statement when they walked in. She was with him. Get over it, boys.

Or maybe that was her wishful thinking and it was simply a habit.

Either way, it worked for her. She didn't shrug it off or pull away.

Having lived in the southwest for the past few months, Tammie wasn't really looking forward to the Mexican food here. She and Robyn used to come here for the atmosphere and margaritas. Not the authenticity of the food.

It didn't really matter. Tammie wasn't hungry. She was tired and irritated and confused.

Inside, thick artificially cooled air engulfed them. Colin took the lead as DJ steered her to the table near the bar that the hostess led them to.

The table was small, which made Tammie feel hemmed in by the two men. She focused on the laminated menu. Looking around, she was mildly surprised to find they were the only patrons in the place.

The bright red walls were decorated with sombreros, ponchos and fake parrots. "Interesting choice of restaurant," DJ said.

"They do mostly lunch," Tammie explained. "I picked this place because there's never a crowd at night."

The door opened then and Robyn stood silhouetted for a second in the sunlight before spotting them. She wove through the tables toward them.

Robyn had always been a beautiful woman, turning heads whenever they went out. Tammie wasn't even surprised when both men watched her every step. Good thing DJ was the first one to look away, or she might have been upset.

"Hi." Robyn pulled the chair out. "We haven't been properly introduced yet." She faced DJ. "I'm Robyn Carpenter."

Tammie almost rolled her eyes. She knew Robyn too well. The business facade was a protective shell for her friend. She was definitely uncomfortable.

"Sorry. DJ Hawkins. And this is Colin McCray." With formalities done, they all focused on the menus in deliberate silence.

"Nice apartment you used to live in," Colin spoke without looking up. "Why'd you move out?"

"What?" Robyn's menu fell forward, nearly landing on the candle in the center of the table. Shock covered her face.

"When I couldn't get ahold of you yesterday, Colin went to check your old place," Tammie hastily explained.

Robyn nodded and visibly relaxed, returning her attention to the menu. "Oh."

"Robyn?" Tammie reached out and touched her friend's hand. "Something happened. Tell me." A shiver of premonition sneaked up Tammie's spine.

"It's not that big of a deal."

"You loved that apartment. You moved because of whatever happened, didn't you?" Tammie wished they had time, just the two of them, to talk. She needed a good girl talk. Looking over at DJ and Colin…*yeah*, that wasn't happening.

"What can I get you, folks?" The waitress appeared out of nowhere, tapping her foot as if she were impatient.

"Margaritas all around," Colin spoke, with a broad grin.

"I'll pass, thank you," Robyn snapped, and Tammie frowned at her friend. "I'd like water. Without lemon, thanks," Robyn ordered.

"You didn't say your friend was a teetotaler," Colin teased Tammie.

What was wrong with him? Was he trying to tick off Robyn?

"Can you give us a minute? We're not decided on our order yet." DJ took control and the girl strolled away, looking back at them a couple of times before disappearing into the kitchen.

Tammie wondered if they'd ever see her again.

"Robyn, why did you move?" DJ asked.

Robyn looked around, much as she had at the bank. The flash of fear in her eyes surprised Tammie. Robyn was the most fearless person she knew.

"Robyn?" Tammie prompted.

"Someone was stalking me," she finally said. "The cops never figured out who it was. The apartment management couldn't keep whoever they were from getting in, and the police didn't have any leads. It lasted about three months. After I moved, everything stopped, thank goodness. Nothing's happened since."

"What *did* happen?" DJ asked.

"He, I assume it was a he, broke in and tore up the place. After I got everything cleaned and fixed up again, I'd find these weird, random "things" sitting inside when I came home from work. Like a child's toy sitting on my dining room table. Or a blouse that wasn't mine on the back of the couch."

"Oh, no." Tammie was almost afraid to ask, afraid she knew who the intruder was.

"A child's toy?" Colin surprised them all by asking, and saving Tammie the trouble. "Like something of Tyler's?"

"I…I don't know." Robyn stared at Tammie. "I wouldn't know. But— Why? You're not making sense." Then suddenly her eyes widened with realization. "You think it's related to you, Tammie? To why you disappeared?"

"I don't know," Tammie admitted. She couldn't

"Is it possible," DJ interrupted, "that Dom made these payments instead?"

Robyn shook her head. She looked at a loss. "I don't understand." She met Tammie's gaze. "Someone really needs to explain."

The waitress reappeared and all conversation shut down while they ordered. As she left, the hostess seated an older couple at the next table, essentially ending the privacy they'd had.

"Come on." Robyn grabbed Tammie's arm. "I need to use the ladies' room."

"Why can't women do that alone? I've always wondered." Colin smiled as the waitress delivered his margarita.

"We'll never tell." Tammie didn't resist her friend's tug, though she should have—she wasn't up to answering the questions lurking in Robyn's eyes.

Once inside the minuscule room, Robyn didn't step into either of the stalls. With the door closed, she turned the lock then faced Tammie. "Would you please explain in simple English what the hell is going on?"

"I—" Tammie hadn't a clue where to begin. Instead, she turned around and rummaged in her backpack to find her hairbrush. She focused on fixing her hair in the distorted mirror.

"You need to explain. Dom has been worried sick about you."

"What?" Tammie spun around. "What is that supposed to mean?"

"I called him before I came here and told him you were in town. He comes by the bank a couple times a week to see if I've heard from you. I told him I'd let him know if I did."

Tammie's stomach churned, nearly bringing up the few chips she'd nibbled on. "No," she whispered. "You can't tell him anything."

"Why not? You better start talking. And don't you dare leave out why you didn't tell me all of this before."

Tammie didn't blame Robyn for being ticked and confused. "It all happened so fast. I…I thought that he was real…" Her words trailed off as she struggled to frame her thoughts without hurting her friend. "I thought it was a real relationship, but it was all a lie. You have to stay away from Dom. I'm certain he's who was stalking you. I'm sorry—I didn't think he'd go after you once I left." Tammie's mind filled with all the hurt and disappointment he'd brought into her life. "Robyn, he's a jewel thief. He forced me to hide stolen jewels by designing jewelry for them."

"How did he make you do that?" She wasn't buying any of this.

"He hurt Tyler." Tammie's voice broke. "I ran. I had to hide Tyler. And I couldn't put you at risk, too. For this last year I've been running from him. That's how Tyler ended up with DJ. DJ's brother is protecting Tyler now." She turned away, focusing on the mirror again.

Robyn stared at her, wide-eyed. "Holy—"

"Yeah." Tammie tried to hide her tears. "I had to give up custody to keep Tyler safe." Her heart broke all over again. She missed him. "I don't even know if I'll ever get him back."

"Oh, hon. Of course you will." Robyn wrapped her arms around Tammie. She'd missed her friend. Together they cried, there in the restroom. Not caring that their food grew cold, not caring that the guys were probably out there tapping their toes in impatience.

Finally, after they'd used nearly half a roll of toilet paper to mop up their tears, they looked at each other. Tammie started laughing first. "I have so missed you."

"Me, too."

"What do we do now? He's going to expect me to call and update him on you."

"Do you know where he lives, where he is now?" It couldn't be that easy to find him, could it? They could call Sam and his buddies to go pick him up.

Robyn shrugged. "He just shows up at the bank."

The sound of knuckles on the door startled them both. "Hey, you okay in there?" DJ's voice came through the wood. Tammie nearly started laughing again, but made herself straighten her shoulders.

"He's in this with me, Robyn. He and Colin both agreed to help. We need to tell them about Dom."

Robyn unlocked the door. "Your guy's okay, but the Neanderthal with him…I'm not so sure about."

"What's the problem with Colin?" She was puzzled by Robyn's reaction to him. But with DJ on the other side of the door, waiting for them, that answer would have to wait.

Robyn opened the door and sailed by with a smile. "Thanks for your concern, but we're fine."

As Tammie went to pass him, DJ stopped her with a hand on her arm. "What's the matter?"

"Nothing," she lied. "Why?"

"Because you've been crying."

She didn't want to tell him, not here. She glanced around, hoping he'd take the hint. "Not now."

He followed her gaze to the nearly empty restaurant and reluctantly nodded. Once he heard what Robyn had to say, he wasn't going to be worrying about her few wayward tears.

"I'm starting to get a complex," Colin said as he dug into his meal. "You all keep abandoning me." Their absence hadn't affected his appetite. Half his burrito was already gone.

"Maybe it's a hint." Robyn stared at him. His only response was a raised eyebrow.

Tammie watched them, intrigued, momentarily distracted from her own problems. Reality came slamming back when Robyn began explaining about Dom's visits to the bank.

"Anyway, I don't think he's even in town right now. He's on vacation supposedly." Robyn took a bite of the burrito steaming on her plate.

"Where'd he go?" Suspicion hung heavy on DJ's words and Tammie saw the thoughts in his head and followed. Whoever had been in their room must have been someone he hired.

"A place called the Crater of Diamonds in the Ozarks. Sounded like a tourist trap to me, but he said he's always wanted...to...go...there."

Everyone put two and two together and definitely came up with four. Her parents.

Tammie cringed when both DJ and Colin swore. In stereo.

For the first time in her life, Tammie felt as if hysteria was a legitimate option. Robyn's words hung in the air above the table like a guillotine blade.

"He's in...Arkansas?" Tammie put her fork down. She was done. She looked across the table at DJ. "That can't be a coincidence."

His stern frown told her he agreed. He pulled out his phone. "Let's call them."

Tammie's heart hurt. "I...I don't know their number."

"It's here in the file." Robyn opened the folder and read the number to DJ as he dialed.

Tammie couldn't face any of them, could barely face herself. Staring down at her half-empty plate, she struggled to keep her dinner down. The nightmare continued. Was no one safe from Dom's evil determination? Her guilt grew. Everyone she loved was at risk, everyone she cared about was suffering because she'd done one stupid thing in her life. She'd dared to dream.

No one spoke, listening as the ring of the phone

was loud in the nearly empty restaurant. DJ's frown grew. "There's no answer." He hung up. "Don't they have voice mail?" He looked at Tammie with a frown.

"I don't know. I haven't talked to them in a long time. I doubt it."

"Is there anyone else?" Colin finally joined the conversation after finishing his food.

"My sister."

"You know her number?"

Tammie nodded and DJ handed her the phone. Her hands shook as she pushed the buttons. Even if she didn't answer, Tammie knew Nancy had voice mail.

"Hello?"

It had been nearly a year since Tammie had talked to Nancy. They'd been close as children, but when Tammie ran away, that had ended that. She'd only reconnected with Nancy a couple of years ago and the distance was still there.

"Nancy, it's Tammie."

"Hey! It's been a long time."

"I know. Look, I need to get ahold of Mama. I tried the house, but no one answered."

"Yeah, they won't be back until later tonight."

"Back? They actually went somewhere?"

Nancy laughed. "Yeah. They went over to Missouri for a weekend."

"They never do that."

"I know. Mama won some contest on the radio and they got a free night over at the Daisy Inn."

"Since when do they call in for radio contests?"

The silence stretched out. "There's a lot of things they do that you don't know about."

That hurt, which the truth often did. "I know," she whispered. Maybe they were safe. Maybe Dom wasn't going there to hurt them. Maybe. But Tammie wasn't buying it.

"Thanks, Nancy. I'll...I'll try later." No sense in scaring the living daylights out of her sister.

"Sure. Hey, Tammie, I'd love to chat, but Willie is taking me and the kids to the movies tonight."

Willie was Nancy's good-for-nothing should-be-ex-husband. "You okay?"

"Of course, I'm fine. I just need to get the kids ready."

"Sure." She didn't want to tell Nancy what she was thinking—she'd learned that her opinions weren't any more welcome with her sister than they'd been with Dad. "Talk to you later."

Three sets of eyes stared at Tammie as she hung up the phone. She only looked back at one. DJ's gaze was full of concern and something else she couldn't quite read.

"They aren't home. For the first time in their lives, they went away for a few days." She handed the phone back to DJ. "Nancy said they'll be back tonight sometime."

He stood and tossed several bills onto the table. "Did they go on their own?"

"I...I think so."

"Let's go. Odds are they're safe. But we need to find out."

AN HOUR LATER, Tammie stood in the cool, dimly lit hotel parking garage. DJ had led the way to the truck, carrying their suitcases.

"Where's Colin?" she asked.

"Right behind you," DJ said without turning around. She glanced behind and sure enough he was there, his duffel bag thrown over his shoulder. How had DJ known Colin was there?

At the truck, DJ set the suitcases down and dropped the tailgate. Hopping into the bed, he started unbuckling the straps holding the motorcycle in place.

"Hey, let me help." Colin threw his bag down and jumped in beside DJ. "We have time to be careful."

Together they unloaded the bike and Colin palmed the keys DJ tossed to him. He straddled the bike and fired up the engine. The roar echoed to every inch of the deserted space.

"What are you doing?" Tammie asked.

That bike was his pride and joy. He'd bought the truck to keep from putting too many miles on it, to protect it. He loaded the suitcases into the bed beside Tyler's chair and the few things she'd brought from the house.

"Colin's going to stay here and see what he can find on your hard drive. *And* keep an eye on the house."

"Did it ever occur to you to include me in the discussion?"

DJ stopped beside her. Was that a smile he was trying to hide? "Yeah, we thought about it. But you'd have said no, so why bother?"

"I wouldn't have."

"Yes, you would," Colin said, joining DJ with a grin. "But we'll forgive you." He killed the loud engine and climbed off the bike. "It sounds great." He walked back to where Tammie stood still staring at them. He leaned in close. "Hey, he must really care about you if he's letting this bike out of his sight. Don't question it."

"What do you mean?"

Colin laughed. "He doesn't let anyone ride that thing."

DJ approached and after a few last-minute details, they shook hands and did that male fake-hug/shoulder-bump thing. "Stay safe," DJ said.

With a nod, Colin returned to the bike and was soon going up the ramp toward the sunshine at the top. Once he turned onto the street, the roar of the engine faded.

They were alone. The buffer was gone. And the close confines of the truck cab loomed beside her. The idea of sitting in the cab, just her and DJ traveling down the road, just the two of them, was unsettling.

"Well, let's hit the road." He wasn't moving any

faster than she was. With a shake of his head, as if to clear his thoughts, he walked over to the passenger door and opened it. She moved to the space between the door and the frame and stopped. The truck surrounded her and DJ stood there, his strong arm holding the door. He looked dangerous and serious.

"I know you hate when I say it, but I'm sorry." She met his gaze. So close, and cold.

He didn't say anything for a long moment. He took a step closer. "I told you when we started this that it was an all-or-nothing deal."

"But you are giving up so much."

"Am I? Get in, Tammie. We've got a long trip ahead. We need to get going."

The cool distance between them was all her fault, she knew that, but she wished… Biting her lip to keep herself from asking him to forgive her, and opening that whole can of worms, she climbed into the truck and let him shut the door behind her. She watched as he strode around the hood and climbed in.

A man in control. A soldier on a mission. She felt the distance he put between them. Colin was wrong. DJ wasn't doing this because he cared so much for her. No, this was for Tyler. He surely just wanted to get the whole thing over with.

The engine of the truck came to life as DJ turned the key. Not the loud rumble of a motorcycle, but the even roar of a determined predator. She swallowed. And buckled her seat belt.

They headed west, toward the lowering sun, away

from the civil confines of the city. Soon they were flying through the countryside, heading toward somewhere she'd sworn to never return to. A place she hadn't seen in over years. A place she'd once called home.

"You okay?" DJ's harsh voice broke into her fears.

"Yeah, fine."

"You don't look fine."

"Thanks," she said sarcastically and ended the conversation. She didn't look in the mirror, not wanting to see the truth.

They drove a few more miles in silence, the hum of the tires on the pavement the only sound. DJ finally broke the quiet. "Can I ask you a question?"

"Uh, sure."

He stared intently out the bug-splattered windshield as he drove. Finally, he asked softly, "Why did you run away from home?"

Since no one knew she had been a runaway, no one had ever asked her that question. And she'd never had to answer. Miles passed, fields flew by coated in sunset gold and red. She stared at them, watching the late-day bugs rise up from the remainders of the mown crops.

"I was seventeen. Stubborn and stupid," she whispered, not daring to look at DJ. "When you meet Dad—" dread made her stomach heave "—you'll understand why I left home."

CHAPTER SEVENTEEN

TAMMIE CRINGED. SHE'D bet these hills had never heard the roar of a truck like this one. With the sun falling below the horizon, DJ had turned on the headlights and the beams reached beyond the edge of the road, into nothing, outlining every hairpin turn.

The narrow mountain roads weren't made for a big vehicle like this one, yet DJ maneuvered the truck through the ruts and wash of the ancient road like an old hand. With each mile, her stomach knotted.

"Relax," DJ said as he glanced at her, swapping hands on the wheel so he could take hers. The miles on the road seemed to have relaxed him. She turned her hand into his, taking what comfort she could.

"I'm fine," she lied. Relax? The man was insane. She'd only been back home once since she'd run away all those years ago. And that visit had been a disaster.

She'd brought Tyler here when he was two. Her father had thrown them out of his house and she hadn't seen her sister nor her mother since.

At least she had talked to them over the phone and had sent Christmas cards and pictures of Tyler each year.

But come face-to-face with them? No. And she wouldn't be doing it now if DJ wasn't forcing her to…and if Dom wasn't a manipulative jerk. What if her parents weren't there? What if they decided to stay longer on their trip? How would she know if they were okay? If they were safe?

Or what if they were there and she actually *did* have to face them?

The dirt road they were on led straight to her parents' house. They were already on their land, and if she knew her father, if he was here, he'd already heard the engine's roar.

Tammie's stomach churned. She stared out the window at the lush vegetation, where the last of the sunlight struggled to shine through. She tried to slow her breathing. "Turn the truck around, please," she said.

DJ's laugh was soft and gentle. "I can't, Tammie. You can't go on without doing this." His voice was tight, so she knew he was aware how difficult this was for her. He didn't care enough to let her off the hook, though, and that really ticked her off.

Determined to show her family, and herself, her strength, she lifted her chin as the turn-in to her parents' drive appeared. But she didn't loosen her grip on DJ's hand. "This is it," she directed him.

Finally, they rounded the corner. It looked just as she remembered. The house sat there against the hill, leaning into the ridge as it always had. The thick stone walls looked as strong as ever. She frowned. It was quiet. Even the animal sounds she remembered were gone.

"There aren't any lights." DJ leaned forward to look through the windshield.

"Still too early. Dad doesn't waste energy. It doesn't mean they aren't there."

As they drove closer, Tammie looked to the front door. It was ajar and in the wide opening her father stood, his shotgun ready, and not a drop of joy on his face.

Tammie trembled and DJ squeezed her hand before letting go. Relief quickly gave way to trepidation as DJ pulled the truck right up in front of the porch. "Go ahead." He urged her to get out.

There wasn't a yard or lawn. Never had been. Tammie stepped out into the silence and looked around.

Slowly, DJ climbed out and came around to stand beside her on the dirt drive, seemingly oblivious to the shotgun aimed at them. She realized suddenly that that was why he'd suggested she climb out first. He was banking on her father recognizing her.

The ratcheting sound of the shotgun being cocked broke the quiet. Tammie stilled. "It's me, Dad," she spoke up. "This is my friend. DJ."

The man who stepped out of the shadows was physically the same as when she'd left. But his face was different. Her father's eyes sank deep into his face, where dozens of lines broke his skin. He blinked several times, but didn't bother lowering the gun aimed directly at DJ.

So much for her hope that he'd mellowed with age.

"Tammie?" Her mother's voice came from the shadows inside the house. "Is that really you?"

"You stay in there, Elizabeth," her father barked, lifting the gun higher. "She ain't alone."

"Oh, Silas. It's Tammie." Elizabeth rushed past her husband, running down the steps. "Oh, Silas, she's come home!"

"Go ahead," DJ encouraged her, smiling. Their gazes met and for an instant she wanted to reach over and kiss him. He'd done this for her.

Ignoring the waves of anger flowing from where her father stood, Tammie headed toward the worn front steps. The gun was still aimed at DJ.

"Mama!" Tammie rushed to her mother, feeling for the first time in a dozen lifetimes the warmth of her mother's hug. Ten years of bottled-up loneliness stabbed at her heart and washed away with her mother's love.

"Oh, sweetheart." Tammie felt her mother pull away and saw her look over at DJ. "I don't know who you are, but thank you for bringing my girl home."

"What are you doin', woman?" Silas barked.

"Oh, put the gun away. You ain't goin' to shoot anyone," her mother said. "Or I'll shoot you. Come inside, both of you."

DJ slowly walked past Tammie and her mother and faced Silas Easton. The gun lowered, though the man's reluctance was obvious.

"Sir." DJ slipped into the attention stance, his soldier training clear. "I'm DJ Hawkins." He extended his hand. Silas stared at it, then at DJ.

Silas reluctantly took DJ's hand and they shook. "I won't welcome you to my home. I didn't invite you."

"Oh, Silas." Tammie's mom walked past her husband, still holding on to her daughter, and went into the house. "Welcome to our home, DJ. Don't let his bark scare you." Her smile was wide and her eyes kept roaming to Tammie.

Silas stepped aside, but didn't follow them. He walked away, settling on the wooden chair that Tammie remembered always sat there on the end of the porch. The evening shadows soon swallowed him.

Her heart pounded. Little had changed and the sense of home soaked in. The couch was new, but the same style. The big wooden rocker still sat beside the stone fireplace, though the crocheted afghan was a different color. Few knickknacks or pictures decorated the small house, but up on the mantel, Tammie saw a small, framed photo of Tyler. One she'd sent and told them was her favorite. It had been taken when he was three.

She blinked furiously to keep the tears at bay and failed miserably. Walking over to the picture, she wished he was here. He needed to meet his grandparents now that he was old enough to remember them. She glanced out the window at her father's silhouette. Even his grandfather.

"We've missed you."

Tammie gathered her nerves and turned back to

her mother. "I've missed you, too, Mama." DJ still stood in the doorway, looking around with a curious and studious stare. He was assessing her past as well as their safety here.

"Please, have a seat." Elizabeth gestured toward the couch.

Needing DJ near, Tammie sat down, leaving room for him, hoping her mother liked him. Hoping...he liked what he saw.

This was where she'd grown up. This was what had made her. These people, this simple backwoods life, had been what she'd run away from. She'd never felt as though she fit here. And now, she wasn't sure she'd ever tried. That realization hurt.

Stupid. She'd been so young and stupid. But without that stupidity, she wouldn't have Tyler—or DJ.

DJ'S SENSES WERE on alert as he looked around, and they stayed that way as they headed into the house. The backwoods, stone-and-log house was tiny, but well cared for and obviously loved. With night's arrival, the shadows tried to get in his way, but he still managed to get the full lay of the land.

The fact that there was only one road in eased some of his concerns. As did the steep, tree-covered hills that shot up on either side of the house. Probably made farming a challenge, but they provided perfect security.

From his seat on the end of the couch, DJ took it

all in, listening to the women and watching the unmoving shadow on the porch doing the same.

"You ladies mind if I stretch my legs?" DJ slowly stood.

Tammie looked up. "Oh, I should have thought—" Tammie rose to her feet.

DJ touched her shoulder and smiled down at her. "Stay here. I'll be back in a bit."

His back and legs were sore from the drive, but it didn't take long to loosen up his muscles. The night air was cool and when he reached the edge of the porch, the stars overhead, bright and clear, caught his eye. No wonder Tammie loved them. Without the city lights to wash them out, there were millions of them to see.

"You plannin' to stay?" Silas's voice came out of the dark. Thank goodness there was no accompanying sound from the shotgun.

"That's up to Tammie."

"Humph. It's my house, but not like she's ever listened to anything I say," he mumbled. "We only got the one guest room."

"I'll manage. I've slept in some rough places. Floors. Rocks. Whatever it takes."

"Why'd you do that?"

DJ seldom talked about his military time in any detail, but he knew he needed something to prove to the old man he wasn't letting a murdering thief into his house. "Afghanistan. Iraq. Some of the places

I've been to weren't exactly five-star. Until recently I was a marine. We do what needs done."

He hoped the older man got the message. DJ wasn't leaving Tammie alone, unprotected.

"I'll stay with Granny Baye." Tammie's voice startled them both. She pushed open the screen door and stepped out.

"Where's that?" DJ asked. "And who's Granny Baye?"

"Just up the hill." In the dim moonlight, he saw her gesture toward the steep slope behind the house. "She's my grandmother."

"Mom would love to see you." Elizabeth's voice came out of the dark. "Probably have a fit if she doesn't."

DJ heard the sound of a match striking, then saw Elizabeth lighting an old-fashioned lantern. The soft glow grew inside the glass house, illuminating everyone and the porch. "This'll help you get there." She lifted it by the wire handle and handed it to Tammie.

After another brief hug with her mom, Tammie turned to the steps. "Come on, DJ. See you in the morning," she called to her parents as she started across the yard. "This way," she said to DJ.

When they'd gone a few yards, DJ leaned close. "What's wrong with grabbing my flashlight from the truck?"

Tammie laughed. "That's not how they do it. Besides, Granny wouldn't recognize it. She'll know this old lamp. We used it all the time as kids."

"It's a wonder you didn't set anything on fire."

"Who said we didn't?"

DJ heard the smile in her voice. Grabbing her suitcase from the truck, he followed behind. After a few yards, the dark shape of a building separated itself from the shadows. Walking around it, they found the light of a single lamp in the window. Tammie handed him the lantern.

"Why'd you do that?"

"'Cause in Granny's book, the gentleman escorts the lady. Come on." There was a skip of joy in Tammie's step that DJ had never seen before. He liked it. Liked it a lot.

GRANNY BAYE WAS the one person Tammie never let herself think about. It hurt too much. She could have never done the things she'd had to do these past years if she'd thought of what her grandmother would think. Now, standing here, staring at the house that had begun as a trapper's lean-to in the settler days, her heart raced. Granny would either smother her in hugs, or kill her. She wasn't sure which.

She wasn't sure which she'd prefer.

"Where the heck you been, child?" a worn voice came from the shadows of the porch. The unfamiliar sound of a wooden cane on the boards had Tammie squinting through the shadows. The woman who emerged into the lamp's light was bent and older than Tammie remembered. Her racing heart hurt. Time had not been kind to Granny.

"Hi, Granny." Tammie's voice trembled.

"Come on up here and give your granny a hug." Granny's voice trembled, too, and Tammie wasn't sure if it was anger or tears that clogged her voice.

How many times had she run up those stairs as a kid, not bothering to think, not bothering to stop except to fling open the screen door? Now each step was measured. Her tennis shoes whispered on the wood. Her eyes quickly adjusted to the shadows and she saw her grandmother standing there. Her shoulders bent, her arms open wide and a sheen of tears in her old blue eyes.

"Oh, Granny, I've missed you so." She enfolded the tiny woman close and realized they were both trembling.

"Welcome home, sweetheart. This place just wasn't right without you."

"Where would you like me to put this?" DJ's voice broke into their reunion. What would Granny think of him? Tammie gulped.

"Granny, this is DJ. DJ, this is my grandmother Sarah Baye."

"Pleased to meet you, ma'am." DJ smiled and even in the dim light, Tammie felt it hit her. She suddenly realized they were going to be apart tonight. They'd been together only a few days, but she could barely remember being without him.

"Are you staying?" Granny asked, her voice hopeful.

"If you'll let me."

"Of course."

"DJ will stay at Mama and Dad's."

Granny reached out and patted DJ's arm. "You're a brave soul." She laughed and pulled open the door. "Follow me."

The tiny back bedroom was one of Tammie's favorite places in the whole world. It had been her refuge so many times. Bringing up the rear of their small procession, Tammie knew exactly the instant DJ saw it. He froze just inside the doorway. Tammie stepped around him. "Amazing, huh?"

"Uh, yeah." He stared at the wall.

The room looked exactly as she remembered. The old brass bed, with its crystal bed knobs that they used to pretend were magic crystal balls, and the wedding ring quilt Granny had made as a young bride were as beautiful as ever. Soft blue walls matched the quilt's color.

But what always took their breath away—and now DJ's—was the back wall. The house had been built into the mountain and the glitter of mica and other semiprecious stones imbedded in the rock was breathtaking.

"Now you know where I fell in love with gems," she whispered as she walked past him. She walked right up to the wall, looking for and finding her favorite bit of clear stone. She was sure it was a diamond, and now with a more practiced eye, she was positive. Gently, she reached out and touched it. "So nice to see you again," she whispered before turning back to face DJ.

"Beautiful." DJ was staring at her, and Tammie blushed under the intensity in his eyes. If he could stay here with her tonight—

"Gracious, it's getting late." Granny's voice broke the spell. DJ smiled down at the tiny woman and set the suitcase on the end of the bed before heading back the way they'd come.

Tammie followed him to the edge of the porch, where he'd left the lantern. Granny stayed inside, but Tammie felt the old woman's eyes on them.

"She's watching, isn't she?" DJ asked.

"Of course." Tammie felt like a girl again, coming home from a date instead of returning after ten years away.

"She's not going to like this." DJ leaned close and slid his arms around Tammie's waist. The moon and the lantern's glow warred to cast their light around them, with the shadows ultimately winning. "You okay?" he whispered.

"So far, so good." Tammie leaned her forehead on his shoulder for a minute, and then she looked up at him. "Thank you."

"For what?"

"For bringing me here. It's good to know they're all safe and well. And to see them."

"Even your dad?" he teased.

Tammie hesitated. "Yeah, even my dad."

The silence stretched out as they looked at each

other. "How ticked is she going to be when I kiss you? She have a shotgun?"

"You're going to kiss me?" She feigned surprise, widening her eyes at him.

"Oh, yeah." And he did. Holding Tammie tight, DJ found her lips with his. He tasted of the night, determination and unfulfilled promises. She shivered and returned his kiss until footsteps from inside brought the world back. She broke away with a laugh he readily joined.

"See you tomorrow." DJ stepped back and snagged the lantern. She stood there, leaning against the porch post until the glow of the lantern disappeared through the trees.

THE FIRELIGHT FLICKERED, the only light and the only warmth in the tiny cabin. Tammie sat huddled on the end of Granny Baye's couch, the old wedding circle quilt wrapped over her shoulders. She stared at the fire, seeing images, her mind too full to sleep.

Tammie loved this house. Two tiny bedrooms, a kitchen, bath and living room were all it consisted of. The back porch was where Granny did her wash and kept her canned goods. That was all there was. All there'd ever been.

Granny and Grandpa Baye had raised four kids in this tiny house. How, Tammie had no clue.

Soft footsteps surprised her and she looked back to see Granny behind her.

"Sorry if I woke you," Tammie apologized.

Granny laughed. "I don't sleep much anyway. I'm too old for that silliness." She headed toward the kitchen. "Want some hot cocoa?"

"You don't need to bother."

"Suit yourself, but I want some."

Tammie thought about getting up to help her grandmother, but she was so comfortable, and even if she did try, Granny wouldn't let her. No one ever did anything other than peek into Granny's kitchen. It had always been that way, and always would be, as long as Granny was alive. She didn't want to think about that inevitability.

"Here we go." Granny held out a cup and Tammie smiled, taking the warm cup. Cocoa and milk and Granny's love wafted in the air between them. It tasted wonderful and sweet. Tammie couldn't remember the last time she'd had hot chocolate. It had been almost ten years since she'd had Granny's.

After stirring the flames and adding another log, Granny settled on the couch beside her. "You gotta share," Granny said as she tugged on the old blanket, and just like when Tammie was little, they snuggled there together.

Tammie's throat tightened. She'd missed this wonderful woman, and she leaned on her grandmother's shoulder and told her so.

"I've missed you, too, sweetheart." Tammie felt a soft kiss on the top of her head, and she closed her eyes to take in all the joy. "I'm sorry you felt you had to leave."

Those words said so much. Tammie hadn't just left, she'd run away from home, leaving behind no indication of where she was going. She hadn't known where she was going. She'd just known she had to leave.

"I couldn't stay."

"I know." Granny hugged her. "Silas is a tough man to live with, but you know, in many ways you are your father's daughter."

Tammie cringed.

"Now, don't you go trying to deny it. You know I'm right. I never wanted your mother to marry him. He's not a kind man. He's a good man, but *kind* isn't a word I'd use for him. But she wanted to wed, and he asked."

Tammie lifted her head and looked up into her grandmother's face. "That doesn't sound much like love."

Granny sighed. "Not everyone wants love. Your father never has."

"But Mama—"

"She had it once." Granny's voice sounded far-off. She shook her head. "She's got the life she wants. You have to accept that."

"I do." She'd long ago learned that she had enough to worry about just keeping track of her own life. "I didn't really want to leave."

Granny was silent for a long time. "I remember. And, unfortunately, that man ain't softened one bit with age." She paused and patted Tammie's hand. "If nothing else, age has made him even worse."

"Is…is he mean to Mama?" Tammie had always wondered how her father could be so harsh to his daughters and not have it spill over to their mother. Elizabeth wasn't a powerful woman.

Granny chuckled. "Your mama is tougher than she acts. Your daddy don't even think about messing with her."

"Good."

"But what about you. Where have you been? What have you been doing?"

Tammie knew she couldn't keep hedging, or they'd be here all week. Who did she think she'd gotten her stubbornness from, anyway?

"I'm still living in Florida." At least for now. The idea she had no clue where she'd end up wasn't something Tammie wanted to think about right now.

"Lordy. No wonder you don't come home. Them beaches look nice on TV."

Tammie laughed this time. "They are. You could visit sometime." The years melted away and while Tammie spoke, she couldn't look at her grandmother. Not everything she'd done to put food on the table and keep herself safe had been good, or easy. But if anyone would understand, she hoped it was Granny.

Still, she stared out the large picture window as she talked, enjoying the shadowed, moonlit view of the valley framed by the pines and hills she knew so well. She'd missed this place nearly as much as she had missed Granny.

"Oh, hon. You are such a breath of fresh air." Granny's laughter filled the cabin. "I've missed you. Now, I want to hear everything about that little boy of yours."

CHAPTER EIGHTEEN

DAWN WAS SLOW in coming, which fit Tammie's mood just fine. She and Granny had stayed up way too late, talking and laughing. Finally, a few hours ago, she'd fallen asleep on the brass bed inside the sparkling room.

Awake, despite lack of sleep, Tammie hurried outside in record-breaking time. She wore one of the new outfits that she'd bought with DJ in New Orleans. Would he remember?

The white lace camisole left her arms bare, but the flowing, long skirt would please everyone here. Soft, cool dirt felt good between her bare toes.

As a kid, she hadn't worn shoes except when she went into town, which wasn't often. Heck, in the spring they hadn't even worn shoes to school half the time. They hadn't had them to wear.

Outside was crisp and fresh with the approaching morning. The hills were alive already, the night creatures not yet gone to bed and the early-morning birds singing to wake the sun. She hurried along the worn path she knew so well. Cresting the next hill, she found it. The ledge of stone she'd always thought of as her special place. There'd been a time when she'd dreamed of bringing her own kids and family here. To see this place. To know the people here.

But that hadn't happened. She'd left and never looked back. Until yesterday. Until DJ made her.

She climbed up on the stone as the sun sneaked over the horizon, casting red and gold tendrils across the valley, painting the pines and oaks sporadically with light. She loved this view and her eyes blurred as the homesickness she'd ignored over the years hit her full force.

She'd missed this place. The sun-dappled light fell through the thick tree branches in patches of gold and white, reminding her of the combination of metal and jewels she used in her work. She refused to think about the damage to her studio.

Shifting on the wide pillar of sandstone at the edge of the ravine, its surface still cool from the night, she recalled all the hours she'd spent here.

Dreaming, wishing, wanting to see a world she'd only glimpsed on television or heard tales of from people in town. She'd wanted so much more. And she'd almost had it.

The sound of footsteps made her spin around in alarm. It wasn't Dom, thank heavens. Or DJ. Her father stood there, in the middle of the path, glaring at her.

Dear God, when had he gotten so old? His shoulders, the ones she'd thought would always be broad and strong, stooped. His hair used to be black. When had it gone so gray at the temples?

She expected him to berate her. He finally had her alone, without DJ or her mother as a buffer. He'd never resisted the urge to fling angry words at her in the past. But today, he remained silent. He simply stood there, staring at her, not saying a word. Then slowly, his hand curled around his walking stick and she recognized it as the same stick he'd had since he was a boy.

Out of the blue, she remembered him telling her and her sister the story of how he'd found it when he'd gotten lost on a family trip to Louisiana. That was the only time she knew of that he'd left this valley for more than a day trip.

He'd kept the sturdy stick as a reminder and had polished it to a bright patina.

He moved toward her, the soft click of the stick in time with his steps. Like the foolish girl she'd always been, she hoped he'd sit and talk with her. Instead, he kept going, passing her to head across the clearing.

A lifetime of anger and hurt erupted. "You aren't even going to say good morning to me?" Tammie fought to keep the hurt from her voice. He froze, standing there with his back to her for a long time.

"Morning." His voice was gruff and deep. He didn't turn around. After a bit, he took a couple of steps, then turned back to look at her. "You shouldn't have come back, Tammie Jo."

"Why not?"

"You'll just break your mama's heart again. She doesn't need that kind of grief."

She spoke before she could stop herself. "Is that what I am to you? Grief?"

He took several steps toward her. "No, girl. You're my daughter. That's the fact of it. But what you bring with you is nothin' but grief."

Tammie stared at him, confused but not surprised. He hadn't changed a bit in all the years she'd been gone.

Thinking about her son, she frowned. How could he think that all she brought with her was grief? Granted, Tyler was only eight, and the years ahead could be filled with all kinds of teenage drama. But she couldn't imagine experiencing even a minute of not wanting him, not missing him when he left home.

"How can you say that? You don't even know me anymore."

"Know you?" He came back to within a few steps of her. "Know you? I know enough. You had a child out of wedlock and are raising him on your own so he don't even know this family."

Silas took another step forward, and Tammie forced herself to stay put. She wasn't running from him anymore.

"Then last week a fancy city slicker comes here sayin' he's your boyfriend, asking questions like he's tryin' to find you." His voice grew loud, echoing back off the hills. "And lo and behold, here you are, with another man I don't even know."

Her father's outrage blinded her for a minute, and then his words soaked in. "Someone came here? Last week?"

"I just said so, didn't I?"

"What did he look like?" Dread sat like a lead weight in her belly.

"Like some city man. Fancy suit and tie. Drove one of them shiny hot rods that ain't worth a plug nickel out here on these roads. He was lucky it didn't rain."

Tammie might have laughed at how Dom had not impressed her father when she was sure that had been his intent—she *would* have laughed, if the idea of him being here wasn't so frightening.

"Did he have dark brown hair? Brown eyes?"

Silas nodded.

"What questions did he ask?"

"If we knew where you were. When we'd seen you last. Questions like the sheriff would ask." Silas's frown turned to a glare. "You in trouble with the law, girl?"

"Why do you always assume the worst?" Not that he was far-off if Dom managed to pin the blame for this jewel theft on her. She shuddered at the too-real possibility. "No, I'm not in trouble. He's the crook, not me."

"I don't assume anything. I just look at what's right in front of my face." The glimpse of decent human being she'd seen vanished. "How many men you got in your life?"

"Not that it's any of your business, but DJ is Tyler's father and Dom, that's the guy who was here last week, is *not* my boyfriend. He lied to you. So don't go judging me."

"I don't see no ring on that finger."

"That's not always the way this world works." He'd plucked the one nerve she refused to acknowledge. She'd always dreamed of having a home, a family, a husband.

"Don't treat me like I'm stupid, girl. I may not live in your fancy city, but not because I can't. I choose to live here. I've provided a good life for your mother and your sister. I'd have done the same for you. But you left."

"Oh, yeah. Nancy's in a great place. Two kids and a worthless, cheating backwoods hick for a husband." She knew she shouldn't have said that the instant her father's face flushed red.

"You have no room to judge, either, missy. Nancy at least tried to make a home and live a decent life. Your mess is of your own making."

How could he still make her feel so small and incompetent? Tammie watched as her father stepped back onto the path and, without a goodbye or even a glance back, kept walking. She didn't say anything more, either.

What was the point?

As always, she couldn't win with him.

Tammie leaned back against the stone, the joy of the morning gone. Once she could no longer hear her father's steps, the solitude she'd always loved morphed into threatening isolation. Glancing around, she felt the eyes of the woods on her.

The animals? Her father? Or was Dom or one of

his goons out there? She shivered and moved quickly back to the path toward the house. And DJ.

DJ HAD SLEPT in a lot of different places, but never, he had to admit, in an old-fashioned feather bed. And he was proud to say, he'd avoided it yet again. The giant marshmallow threatened to engulf him. But the rough wooden floor of the Eastons' cabin was nice, solid and cool. Perfect.

Respecting her father's wishes that they not share a room hadn't been hard. It gave Tammie an excuse to visit her grandmother, and DJ got a good night's sleep for the first time in weeks.

Lately, he'd slept with one eye open, partially to watch over her, partially to make sure she stayed put and partially…because she was damned nice to look at.

Just after dawn, the twin scents of coffee and bacon had him headed to the small kitchen. He expected to find Silas Easton there, and while DJ wasn't intimidated by the man, he wasn't anxious for an altercation. He was relieved to find only Elizabeth in the room.

She stood at an old-fashioned gas stove, cast-iron skillets steaming on the burners. The ceiling was low, and all the appliances looked generations old, along with the deep soapstone sink that dominated one wall.

"Have a seat." She smiled over her shoulder at him. "I've got plenty of everything." She glanced up at the clock hanging on the wall. “Unless Tammie's changed drastically, she won't be joining us for a couple hours.”

“No. She's not much of a morning person.”

“And you are?”

“It's a habit now.” DJ was still stiff this morning and was glad to see the solid wooden chairs around the table. He walked slowly into the room and helped himself to a cup of coffee. On closer inspection, DJ realized the wooden chairs at the table looked a lot like the ones he'd grown up with. He smiled, recalling Tyler's chair in the bed of his truck. “Are we the first ones up?”

“Oh, no.” She laughed. “Silas's been gone nearly an hour. He's out roaming the hills like he does every morning. Always planning next crop's planting.” Elizabeth looked at him in concern. “Are you okay? I hope the bed was comfortable enough.”

“The bed was fine, ma'am. I'm always a bit stiff in the morning.” He didn't want her thinking a guest wasn't comfortable. “When I was deployed last year, I was injured in a bomb blast. I'm healed now, but still have some scars that tighten up.”

She nodded as she set a full plate of fried breakfast in front of him. It smelled like the heaven his mom used to make, and he hungrily dug in.

“This is great. Thanks.” He watched her smile bloom. “Please, join me. Tell me about Tammie when she was a kid.” He grinned when Elizabeth took the seat across from him, her own full cup of coffee steaming between her weathered hands.

DJ looked for the resemblance between mother and daughter. It was small. Hair color and height, but otherwise, Tammie was her father's child.

Elizabeth smiled at him and took a leisurely sip of her coffee as if savoring every drop. "Tyler looks like you, a'right."

DJ froze midbite and met the woman's stare. "That bother you?" The loaded question hung in the air for a long minute.

She shrugged. "There's a whole lot worse things that could have happened to my girl out there in the world."

"She's done well."

She nodded. "I always knew she would. Even when she was little, that stubborn streak of hers was strong."

It was DJ's turn to smile. "Yeah. She does have that."

"Just like her daddy that way."

DJ stuffed food into his mouth, knowing when to remain silent.

"So, tell me about your family. What kind of folks are looking after that boy?" she asked.

"Good folks, ma'am. Right now, he's with my oldest brother, Wyatt."

"How many brother's you got?"

DJ grinned. "Two brothers. Three sisters. I'm fifth in line."

"Gracious! That's a full house. All your family military?"

"Just me. Wyatt has my grandfather's ranch and Jason is a lawyer out in California." He stopped himself from shaking his head. What a bunch they were.

"And your sisters?"

He laughed. "They are as independent as Tammie. Addie's a teacher, Tara's a chef and Mandy—" *Amanda,* he mentally reminded himself "—is expecting her first child."

"What's her husband do?"

The old-fashioned questions surprised him. "She's not married." Yet. He had a feeling this child wouldn't grow up without a father. That wasn't Mandy's style. He just wasn't sure how she was going to pull it off.

Elizabeth shook her head, but didn't say any more. Instead, she rose and refilled her cup. She offered him another one, but he shook his head.

"Sounds like an ambitious bunch." She sat back down. "Your parents must be proud."

"Mom was. She passed a few months before Tyler showed up. My dad died in a car accident when I was six."

"I'm sorry to hear that. It must have been hard for your mom. Doin' it by herself."

He had to think about that. "Probably was, with six kids. But she was strong. Wyatt and Addie stepped up and helped raise the rest of us."

Tilting her head, she studied him. "Sounds tough."

"Actually? It was a great way to grow up. We're

still close, and when Mom passed away, we were all able to be there."

She smiled, seemingly pleased at his family's closeness.

"Mom worked hard, and we didn't have much. But we will always remember her fondly. After the funeral, we each took one of the dining room chairs home. It's a nice reminder. These chairs remind me of them."

A shadow crossed Elizabeth's face. She averted her gaze, peering deep into her coffee.

"Sorry if I said anything to upset you."

"Oh, no." She still didn't look up. "I wish I'd met your mom. Maybe I could have learned something about being a better mother."

DJ thought carefully before talking. He didn't want to put words or thoughts into Tammie's mouth. "You know, Tyler is the most amazing kid. Tammie's a great mom. I think she must have learned that from somewhere."

She met his stare and smiled. "Now, aren't you the charmer."

The sound of heavy footsteps made Elizabeth jump to her feet. DJ watched closely, noting the lack of fear in her face. When Silas Easton entered the room, he froze for a moment on the threshold at seeing DJ, then walked purposefully into the room. He grabbed a coffee cup and filled it, sitting in the chair at the head of the table. "Morning."

DJ nodded and finished swallowing his food before turning to face the man. "Morning, sir."

"Did you want some breakfast?" Elizabeth returned to stand at the stove. She'd taken her coffee with her and it sat on the counter, out of view. She set a full plate in front of her husband before returning to clean up the dishes.

"Thank you."

"You're welcome."

The formality between them was strange. DJ didn't recall his dad too clearly, but he remembered laughter between his parents. What were these two like when they were alone?

Silas ate in silence until he was nearly done. "So, what kind of stories has that girl told you about us?" He finally looked up from his plate.

"None that I recall." DJ leaned back in the chair with his cup. If the old man wanted a test of wills, he'd gladly oblige—and win.

"So we're not horrible, overbearing monsters?"

Elizabeth spun around, spatula in hand. "Silas! You know she didn't mean that. She was just a girl."

DJ glanced at Elizabeth.

"She said it, didn't she?" Silas resumed eating. "And she ran away from here right after that," he mumbled.

DJ knew better than to touch that comment. Instead, he sat and waited.

Silas didn't disappoint him. The older man glanced

up, pointing his fork at DJ. "We gave her everything she needed. I've provided for my family just fine."

"I can see that." Antagonizing the man probably wasn't the best idea right now. Maybe he'd learn something if he just let him talk.

"Damn straight, I have. Haven't I, 'Lizabeth?"

She nodded. "You've done well by us, Silas."

Again, DJ looked between the two of them, wondering what they were like when no one else was around.

"My girls were taught right. I made sure they knew how to take care of a family the way they should. That's what a good father does."

DJ wondered who he was actually talking to. "I understand that, sir." DJ met the man's angry stare. "I grew up in a large family. After my dad died, we had to take care of each other."

"You the oldest?"

"No. I have two brothers and two sisters ahead of me."

"You join the military to get out of trouble?"

"Silas!" Elizabeth nearly dropped a dish as she lifted it from the table.

"I have the right to see what kind of man is sitting at my table," he defended himself.

"Yes, you do, sir." DJ met Silas's gaze. "And I'll gladly answer your questions, but I'd appreciate the benefit of the doubt."

The old man covered up the startled expression on his face quickly, but not before DJ saw it. Long seconds ticked by as their glares clashed across the table. Finally, Silas nodded. "Fair enough."

"What do you want to know?" DJ knew he'd surprised Silas. He liked to keep his opponents guessing, and at this point, Tammie's father was most certainly the opponent.

"Stop it, Dad."

None of them had heard Tammie arrive. She stood in the doorway, framed by the bright morning light that glowed in the green of the woods behind her and glinted in her hair. Her hands on her hips, she glared at her father.

Silas looked as startled as any of them, and DJ wanted to jump up and intervene in the storm that was brewing between them. Elizabeth turned away, focusing on the sink full of dishes, as if she'd seen too much already.

DJ simply stared at Tammie. He'd never seen her in a dress—other than her waitress uniform, which didn't count—though he remembered them buying this one. The camisole top, over a long, flowing blue skirt, hugged the curves he'd come to appreciate.

She looked pretty—the way he'd expected the girl on the beach to grow up.

"Ahem." Silas cleared his throat, reminding them all of where they were. Tammie blushed and DJ forced himself to meet the older man's disapproving stare.

Everyone settled around the table, and DJ waited to see what would happen next. The silence was nearly deafening, and so foreign to DJ's idea of a family meal.

"I'm sure you know we didn't come here just for a visit," DJ began. Three sets of eyes turned to him.

"So, why *did* you come here?" Silas leaned back in his chair.

"Oddly enough," Tammie said, "to make sure Mom and you were safe."

"Of course we're safe. Unless you did something to change that."

DJ frowned. Something had happened between Tammie and her father sometime this morning. The electrified silence told him that. "We aren't here to solve twenty years of issues, though it probably needs doing." When Tammie opened her mouth to speak, DJ reached out and took her hand in his. Silas's eyebrows lifted but he was prudent enough to stay quiet.

"We have more pressing issues right now. Issues that put your daughter and grandson at risk." He met Silas's glare while Elizabeth's gasp made him wish he could comfort her, too.

"Wh-what kind of issues?" Elizabeth asked softly.

"Like that man you told me about this morning." Tammie looked at her father, then at DJ, not letting go of his hand, clasping tighter, if anything. Silas nodded. "Dom was here. Last week," she told DJ, then faced her father again. "He's the danger."

Tammie launched into the details of the last year. She didn't leave anything out, and both Elizabeth and Silas listened without interrupting. She told them about her job, the trade show where she'd met Dom and how DJ had found her.

"I have a house down in Florida." Tammie looked across the table at her mother. "When we went to the bank where my friend Robyn works, we learned that she'd contacted you. You've been paying the mortgage..." Tammie's voice faded off. "Thank you," she whispered.

"We didn't pay that." Silas's voice was harsh and loud, startling them all. "Why would we do that?"

DJ resisted the urge to roll his eyes. Tactful the man was not.

"You don't know everything, old man," Elizabeth addressed him, a look of defiance and frustration on her face. After several energy-charged seconds, Elizabeth stood and walked over to the counter. She lifted the lid off one of the canisters. Flour spilled over the edge and her white hand emerged, her fingers curled around something small.

A bag. She shook the white flour off, not caring where it landed, and pulled the strings on the bag. She dumped the contents into her hand before stomping back to stand at the table, right next to her husband.

She tossed the contents in her hand onto the table. Loud clatter broke the silence, and DJ peered at the rocks that scattered over the scarred wood.

"Mom!" Tammie gasped and grabbed the small rock nearest to her. She held it up to the light and turned it several times, examining it. "How—"

"The diamond fields. That's how I've been paying your mortgage."

Silas rose to his feet, towering over his diminutive wife. "When the hell have you been doing that?" The darkness in his eyes wasn't anger, and DJ guessed it had more to do with him not having control the way he thought.

"A couple of days a week. I'm pretty good at finding them." Elizabeth tilted her head, proud of her ability.

"At that tourist trap?" He sneered. "They're probably fake or cheap versions."

"No, Dad." Tammie looked up from examining the stone. "These are good quality. Amazing, actually."

To DJ they looked like small, rough rocks. "What are they?"

Tammie handed him one. "These are rough diamonds. Around here they can be found on the ground. The Crater of Diamonds is a surface mine where people can go and hunt for them. We always wanted to go as kids." Tammie cast a glance at her dad as if to remind him what they'd missed out on.

"You've been doing this?" Tammie stood and walked over to her mother. "For me?"

"Of course for you." Elizabeth tried to look perturbed, but DJ saw the spark in her eye. This was what she'd been craving, what she'd mentioned before. Her children to love and appreciate her.

"Thank you." Tammie threw her arms around her mother and held on. "I'm sorry."

"Oh, now." Elizabeth's voice wobbled, and she carefully wrapped her arms around Tammie. Tears shone in her eyes and soon, she was crying just like Tammie. "I'm just glad to have you back."

The familiar chirp of DJ's phone sounded strange in the tiny, old-fashioned kitchen. He pulled it out and looked at the display. Colin.

"Hey, buddy. What do you know?" DJ answered.

"Too much. You and your lady both there?"

"Yeah. She's here."

"Put it on speaker," Tammie suggested and with a nod from Elizabeth, DJ set the phone on the table so they could all hear.

"Go ahead. Tammie's folks are here, too. They know the details." He looked around at the three civilian faces, wishing they were soldiers...and that this wasn't really happening.

"You sure?" Colin's voice lacked the usual positive, teasing note. DJ mentally cursed. Maybe putting it on speaker wasn't a good idea.

Tammie nodded. "Yeah. This affects them, too."

Colin paused and DJ pictured him, walking, talking and thinking with his feet. "I met with Watson this morning. We got a hit. Dom used his credit card." He paused and they all waited. "In Dallas."

Tammie abruptly sat down on the dining room chair. Elizabeth slipped her arm around her daughter's shoulders and looked up at DJ.

"You're sure?" DJ asked.

"He's headed for Tyler." Tammie squeezed her hands together.

"Yeah. Seems like it," Colin said. "Here, talk with Sam."

"Mornin', folks." The rough FBI agent introduced himself to Tammie's parents. He didn't sound any happier than Colin had. "I talked with a couple of guys I trust in Dallas. They're good, solid men. I'm heading there in a couple hours, but they've been briefed and are ready to go."

"Go?" Tammie's voice trembled.

DJ hadn't wanted to take this path. He'd hoped they could find Dom here or scare him enough to force him back to Florida, where the agent and his men would be waiting.

"I'm sending them to your brother's place. How soon can you two head to Texas?"

"Anytime," DJ answered without asking Tammie. He knew she wanted this done as much, if not more, than he did.

"We hoped to get him here in Florida, but doesn't look like that'll work. Your boy's birthday is coming up, right?"

Tammie nodded, her expression distant, distracted, apparently forgetting they couldn't see her.

"Yeah," DJ answered. "What do you need us to do?" The agent sounded as if he had a plan.

The silence wasn't reassuring. Colin spoke. "Robyn's going to call Dom and tell him you're heading to the ranch for the birthday party."

"No!" Tammie shot to her feet. "I don't want him near Tyler."

"Don't worry." Agent Watson's voice was stern, but reassuring. "My guys have been instructed to get your family out of there. We're moving them to DJ's sister Amanda's place. And that's where you two will head, too. The only people Carlyle is going to find at that house are mine."

The air was thick. DJ nodded. "Sounds like a good plan."

"It's solid," Colin said.

"Thank you," Tammie whispered. Several seconds ticked by as the four of them sat there, each lost in their own thoughts.

"It's time, Tammie." DJ stood and walked over to her. "The running is over." Elizabeth and Silas watched closely, holding back to let him handle her.

"We have all our vulnerabilities protected," he tried to reassure her. "Colin is with Robyn. I'm confident your father is capable of protecting your family here." DJ saw Silas's chest puff up with pride before he refocused on the women. "Tyler is with Wyatt and you're with me. Now the battle shifts. *We* take control."

"Oh, God. It sounds so—" Tammie said.

"Planned? Military? I told you we were going on a hunt," DJ said. "The best part's ahead. Where we win."

He watched her swallow and he leaned back, giving her time and space to digest what he'd said.

"So, we're bait?"

Colin's distant laughter helped ease the mood. "She's been hanging out with us too long," he said over the phone.

DJ smiled. "Essentially, but not really. We're going back to a battlefield I know, where we've got reinforcements. And we shouldn't be anywhere near the action when they take down Dom."

"I'll call you later with the information on where to meet my guys," Sam said. "We're close, people. Let's get this done. Go about business as normal. Act like there's nothing unusual about today."

"Easy for him to say," Tammie mumbled after DJ ended the call.

Her mother hugged her tight. "It actually makes sense," Elizabeth comforted her.

"Well, of course it does," her father said. "This time you might have actually gotten yourself a smart one. You might try to keep him." Silas stood and went to the coffeepot, draining the last before turning back to face them. He started to speak again, but Elizabeth cut him off.

"Don't say it." Elizabeth pointed a finger at him before taking Tammie's shoulders in her hands and turning her to face her. "You stay safe, Tammie Jo. Do what DJ says. For once in your life—" she took a deep breath and let it out "—set your stubborn streak aside. We want you, and that boy, to come back here for a real visit, you hear?"

As an olive branch, it would do just fine. DJ watched the two women hug, and even he had to swallow the lump in his throat.

CHAPTER NINETEEN

SAYING GOODBYE WAS harder this time, without anger to propel her out the door. Tammie stood beside the pickup as DJ loaded their suitcases in the bed. Even Granny Baye had insisted on walking down to tell them goodbye. "You be careful going back up that hill, okay?" Tammie hugged the old woman a long time.

"I've taken care of myself longer than you been alive, little one. *You're* the one who needs taken care of." She looked meaningfully over at DJ.

"Will do, ma'am." He laughed and opened the passenger door for Tammie.

"Where's Mama?"

"Right here." Elizabeth's voice came from inside the house. A loud thunk preceded her as she backed out through the screen door.

"What are you doin', woman?" Silas sat in the rocker again.

"You just never mind." She stepped out onto the front porch, pulling one of the wooden chairs from the dining room behind her. DJ hurried over to help.

Elizabeth looked up at him and stepped back with a smile. "You take that with you. Put it with the others."

"I'll take good care of everything," he promised and hefted the chair as if it weighed nothing.

"Show-off," Elizabeth teased.

"What's with the chair?" Tammie asked. He'd taken Tyler's desk chair, too.

He smiled at her. "You'll see."

Stowing the chair in the truck bed, alongside Tyler's, DJ took his time securing the tarp. As Tammie climbed into the passenger seat, she almost wished she could stay. Almost. She'd never felt that way before and decided to analyze it later. Much later.

THE DRIVE WOULD take a little over four hours, not because it was far, but because the roads were full of hairpin turns and narrow passages. DJ shook his head. How the heck had anyone in a covered wagon ever made it through these hills? Most likely they hadn't. They'd come in on horseback. Isolated and independent.

He glanced sideways at Tammie as she slept with her head against the window and saw her ancestors stamped on her face. After meeting her parents and grandmother, and learning a little more about where Tammie had come from, he understood her better.

And admired her independent streak more than ever.

He wasn't sure where their relationship was headed. Hell, he didn't even know what he was going to do after he was fully discharged. But one thing was certain—if he had anything to say about it, he wasn't letting Tammie go back to Florida. He wanted her with him. He wasn't even remotely interested in being a single father.

His cell phone rang, startling Tammie awake. "Can you grab it?" he asked. Maneuvering the narrow road took both hands on the wheel.

"Uh, yeah. Sure."

Tammie shook her head, her hair scattering around her shoulders and face. She grabbed the phone and put it on speaker. DJ had to force his focus back to the road.

"Hello?"

"Ms. Easton? Agent Watson here." The agent's voice came over the speaker of the cell phone, a bit tinny and quiet.

"Oh. Hi. How is everything going?" Her voice sounded even. Controlled.

"Good. Our guys are in place. Is DJ there?"

"Right here," he answered.

"I've sent a team out to your brother's ranch, and I've got another team set to meet you guys. You'll remember them, DJ. They were involved in the joint exercises where I met you and Colin. Hal Black and Nick Mann?"

"Yeah. Texas Rangers, if I recall."

"Good guys."

"Lousy at poker, though."

The laughter helped and DJ watched Tammie lean back. She closed her eyes—was she saying a prayer? One sure as hell wafted through his brain. *Please, let this work.*

DJ frowned, intently focused as the big truck tires left the side road and hit the open highway. Speed felt like urgency, like progress.

"Colin's confirmed that Ms. Carpenter made the call to Dominic Carlyle about four hours ago. He's confident Carlyle bought it and is headed to the ranch."

DJ took a deep breath and blew it out. "So what now?"

"As planned, we're sending your family to Dallas—to Amanda's house—with an escort."

"What about us?" Tammie had opened her eyes and was leaning forward, listening intently.

"You are to stick to the plan and make your way to Amanda's, too. But in the meantime, we want you two to act normal. Do exactly what parents would do in preparation for their son's birthday party."

Tammie glanced at DJ. He nodded.

"Like what?" she asked.

"Go buy him a gift. Go shopping. Something very public. Very normal."

DJ met her stare, hoping to ease some of her stress with a reminder of their earlier conversation. "Like buying him a bike?"

"Yeah, like that."

The agent knew nothing about their disagreement, but the frown Tammie threw him told him she remembered it. Good. Distraction accomplished. The sound of someone typing on computer keys came through the phone.

"There's a bike store on the north side of Dallas, near your sister's place. Bike Heaven. My guys will meet you there. Three hours. They'll fill you in on the final details."

Tammie took a deep breath. "You really think this will work?"

"We hope so. We'll be ready." The agent's voice was quiet. "Okay, I'm headed to my concourse. My flight lands in a couple hours. You folks drive safe. We *will* get this guy." The line went silent—a silence filled with the whine of the tires on the pavement and the pounding of her heart in her ears.

"You okay?" DJ didn't take his eyes off the road, but she saw the concern on his face. "You say the word and we'll call it off."

"No. I want it done."

"Me, too." He reached over and put his big hand over hers, warm and comforting. His strength helped, as did the calmness in his face. She wanted to curl up into a ball and whimper. He was calmer than she'd ever seen him.

"Is this—" She took a swallow to clear her dry throat. "Is this what it was like when you were fighting in Afghanistan?"

"A little. Same adrenaline. Same planning." He took his eyes off the road and met her gaze. "Very different, though."

"How?" Did she really want to know?

"You. Tyler." He took a deep breath and put his hand back on the steering wheel.

She immediately resented the loss. "I'm sorry—"

"No, not like that." His frown deepened. "When we were on a mission, it was always for the cause. For God and country. For the masses." He fell silent for several long minutes. "When that bomb went off," he whispered. "It was about Reed and Kauffman. It was about Colin. My back and legs."

She gasped. He'd seen too much. He didn't deserve this. Guilt washed over her.

His voice was softer even when he spoke again. "I finally realized why I went off to that war. Why it was right."

"Why?" Her voice wobbled and she fought to control her emotions. He didn't need to take on her feelings, though she knew he would.

"For the same reason we're going to do exactly what Sam says. To keep you and Ty safe. To beat the bad guys."

DJ didn't say anything for a long time. And she was afraid to say anything herself—afraid of the thoughts and fears racing through her brain. If this worked, she'd be free to rebuild her life. If it didn't? If someone was hurt? What if Dom got away and continued terrorizing her?

Would the goal DJ described ever really be possible? Or was she trapped, never again able to go home and have a dull, boring safe day?

"You'll recognize these guys, right?" she asked, needing to pull herself from her troubled thoughts.

"Yeah, but I won't have to. They'll find us."

"Are you sure?"

He turned his head, looked at her with that intense stare, and then smiled. "Trust me. And if you can't do that. Trust Sam and his team."

"I'm not very good at that. At trust."

"I know." The conversation they'd had a couple days ago at the hotel echoed around them. "It's time you try."

All she managed was a nod.

THE SKYLINE OF Dallas, Texas, lay on the horizon when DJ's phone rang again. Tammie answered and the loud squeal of a voice coming through the phone told DJ who it was. Tyler. Had to be. Tammie was smiling too wide for it not to be.

"Can I put you on speaker? I think your dad would like to hear, but he's driving." She listened for a minute. "Yes, silly, we're driving down a road. Hold on."

She thumbed the speaker button and settled the phone in the cup holder, where they could both hear. DJ smiled at her.

"Dad? You there?"

"Yep. What's your news?"

"I get to take Hamlet and Pork Chop to the fair." Only in Tyler's world did that sound even remotely normal. "Uncle Wyatt got the papers today."

"That's great, sweetheart." Tammie might not understand how the whole fair thing worked, but she knew how to be a mom. DJ could almost hear the smile in his son's voice.

"Wow, that's a big deal," DJ added, feeling strange. *Act normal,* he reminded himself.

"I think so." Tyler fell silent. "Where you guys going?"

DJ looked over at Tammie, hoping she could read his question.

She did. She shook her head and mouthed, "Don't tell him." Aloud, she said, "We've been visiting your Grandma and Grandpa Easton. They said to tell you hi. Hopefully, we can come visit them together soon."

"What are you up to?" DJ broke in, hoping the boy wouldn't ask any more about them coming back to Texas.

"Oh, nothin'."

"You called for nothin'?" DJ asked.

"No. I just—" The silence stretched out.

"Good thing we don't pay for minutes, buddy. You're burning them up," DJ teased, hoping to head off the emotions he heard in that *nothin'*.

"I…I miss you guys."

Tammie gasped and turned away from DJ and the phone to stare out the window. "We miss you, too," she said to the glass.

"Are—" The gulp was loud in Tyler's voice. "Are you gonna be here for my birthday?"

Now everyone was silent.

Finally, Tyler's words came out in a rush. "See, Aunt Amanda wants to have a party for me, but since she's having a baby she can't come here to the ranch. At first Uncle Wyatt said we can't go to her house in the middle of the week, but now we're going there for a barbecue."

DJ smiled. "But you don't want to do it without us."

"Uh-huh."

Tammie stared at the phone, stricken. She opened her mouth to speak, but DJ put his hand over hers and gently shook his head.

DJ had learned to watch his words with Tyler since the boy could twist just about anything into a promise. "Here's the deal. I can't promise anything, but we will do everything in our power to be there. Fair enough?"

"Guess so." There wasn't any enthusiasm in his voice. "I promise I'll be good. And it doesn't matter about the dirt bike. I'd rather have you guys."

"Oh, sweetheart. We want to be there." Tammie's voice cracked, and DJ could tell she wished she could crawl through the phone.

"We're gonna do our best." DJ winked at Tammie, hoping to lighten the mood even a little.

"Mama?" Tyler whispered into the phone.

Tammie frowned. "Yeah?" She looked over at DJ, who stared at the road and frowned, as well.

"When you get here, are you gonna take me home?" he continued to whisper, as if DJ couldn't hear him.

Heavy, thick silence filled the cab. DJ's jaw clenched and he didn't bother looking over at her. His knuckles were white on the steering wheel.

"We'll go over everything later," she finally answered, failing to erase the awkwardness.

"Hey, Tyler? Is your uncle Wyatt around?" DJ asked. He had to end this conversation. Now was not the time for it—he hoped it never would be.

Tyler hesitated. "Yeah. Wanna talk to him?"

"That'd be good."

Voices in the background mixed until finally Wyatt came on the line.

"Hey, what's up?" DJ asked. "What's got Tyler so upset?"

Wyatt was quiet, and DJ thought he heard footsteps and the screech of the screen door. "Let me get outside," Wyatt said.

DJ looked over at Tammie, who stared at the phone as if she could will it to show her what was happening. It was getting easier to read her. He wondered if she could read him as easily.

"Why are two Texas Rangers at my house?" Nothing but the wind crackling over the phone followed Wyatt's question.

DJ relaxed. "Good. They're there."

"Yeah, they're here. I thought it had to do with the incident at Tyler's school. Guess not." DJ could tell Wyatt was ticked, and very confused.

"What incident? What happened?" Tammie asked.

"A stranger managed to get into the cafeteria. The teachers were on top of it, but the guy ran when the security officer approached him. They were in lockdown all afternoon."

Lockdown? The things kids had to deal with these days. DJ had never thought about it before. But he never had to deal with being a parent before, either.

Tammie had. "What did the stranger look like?" she asked.

"There's a sketch on the school's website. You think it's related to Tyler? Or you?"

"I don't know." She paused. "Probably."

The silence in the cab was heavy. Tammie looked over at DJ and the guilt in her eyes ticked DJ off. Not at her, but at Dom, all over again. "We're headed that way. Should be there tonight. Wyatt?"

"Yeah?"

"I can't explain everything, but do what the Rangers ask you to do."

"Why?" The alarm was loud in that single word. The following silence was nearly as loud.

"I'll explain later. Promise."

"You'd better. It's that serious?"

"Yeah." DJ wanted to explain, but he couldn't put Tammie through another rehashing right now. The Rangers would explain and hopefully they'd soon be on their way to Dallas. Away from the threat that was headed toward the ranch.

"Be safe," Wyatt whispered.

"Yeah. You, too."

Neither Tammie nor DJ spoke once the call ended. The big tires ate up the road yet the miles disappeared all too slowly.

"I never meant to give Tyler the idea—" Tammie started.

"Don't." DJ uncurled his hands, then gripped the steering wheel tight again. "I know how Tyler's brain works. You don't have to explain." He looked over at her then, and saw her shiver. She wrapped her arms around herself, and DJ reached over to turn down the air-conditioning. "We'll deal with it later."

She nodded, staring unseeing out the window for the next few miles.

"We should have decent service from here on," DJ said finally. "See if you can find that picture on the school's website. Send it to Watson."

Tammie wasn't familiar with his phone, but she navigated quickly with his instructions. Her curse minutes later hurt his ears and heart.

She gasped at the image that lit up the phone's screen.

"Is it Dom?"

Tammie shook her head. "No. Worse." She turned the tiny screen so he could see the sketch. Nope, not Dom. The man's face was familiar, though. The same guy who had tried to grab Tammie in that alley. And he remembered that the guy had come with friends.

DJ reached over, took the phone and disconnected. "Don't stress out on me now, Tammie." He curled his hand around her fist.

"If Dom's there, and this guy brings his buddies—"

"You heard Sam. No one will be at the house. We'll be prepared. We'll be careful. And, hey, Dom tipped his hand. We know what to expect. If he's sending his thug to a school, he must be getting desperate."

"Desperate people do desperate things," she whispered.

"Which also makes them do stupid things." DJ lifted her hand to his lips and softly kissed her fingers. "Besides, we need to focus on our next task. We've got Rangers to meet at the store and a birthday present to buy."

He watched her try to smile. Damn, he wanted this over.

Less than an hour later, DJ's senses went on high alert as he drove into the parking lot of Bicycle Heaven.

As they headed toward the entrance, where an old-fashioned bicycle was welded to the roof, he frowned. He didn't see anyone familiar, but he kept scanning the area.

"Why doesn't Tyler already have a bike?" he asked, going for as normal as he could. The question made sense. By that age, DJ had learned to ride and was tooling around the neighborhood and jumping that ramp he and his friends had built.

Tammie shrugged. "We live on the beach. Where's he supposed to ride it?"

DJ looked at her. Made sense. Sort of.

Inside the store, DJ stopped. And stared. Rows and rows of bikes stretched nearly as far as he could see. Neon signs hung from the rafters. "Repairs."

"Racing." "Attire." They were definitely in over their heads. At least, he was.

"Can I help you?" A young man—amend that—a teen approached them. DJ looked close and wondered if he was even remotely ready to shave. Definitely not a Ranger.

"Uh. Yeah." But DJ hadn't a clue what to ask. He looked around, hoping for contact. Wanting to get this whole show on the road.

Tammie stepped forward, taking over. "We need help. Our son is turning nine and we need a nice, simple beginner's bike for him. But something he'll be impressed with, too."

"Sure. Follow me."

Bikes had come a long way since DJ was a kid. Every color, every size. As they wound through the aisles, the clerk led them to a section of smaller bikes. Rapid-fire questions came out of the kid's mouth. Age? Experience? Height? DJ watched as Tammie supplied all the information off the top of her head.

It reminded him a lot of those nightmares he had in high school just before finals, where he knew none of the answers on the test. He couldn't even guess.

She had memories of Tyler he couldn't even begin to try to build. Even if he had Tyler with him until he turned eighteen, there was no going back and retrieving those lost memories.

"What do you think?" Tammie's voice broke into his thoughts.

"What? Oh." Three bikes had been pulled from the racks as he'd stood looking for familiar faces. Each bike looked insanely expensive and, surprisingly, similar to the dirt bike Tyler had shown him. The neon green was nearly the exact same color as the Dirt Rocket in the magazine picture.

"Which one do you think he'd like?" Tammie was trying to defer to him, but he could see in her face that she'd already made a selection.

"Which one do you think?" He wanted her to pick the green one. He needed some type of reassurance that he knew *something* about his son—that he'd learned some of his idiosyncrasies during the past few weeks.

"I like the blue one. But if it's for the ranch, the green one is sturdier," she said.

"What else would it be for?"

Their eyes met. She looked as shocked as he felt. "Where are you going to live?" she asked.

"I—" How the hell did he know? He'd just been discharged, and had spent over a week traipsing around four different states. He didn't even know what kind of a job he could get.

"He won't need it when he's at the beach." She turned back to the clerk. "I think the green for the ranch."

The clerk wheeled the bike through the store to a counter, where Tammie pulled out her small stash of money.

"What are you doing?" DJ asked her.

"It's partially from me."

"You can't afford—"

"Don't even." Her temper rose bright red in her face as she slapped the precious bills on the counter.

He threw down his credit card with the same intensity. The clerk looked totally confused. For the first time, DJ found something in common with the kid. But aside from arguing with her here and now, what else could he do?

"Put the cash on it and whatever that doesn't cover can go on the card."

As they waited for the kid to complete the transaction, DJ slowly, carefully looked around the store. A dozen people were shopping, in addition to a few clerks not much older than this one helping them. No one looked familiar, and no one seemed to notice them.

Finally, DJ wheeled the bike out to the truck and loaded it in the bed along with all the other things they'd packed.

He stood for a moment, looking at the boxes. At Tyler's desk chair. At the dining room chair from Tammie's mother. At the newly added bike. All the bits and pieces of *her* life that he'd gathered up were nestled in the bed of *his* truck. And it felt right.

"What's the matter?" Tammie asked, standing a few feet away.

He looked over at her. She looked so small standing there. Small yet strong. Smart and yet vulnerable to people like Dom.

DJ had no clue how to answer her. Instead, he walked to where she stood and without warning of what he intended, he swept her into his arms and kissed her. Hard and swift.

If anyone was watching, they'd see a couple kissing, involved in each other. Normal, everyday stuff.

Except, it wasn't normal, everyday stuff. DJ lost himself in the sweetness of her taste. He hoped and prayed she could decipher the message he couldn't put into words.

He'd done the one thing he'd never thought he'd do. He'd fallen. Fallen hard, for a tough, beautiful woman.

And, damn it, he had no clue what the hell he would do if anything happened to her.

She didn't need him. She'd proven that. Other than the situation with Dom, she could, and would, go on her way once this was all over. She'd mentioned going back to the beach. Taking Tyler with her.

He had to figure out how to convince her to stay.

THE SOUND OF someone clearing their throat had Tammie blushing and pulling away from DJ. He simply laughed at her.

"You think they got the word? Think they're celebratin'?" the taller of the two cowboys standing there asked. Both men wore Stetsons, finishing the look with jeans and worn cowboy boots. Not everyone in Texas was a cowboy, but these guys couldn't prove it.

DJ laughed, extending his hand to shake each man's hand. "Good to see you, guys."

These must be the Texas Rangers Sam Watson had told them about. She hoped so. She'd had a hard time concentrating in the store, expecting someone to walk up on them any second. Half expecting it to be Dom, and hoping it would be a Ranger.

"Sorry we're late. We just got off the phone with Watson. He said he tried to call you."

DJ pulled out his phone. The battery was nearly dead. "Sure enough, two missed calls," he said. He leaned into the truck and connected the charger.

"Oh, this is Tammie Easton," he said, introducing her. Both men shook her hand, doffing their Stetsons for an instant and smiling bright and warm.

"Is everything okay?" Did they think she hadn't heard them? That she'd been too involved making out with DJ? Okay, maybe that was the logical conclusion, given the position she'd been in when they arrived. Her blush returned.

"Yeah. Going just as planned. Your brother is about an hour out," the other man spoke for the first time. "Our guys are with him. He and Tyler will be fine."

It all sounded too good to be true. Was this really going to be the end? Would she really be free?

"You ready, Tammie?" DJ opened the door of the truck.

"We'll follow you over to the house," the first

Ranger said, the truck next to theirs beeping and flashing its light as he hit the key fob.

Tammie nodded and climbed in. Her stomach fluttered. Her heart pounded. This was it. The end…and hopefully the beginning. She smiled at DJ then, for the first time feeling the hope she'd ignored for so very long.

CHAPTER TWENTY

TAMMIE STARED OUT the pickup's window as DJ pulled to the curb across the street from a small, craftsman-style house.

Painted a pale blue with white trim, it looked homey and inviting—except for the crowd of people she could see through the front window and open door. Her heart sank.

"Don't worry. Everyone's safe. They'll get Dom soon."

"I know." He'd managed to convince her to trust Watson and the authorities who were involved. "That's not what scares me right now."

"It's not? Then why are you so nervous?"

She wanted to laugh, but the hysteria was too close. "That's your family in there." She looked down at her hands, no longer able to look into his eyes. "They're not going to be too thrilled to meet me."

"Once they get to know you, they'll love you."

Tammie looked over at DJ and almost asked him the question on the tip of her tongue. *Like you do?* Except she was afraid of what he'd say. Or wouldn't say.

"Hey, at least none of them will greet us with a shotgun," he teased.

"Good to know." She didn't move, just sat there, staring. Waiting.

The Rangers had parked across the street. The tall one, who DJ had explained was Hal Black, got out. He ambled across the pavement, looking more as if he'd just climbed off a horse than from a truck. He stopped at DJ's window, which DJ promptly lowered.

The man's smile was nearly too bright. "Good news. The team at your brother's ranch called. They got him."

"Who? Dom?" Tammie asked, leaning toward the open window, needing to see the man's face, needing reassurance this was real.

"Yes, ma'am. Carlyle. He's in custody. Agent Watson is headed that way to take over the case."

DJ leaned back against the seat, a smile blooming on his face. She leaned back and looked at DJ. "Really? I..." This was too easy, too quick. And yet—the past year seemed to stretch out eternally behind her. Nothing quick about any of it.

"Yeah, really." Hal grinned at them. "I think you've earned a right to that party, ma'am."

"Damn right." DJ opened the door and climbed out. "Join us, guys. You've earned it, too."

"Thanks for the offer. We'll come inside, but we're still on duty, so we won't be doing much partying." Hal grinned and waved at his partner to join them. "We're here until they're sure all the parties have been rounded up."

DJ nodded, accepting their company. He came

around the truck's hood and opened her door. "Come on." It wasn't a command, more of an invitation, but her dread was just as strong.

She was stunned. Dom was no longer a threat? If this was a dream, she hoped she didn't wake up anytime soon. She'd turned to climb out, when she glanced at the house again.

She still had to deal with the people in that house.

His brothers and sisters. And some friends. Too many new faces—too many people she didn't know. She could feel their judgment from here. "Is Tyler here yet?"

"I don't see Wyatt's truck." DJ stepped closer, leaning on the door frame. Their faces were level as he stood on the street, and she remained seated. The air between them stilled and their eyes met. A smile filled his face, and her heart squeezed.

DJ would cringe if she said it, but, Lord, he was beautiful. All rough, tough soldier, anxious to be home with his family. She wished he wanted her as much.

Shaking her head, she broke the spell before he kissed her in front of all those nosy people inside—and they were nosy. She could feel them staring at them through the windows, watching and wondering.

"I don't give a damn what they think," DJ said when she cast her glance toward the house. "And since when do you?"

Since she'd let them be a part of her son's life. Surprised at her own realization she could only stare.

Until DJ's lips found hers. And then it was just him. All the rest melted away.

DJ's arms went around her, pulling her off the seat and into his arms. Her feet landed on soft grass, and DJ stepped back with a grin on his face.

"There. That should do it."

"Do what?"

"Get us over that hump. You're out of the truck, and they know where you and I stand."

Great. They knew more than she did.

DJ led her up the walk, making her feel as if she were the proverbial sacrificial lamb being dragged into the lion's den.

"Relax," he whispered in her ear.

"Uh, yeah." Easy for him to say.

"Hey, look who's here." A man's voice greeted them at the front door and the introductions began. A blur of faces and names swirled in her head. They were all too polite to say anything outright to her, but she saw the stares, the sideways glances.

"Hey, little mama." DJ bent down to kiss the cheek of a very pregnant woman seated in a recliner. Despite looking uncomfortable, the woman's skin glowed and her dark hair hung long and pretty to her shoulders. "How you doin'?"

"Fat and grumpy. Don't tick me off."

"Ha. Your threats are empty. You'd have to catch me first, and I can still run faster than you, sis."

"Doctor says she can't get up, so quit baiting her, Deej."

A tall, well-dressed man appeared beside DJ. They shook hands and pseudo-hugged.

"Tammie, this is my sister Mandy. This is her house. And my brother Jason."

Tammie nodded, barely catching herself from sidling closer to DJ. Disgusted with her behavior, she lifted her chin and reminded herself that she didn't care what people really thought.

"Where're Addie and Tara?" DJ asked.

"In the kitchen." Jason pointed to a swinging wooden door with his beer. "Where else?"

DJ led Tammie to a small dining room, where she froze and stared, convinced she was going to throw up. A white-and-blue birthday cake sat in the center of a table where a paper tablecloth decorated with video game characters had been spread. Balloons bounced on the ends of ribbons tied to the backs of the chairs.

Tyler was going to love it.

And Tammie'd had nothing to do with it.

"Hey." DJ walked over to a blonde woman spreading out video game character napkins.

"You're back," she cried and smiled as DJ wrapped her in a hug.

"Of course I came back."

Her smile faded as she caught sight of Tammie. "Hello."

From what DJ had told her about his family, this had to be Addie. There was no warmth for Tammie in Addie's eyes.

Reprieve came in the form of another woman poking her head around the door. "Who's helping with the grill?" She saw DJ in the same instant and grinned. "Great timing."

"Not letting the suit near the fire?"

"Nope."

"I heard that," Jason called from the living room.

DJ caught Tammie's eye and smiled at her. "She doesn't really trust me, either. But she doesn't have a choice."

The camaraderie and inside stories declared them family, and Tammie felt like the outsider she was. Torn, she waffled back and forth between wanting to run and staying here to wait for Tyler.

Taking a deep breath as DJ headed into the kitchen, Tammie walked over to Addie. She'd done all this for Tyler. "Thank you. He'll love this."

Addie nodded, still unsmiling. "You're welcome, but I didn't do it for you."

"I know that."

"Ladies." Jason swept into the room and slipped an arm around Tammie. "I do believe we should adjourn to watch the master at work."

"If you mean DJ…how much have you had to drink?" Addie asked, letting herself smile. "I'll be out in a minute." She returned to finish the table.

Before Tammie could say a thing, Jason led her through the kitchen and out to the deck, where DJ was lighting the grill under Tara's close direction. DJ smiled at her, and Tammie relaxed a little.

"The government lets me handle lethal weapons, you know. I think I can handle a civilian grill."

"Uh-huh." Tara turned to Tammie. "We know the truth. We were there when you set the barn on fire. Here, let me do that."

"Hey, that wasn't on purpose. Why'd you even ask if you're just gonna do it yourself?"

"Gotta keep that male ego polished."

Tammie liked Tara, and she couldn't help but smile at the siblings' easy banter.

"Sorry about Addie." Jason leaned on the rail a few feet away. "She's gotten attached to Tyler. She's afraid you'll take him away."

Tammie didn't know what to say, and at her silence, three sets of eyes turned to her. What did they expect of her? She'd given Tyler up only to keep him safe, not because she was willing to lose her son.

The others looked away before DJ did. He frowned but didn't say anything, either.

Shrugging, Tammie focused on the spacious backyard. She needed something else to think about. Her nerves were stretched tight and her stomach twisted. She wished she could step off the deck and disappear into the yard. Instead, she just stood and looked around. It was the best she could get right now.

Trees and shrubs grew thick around the perimeter, creating a private oasis. Big arching branches formed a canopy overhead that shaded most of the yard.

The gravel driveway that ran along one side of the house ended abruptly at an old wooden garage with a battered door and darkened windows. A compact car shone in the dappled sunlight.

It was a pretty place. Comfortable and safe.

Laughter and male voices erupted from the doorway as more guests arrived. Tammie turned around, her hopes rising. A group of cowboys had arrived, carrying a barrel filled with ice and long necks. They plunked it down on the wood with a thud. Several grabbed a bottle for themselves before stepping back to take a seat, or lean on a rail. A few women were sprinkled in the crowd.

No little boy.

She didn't know how much any of them knew, but they knew enough. Or at least they thought they did. She lifted her chin and walked purposefully over to where DJ stood near the drinks and yanked a bottle from the ice. She met his gaze, silently daring him to question her, or try to be all macho and open the bottle for her. She twisted off the top and took a deep swallow of the liquid courage before strolling away.

Voices drifted around her, and she tried not to identify them, or to guess if the whispers were about her. Instead, she focused on the sound of the breeze in the branches. On the faint roar of traffic on the street.

DJ had warned her that Wyatt and Tyler had a long drive, so she tried to be patient. Anticipation won over worry and fluttered in her stomach.

Another car door slammed. This time, she didn't turn around, didn't let her hopes lift. She couldn't take the pain anymore. She closed her eyes and focused on everything else. It would have been nice if it had worked.

The sliding glass door of the house rattled open again. Tammie held her breath. She heard footsteps. Fast, small footsteps.

"Mama!" Tyler's voice rang out over everything. His tennis shoes pounded down the steps.

"Tyler? Ah, baby," she whispered, spinning around and falling to her knees. He ran into her arms and she clung to him. Tears ran down her cheeks. So much for her resolve.

Pain cut through Tammie's chest, choking her. She didn't dare give in or she'd turn into a blubbering fool. She was an adult. She had to be strong. Had to hold on to—

He felt so good, his little arms tight around her neck. Warm. Sweet.

She knew the crowd at the house watched her, judged her, but none of it mattered now. Nothing mattered except the feel of her son in her arms.

"Don't cry, Mama." Tyler hugged her tight, patting her back as he buried his face against her neck.

"I missed you so much." She hoped he never knew how much.

"Me, too."

The silence coming from the house made Tammie open her eyes and look over her son's head. Everyone had gone back inside. She couldn't even see them peering through the windows.

DJ had done this. She'd have to thank him later for giving her this time alone with Tyler. For letting them have some semblance of privacy.

She didn't ever want to let go, but she knew everyone's curiosity would soon overwhelm even the best of intentions. She leaned back from Tyler, hugging him with her gaze now in addition to her arms. "You've grown." She smiled through her tears.

"Yep. A whole inch!" Pride shone in his voice. "I gotta show you." He pulled out a handful of junk, different from what he used to carry in his pockets. He had a coin and the plastic lizard she'd given him before they'd left Florida.

"Look." And a tooth. Not his, thank God. She remembered the call about the pig's tusk he'd helped Wyatt remove. She groaned but didn't say anything. He was so proud—proud as only an almost-nine-year-old could be.

Heavy footsteps sounded behind them on the gravel, breaking into their reunion. Another arrival for the party. Tyler looked up and over her shoulder. His smile vanished as the color drained from his face.

Strong, hard hands closed around Tammie's shoulders, painfully biting into her skin. Before she could move away, someone grabbed her arm and twisted it tight.

"Unless you want the two gentlemen who just joined the party to help that pretty little pregnant one with her labor, you two are coming with me." Dom's voice ripped out of her memory and into reality.

He shoved Tammie hard, not letting go of her arm and wrenching her shoulder. "Make a peep, kid, and I'll hurt your mother. Hurt her bad. You understand?"

Tyler nodded and silently fell into step.

"You do anything," Dom breathed in her ear, "and the kid will more than hurt. I'll break his neck this time."

No! No! No! What should she do? What had she done? The Ranger's words echoed in her mind. They'd caught him. What had happened? The pain screaming in her shoulder drowned out any clear thoughts.

Dom dragged her along the side of the house. Vaguely, it registered there were no windows on this wall. When they reached the front, she prayed someone was out on the porch, but it was empty.

"Move it. Now." He shoved her arm hard and Tammie saw stars. She had to do something. *Think.*

If she screamed, the men would go for Mandy. If they saw Tyler run, they'd—

Pickup trucks lined both sides of the street. Behind DJ's bright red truck sat a black car.

Crossing the street, Dom led them in front of the truck. Had DJ locked it? She didn't remember. She had to try. Had to save Tyler.

At the passenger door, Tammie put everything she had into pulling free. She had a split second, but it was enough. Taken off guard, Dom stumbled.

Tammie yanked the passenger door open and shoved Tyler inside. "Lock it!" she screamed.

"Mama!" Tyler yelled from inside, his voice muffled.

"You'll pay for that, bitch."

Tammie tried to run, but Dom caught her. The pain in her shoulder felt as if he'd dislocated it. Panic nearly overwhelmed her as he dragged her toward the car. She couldn't let him get her inside.

She heard Tyler's cries. When the truck horn went off, she hoped and prayed the family and friends in the house could protect Mandy.

"Why are you doing this?" Could she reason with him? They'd spent hours in the restaurant that first night, talking and laughing.

"You're not that stupid." He pushed her. A few more inches of freedom disappeared.

"Maybe I am." She stumbled. "I've had a rough year."

"*You've* had a rough year?" He stopped and pulled her back so he could glare at her. He shook her. "*You've* had a rough year?" he repeated, louder.

"Dom, stop. I'm telling the truth."

"Then tell me where you put the diamonds."

"I…I put them in the necklaces. Just like you told me to." She remembered every painstaking, painful piece she'd created.

"Not all of them. Four were missing—the ones in the display necklaces. You stole them and my boss is *not* happy."

Anger surged through her. "Stole? How do you steal stolen diamonds?" *He'd* put them in the display pieces, not her. "I didn't even know there were real diamonds in *those* necklaces, Dom! Anyway, I don't have them anymore. But I know where they are." That was the truth, but she didn't dare tell him the FBI had them. Then she and Tyler wouldn't have any value to him.

CHAPTER TWENTY-ONE

THE HOUSE WAS full of family and friends. Packed to the gills, and DJ was pretty fed up with all of them. Wyatt and Emily were disgustingly lovey-dovey, which for them was just plain weird.

Addie and Tara were busy carrying enough food for his whole division from the kitchen to the table, and Mandy looked about ready to pop—if not to have the kid, to deck one of her siblings. Jason was DJ's only sibling he liked right now—and only because he wasn't here at the moment.

Who gave a birthday party and forgot the candles? Apparently, his siblings were a bit out of practice. Good thing the store was only a few blocks away and Jason was willing to go buy some.

In addition to his family, half the hands from the ranch were here, as well. It was a relief to know everyone was safe, but the only people he really wanted anything to do with right now were Tammie and Tyler.

The way Tyler had run into her arms the instant he'd seen her told DJ the whole trip had been worth it. But he tried not to feel left out when they seemed to forget he was there. He understood that mother and son deserved time together.

Still, he thought they'd have come inside by now.

There were, after all, presents and cake. And Tyler was…Tyler.

Trying to be casual, he strolled to the back door and looked out. Where were they? He pulled open the door and stepped out. Empty.

Back inside, he found Wyatt. "You see where Tammie went?" His heart sank. He trusted her. Really, he did. She wouldn't take Tyler. She wouldn't—

He broke off his thoughts and moved away from his brother. "What do you mean, where are they?" Addie's voice was the first he heard. "I just looked and they were there. She can't take him." Heartache filled her voice.

For an instant, DJ's heart sank. An instant he'd forever regret. "She didn't." He cursed and reversed course. She'd earned and deserved his trust. He wouldn't let her down.

Halfway through the living room, he froze. "Who the hell are you?" Two cowboys he'd never seen before suddenly stuck out. They hovered too close to Mandy. The crowd was big enough that no one had noticed them. Wyatt's crew picked up on DJ's reaction. Then Hal and Nick appeared, no longer relaxed but on full alert.

DJ had just reached the front door when a loud car horn broke the air outside. Every nerve in his body went tense.

He sprinted out the front door. A scream pushed him even harder. The sounds of pounding feet behind him told him his brother, and the rest of his family, weren't far behind.

Where the hell was Tammie?

The flashing lights on his truck and the blaring horn made it all too clear.

DJ's heart beat in his chest, sending the blood racing through his veins. He'd missed the adrenaline rushes of war. But the fine edge of fear that made the world much sharper and clearer had never before been so double-sided.

This wasn't a village under attack. Or some unidentified cache of weapons to destroy. This wasn't a mission where he could emotionally distance himself. Not business as usual.

This was Tammie and Tyler. His family. His life.

Wyatt was close at DJ's heels as they edged along the line of trucks parked at the curb. God bless Texas cowboys who drove trucks. Half a dozen of them along the street gave them plenty of cover.

Dom had Tammie. He could see, even from here, that she was in pain. Tears glistened on her cheeks in the late-afternoon sunlight. Where the hell was Tyler? Panic clouded DJ's thoughts.

With a curse, he refocused. He was their only hope. He could not, would not, let fear put them all at risk.

He wasn't afraid of this guy. Wyatt was a step behind him, and DJ was thankful for his brother's presence. Though he prayed he stayed safe, he knew Wyatt could take care of himself.

The soldier came alive.

Sunset had settled in, and the shadows reached out to cloak the landscape. It gave DJ an advantage. He hoped.

Slowly, he inched around his truck. At the front bumper, he cautiously leaned forward.

Tammie struggled against Dom's hold. Dom was a big man and had her arm twisted. Thanks to Tammie's resistance, their progress toward a parked sedan was slow.

The passenger door of the truck stood open for some reason, and DJ used it for cover.

Where the hell was Tyler?

"Where do you want me?" Wyatt whispered behind DJ.

Back home. But that wouldn't get the job done. DJ gestured for Wyatt to head around to the other side. Wyatt nodded and moved into position. DJ hoped his brother had sense enough not to get between the vehicles. Last thing he needed was Emily watching Wyatt get mowed down.

Wyatt's boots were quiet in the twilight, but DJ knew exactly where he was.

"Let my mom go." Tyler's voice startled DJ. Dom froze, too, looking back, seemingly right at DJ.

What the…

Ah, hell.

Tyler stood there, his child's hands curled around Tammie's gun. He had it aimed straight at Dom. And as DJ watched, Dom shifted positions and shoved Tammie in front of him. The gun was aimed at her.

"Tyler, no," Tammie cried. "Please, sweetie, put it down."

Dom laughed. An evil, angry laugh. "Go ahead, kid. Shoot. Shoot your mom."

DJ saw Tyler's hands shake, but he didn't put the gun down. Another curse, long and loud, echoed in his brain. The air remained quiet and still. A slight movement told DJ Wyatt was in place between the trucks, behind Dom.

DJ's mind reeled with images of Tammie bathed in blood, like so many bodies he'd seen. Of Tyler lost to the ravages of his guilt. DJ stopped thinking. He had put himself in harm's way for total strangers all his adult life. This was his life and theirs.

Time to move. Stepping out from behind the door, DJ plucked the gun from Tyler's grasp. "Give me that." Thank God the thing had never been loaded.

But Tyler didn't know that.

And neither did Dom.

It was still a deadly weapon in the hands of an eight-year-old. DJ shuddered, letting his anger loose.

"Kids and women are easy," DJ roared at the fool who held Tammie tight, her arm wrenched behind her back. "Let's see how you do against me."

DJ lunged, and in the same instant, Wyatt grabbed Tammie. DJ's fist connected painfully, but solidly, with Dom's jaw.

Dom stumbled backward, but he didn't go down.

Good. DJ wasn't done with him. The useless gun landed in the thick grass and he faced off against the other man. Fists clenched, DJ let the adrenaline rise. Let the anger take over as he hit Dom again…and again…and again.

If anyone was going to die today, it was *not* going to be his family. But DJ wasn't against Dom taking the honors.

"Dad!" Tyler's voice broke through the haze of anger, clouding DJ's thoughts.

"Whoa, boy." Chet, the ranch foreman, took hold of DJ and two of the ranch hands had no trouble subduing Dom. None too gently, either. Cowboys and beer always equaled a bar fight in these men's world. And they were spoiling for that fight.

Deep breaths did little to slow DJ's heart or his breathing, but slowly, the fog receded. Where was Tyler? Tammie? He looked around, and Chet loosened his grip. DJ jerked away.

Wyatt sat beside Tammie on the curb. Her head was down and she cradled her arm. Tyler was at her side, leaning against her, his arms wrapped tight around her.

"Come on, boys." Chet gestured to his men. "Let's get this scum outta here."

Dom struggled. Chet leaned close to the man's face. "My boys are just aching to beat the shit out of you. Want me to let 'em?"

The sound of footsteps behind him had DJ spinning around ready to defend Tammie. He only slightly relaxed when he saw Hal headed toward them. "What the hell happened? I thought you guys had him?"

Hal shook his head. "I won't apologize, as I don't know all the details. But the team at the ranch has three in custody, but none of them was Carlyle. We've got him now. I'd feel better if you'd head back to the house. Just in case there's anyone else."

DJ nodded, knowing the lawman was right, but needing time. "Just a sec." Hal settled into the shadows, close, but not really there.

DJ stopped paying attention then, his mind seeing only the ones he loved. He hunkered down in the street before her. "Hey."

Wyatt stood. "Come on, kiddo. Let's give your folks a minute. Besides, we've got a birthday cake waiting."

"Not without Mama and Dad."

"Nope. Don't worry. We'll wait for them inside." Wyatt guided the boy toward the house. DJ threw his brother a thankful glance. The evening had grown quiet, only distant approaching night sounds intruded.

She looked up and his heart broke. Tears flooded her eyes. "I'm sorry," she whispered.

"Sorry for what?"

"Bringing him here. Putting you all at risk."

DJ forced himself to smile at her. Slowly, he reached out and pushed her tangled hair away from her eyes. A few stray strands clung to the tears on her cheeks, and he gently moved them away. Finally, when she could see him clearly, he caught her gaze. “We knew there was every chance he’d be here, didn’t we?”

She nodded. “But I never thought—” She stopped and looked away.

“Never thought what?” DJ reached out carefully and tilted her chin back to him.

“Never thought it would be so awful. Oh, God, DJ, I’ll never get the image of Tyler with that gun out of my head.” A sob shattered the air. “I can’t do this. I’m not that strong.”

“Oh, honey.” DJ carefully pulled her into his arms, settling on the curb where Wyatt had been. She buried her face in his chest, and he let her cry. “You are the strongest woman I know. Bar none.”

“No, I’m not.”

“Could have fooled me.” His heart hurt, and he searched for the right thing to say to her. “Let’s see. You ran away from a shotgun-totin’ father. You lived on the streets yet managed to start a business and support our son. You put up with me—”

She pulled back and glared at him. “Oh, now you’re being ridiculous.”

There was the girl he knew and loved. DJ stared. Loved? He felt himself smile. Yeah, loved. The words were on the tip of his tongue to tell her when the wail of sirens cut through the night.

“Wonder who called them?”

They both looked at each other and said, "Addie," at the same time.

Neither of them moved.

"Guess what?" he finally whispered, brushing her cheeks with his thumb and wiping away the tears.

"What?"

He paused again. "We won. We got the bad guy."

She stared up at him and her eyes widened as realization dawned. With a cry, she threw her arm around his neck.

He heard her whisper against his chest, "We won."

DJ held her tight—thanking God over and over again that he was able to.

"We've got a birthday to finish."

"Yeah." She pulled back and looked up at him. "Thank you." She reached up then and kissed him. Long and sweet. Finally, she pulled away. "Let's go!"

DJ carefully stood, reaching down to give her a hand.

She hesitated. "No. Your back."

He frowned at her and reoffered his hand. "Just once, pretend to be the damsel in distress. Humor me. You can be the independent one again tomorrow."

She struggled to her feet, even with his help. She grimaced when she let go of her injured arm.

"Tammie, let me take care of you." Before she could answer, DJ bent and scooped her up into his arms. "Argue and I might drop you," he warned.

She tried to laugh and looped her good arm around his neck. "Yes, sir."

Cowboys and family mingled out on the lawn as DJ carried her toward the house. Relief warred with the surprising sense of belonging that she felt.

The birthday party had moved outside. When had the ambulance arrived?

Every light in the small house was on, and DJ strolled through the crowd, ignoring the concerned and knowing glances. Tammie blushed. Finally, at the front door, he let Tammie slide down to her feet.

He opened the door for her, and the activity inside hit her, loud and bright.

Dom was sitting in a sturdy wooden chair, his arms pulled back and secured with—she looked closer—bungee cords?

"Mom would so kill you," DJ said to his siblings.

"It wasn't my idea," Mandy said from the recliner, where an EMT was busy taking her blood pressure. Fear shot through Tammie. Had Dom's men hurt her?

"Like there's any other choice, DJ?" Wyatt indicated the room full of soft, cushy furniture. "She'd appreciate our resourcefulness."

Confused, Tammie looked up at DJ as he walked her over to sit on the couch near Mandy. Tyler was leaning against Addie's side, much as he had hers outside, but as soon as he saw her, he came running. She gasped as he bumped her arm, but she did everything she could to wrap her good arm around him. She wasn't sure who was trembling—Tyler or her.

"Here." Addie came over and helped move Tyler so he was next to her, but not leaning on her injured arm. "She's hurt," Addie told the EMT. The animosity of earlier was gone. "I'm sorry—"

"Shh, no apologies necessary—right, Tyler?"

"Right." Tyler nodded and smiled up at his aunt from where he nestled against Tammie.

A pair of EMTs came through the front door just then, a gurney between them. Suddenly, Mandy gave a cry of pain and Tyler leaned harder against Tammie's side. "Mama, what's the matter with Aunt Amanda?"

The EMT turned to smile at Tyler. "Nothing's wrong. She's just having a baby."

Tyler's eyes grew wide. "Now?"

Voices around the room laughed. "Not quite yet," the EMT explained. "But soon." Turning, he focused on Mandy again. "Okay, let's get you on your way to the hospital."

Once Tammie's arm was treated, with instructions to see an orthopedic doctor the next day, the EMTs loaded Mandy into the ambulance and sped away. Tammie noticed then, the Texas Rangers preparing to take Dom away, even as they complimented Wyatt and Chet on their makeshift handcuffs.

"Oh, Lord," Tara whispered from the recliner, where she'd taken Mandy's seat. "Don't encourage them, Officers." She looked over at Tammie. "The male egos are going to be huge for the next few days."

Addie was busy trying to encourage the party guests to head home, but no one seemed inclined to leave. They were too busy watching the show.

If the pain meds hadn't started to take hold, Tammie thought she might be embarrassed by the whole thing.

Tammie leaned in and kissed the top of Tyler's head. Her sweet, brave boy.

"Mama?" Tyler whispered.

"Yes, sweetie?"

He paused for a second, and all kinds of motherly fears rushed to the surface. How would he handle all the trauma he'd been through?

"There was a green bike in the back of Dad's truck." He looked up. "Is that mine?" All the hope in the world echoed in his voice.

Tammie laughed and cried. She looked over at DJ as he headed out the door to retrieve their son's birthday gift. "Maybe," she said.

"Cool!"

CHAPTER TWENTY-TWO

Two months later

DJ PACED ACROSS his brand-new living room. Finally, he'd used the money from his hazard pay and what he'd saved over the years to get a place away from the ranch. It felt new, but good. His.

Tyler was in his room, getting his things packed. Lord, had he really agreed to this? Tammie would be here any minute and was taking Tyler for the weekend. It would be the first time she'd had him to herself since the custody hearing. He knew from what she'd said on the phone last night that she was nervous about it.

He'd miss having Tyler around. Already the house felt lonely. With any luck, it wouldn't be for long.

"Are you ready?" Tyler said as he raced out of his room. He flung his backpack onto the floor by the door. "You're not gonna choke, are you?" Tyler was so serious.

"Hey, I'm a marine. We don't choke." DJ tried to glare at his son.

"Yeah, you do." Tyler giggled and headed to the kitchen. DJ followed him. He needed to check on the food. Tara had happily agreed to make tonight's meal for him and his mouth watered with anticipation at the lasagna baking in his brand-new oven.

Everything was new in here. Almost everything. DJ walked over to the dining room table in the small alcove off the kitchen to make sure everything was perfect.

A wooden table with one matching chair sat centered in the room. The other chairs were from his mom's house, from Elizabeth Easton's house and from Tyler's wooden desk in Florida. The other chairs that came with the table were stacked in a corner. He'd figure out what to do with those later.

The table was set, thanks to Tyler's help. "Mama showed me where to put everything. It's not really that hard," he'd said as he jabbered and moved around the table. The bouquet of flowers in the center was bright and livened up the rather dark interior.

DJ had never owned a house before. It scared the hell out of him. He'd always thought he'd be career military, living in base housing or apartments. He hadn't really planned on settling down. But here he was, in his own place.

The doorbell rang, and Tyler ran off to answer it. DJ followed more slowly, still hindered by the scars on his legs and back. He'd healed, but he wasn't going to get much better than this. He'd learned to deal with it, but that didn't mean he had to like it. Buying a house without any stairs had helped, though.

"Hey, sweetie." Tammie's voice filled the house,

and DJ swore he could hear the hug she gave Tyler. They came into the kitchen a few seconds later.

"You look great," DJ said to Tammie, and he felt himself grinning. The stress was gone from her face and she was wearing one of the outfits he'd bought her that day in New Orleans. He couldn't look away. He didn't want to, and finally, he didn't have to.

"Thanks." She blushed and looked around the sparse kitchen, instead of at him.

Tyler grinned up at her, then looked up at DJ. "Is this the part where I'm s'posed to make myself scarce?"

"Uh—"

"No." Tammie peeked into the oven. "Looks like dinner is about ready. Please tell me that's Tara's lasagna."

"It is."

Such scintillating conversation. DJ nearly groaned. "Let's get washed up." He guided Tyler down the hall. At the bathroom door he stopped his son. "I said act natural."

"I am. You're the one who's gonna choke." Tyler turned on the water.

"I am not," DJ said in a harsh whisper.

Tyler met DJ's gaze in the mirror, rolling his eyes only as a nine-year-old could.

The aroma of the lasagna, the wine and Tammie's perfume filled the kitchen. DJ inhaled, savoring it all. They sat down to their first meal together, just the three of them, in his house. Almost a family.

The meal finished, DJ leaned back, relaxing for the first time in days. He looked over at his son. He'd never seen him so happy, so at ease. It all felt right.

Finally, Tyler turned to meet DJ's gaze. "Now?" the boy asked softly.

DJ couldn't speak. He nodded and slowly stood. Tyler ran around the table and grabbed his mother's hand. "Come on, Mama."

"Where are we going?"

"It's a surprise." He pulled harder on her hand. She frowned at DJ, and he simply smiled. "Come on."

Tammie let Tyler drag her down the hall and glanced over her shoulder a couple of times to see DJ following. They stopped at the end of the hall to a closed door.

"Okay, close your eyes," Tyler instructed.

"What?"

"Don't you trust us?" DJ whispered in her ear, and they both laughed.

"Fine." Tammie closed her eyes, frowning as she did so. "What are you two up to?"

"Just keep 'em closed, Mama."

SHE HEARD THE DOOR open and could see light, though her eyes were closed. She stepped into the room, her heels echoing on the wood floor.

"Okay, you can look." Tyler's voice was full of excitement. It was so good to hear his joy, instead of the worry and hurt she'd grown so accustomed to over the past year.

She was nervous, afraid to look. Slowly, she opened her eyes. And gasped. The late-afternoon light bathed the room in brightness. Brightness that bounced off the shiny surface of the wood floor, a set of new cabinets and counters, a desk—and a drafting table.

A very beautiful, familiar drafting table. "How—" She gasped. Her eyes burned as she turned to look at DJ.

"Robyn helped. She had it restored with the help of historical photos."

"Oh…oh…" She hurried over to the table, running her hand along the smooth, clean surface. For an instant, images of the damage she'd seen in Florida flashed through her mind. She felt her heart break again and then shoved away the images. All that pain had been erased. The table looked beautiful even through her tears.

And then she saw the black velvet box sitting in the center. All by itself. "What…what's that?"

"Now?" Tyler whispered.

"Wait," DJ whispered back.

Tammie's hand shook as she reached out for the box. Out of the corner of her eye, she saw DJ's strong hand pick it up. His fingers, with all the white scars against his tanned skin, curled around the box. She turned to face him, afraid of what she was going to see when he opened the box.

"Now," DJ said out of the side of his mouth. Tyler stepped forward, standing beside his dad.

"Dad said I could do this part since his knee won't let him." Slowly, Tyler got down on one knee.

"Oh." Words escaped her.

DJ opened the box. Instead of the customary solitaire diamond, a rough, uncut, unpolished diamond was nestled in the velvet. "We figured you'd make a better design than anything we could ever find," DJ whispered. "Your mom thought you'd like this one."

She stared.

"Mama?" Tyler said softly.

"Y-yes, sweetie?" Tammie whispered, never taking her eyes from DJ.

"Will you marry us?"

"I—"

"Tammie." DJ stepped close, his hand coming up to cup her chin. "I love you. I am so damned proud of you. So impressed by your strength. By your creativity. Everything that you are. I want you to be a part of my life. Our life. Always."

The sincerity in his eyes surprised and pleased her. "Oh, DJ. I love you, too."

"Say yes," Tyler prompted.

Tammie laughed and smiled up at DJ. "Yes," she whispered. And then he kissed her.

"Oh, jeez. Not the mushy stuff." Tyler sighed, then laughed as he left the room. "I'm gonna unpack."

* * * * *